MW00831523

blissbody

ADVENTURES IN TANTRA

CATHERINE AUMAN

Green Tara Press

Green Tara Press

Green Tara Press
Los Angeles, CA
www.greentarapress.com

© 2010, 2023 by Catherine Auman

All Rights Reserved. Published 2023.

Auman, Catherine I.
blissbody: adventures in tantra
   1. Fiction 2. Action and Adventure 3. Romance

ISBN: 978-1-945085-40-6   Paperback
ISBN: 978-1-945085-41-3   Electronic Book Text

Cover designed by Catherine Auman and Lilly Penhall
Interior book design by Catherine Auman and Lorie DeWorken
Author Photo by Alexis Rhone Fancher

" . . . the ecstasy is holy . . ."

Patti Smith, "Spell," lyric by Allen Ginsburg

"The world's a mess; it's in my kiss"

Exene Cervenka and John Doe, *X*

t_here's nobody here,_ LEELA THOUGHT AS SHE
scanned the crowd on the bulwark below. Hundreds of
writhing dancers strutting and swaying but not a single one
who might qualify as her Beloved. She saw a man looking up
at her: dark hair, medium height, attractive in a boy-next-
door kind of way, maybe ten years younger. Momentarily
mesmerized by him and his T-shirt with its _om_ symbol, she
shook her head. Definitely not her type.

Everywhere a riot of tattoos, pierced body parts, wild
techno dayglo clothes, bell-bottoms that zipped off at the
knee. Perfect girls with perfect bodies, showing off their
breasts in tiny string tees. _How could they have such breasts
when they have no body fat?_ Leela wondered. Perfect boys with
six-pack abs, careless, not yet knowing how much effort those
bodies would later take to maintain. Most everyone was in
their twenties or early thirties, with not a single poseur dressed
all in black as there would have been in the West. No sign of
any women her age, home tending children or careers.

Not quite knowing how to behave at a morning rave, or any rave for that matter, Leela walked over to a makeshift bar with sweaty cold *Kingfishers*, quart-sized Indian beers, and although they were at ridiculously inflated prices, bought one to punctuate the fact that she too was still a rebel, in a Kerouac sort of way.

"We got in last night around eleven," Leela overheard a girl in front of her say. "We never miss a full moon party. Are you guys still going up to the ashram?"

Her friend was Japanese with bleached-blonde hair. Both girls were unselfconsciously sexy with exposed midriffs, tiny hot pants, and four-inch moon boots. "We're leaving tonight after we sleep this off. Most of the crew is headed up to the foothills. Me, Dylan, Brandon—we're going to the ashram. Besides, I'm due for my Andrew fix."

"Rebecca, you are the conniving one," her friend said.

"I take my pleasure seriously!"

Leela felt the beer buzz coming on as she sat down on the bulkhead separating the dance floor from the cliff plunging into the sea. On the sides were neon-colored banners of psychedelic buddhas, Shiva meditating with a serpent on his shoulder, *yin yangs* symbols, and Stars of David floating above his head. The music streaked through the air from one side of the planet to the other like alien communication. The beat pulsed through her nervous system, now ready for takeoff.

The man she had examined before appeared on her left. "Dance?" he gestured.

She sized him up. Still too young and not her type. "No, thanks," she mouthed.

"C'mon," he said. "It'll be fun."

"I don't feel like it. That's all."

"Don't feel like it? Really? I saw you tapping your foot and nearly jumping out of your skin." He grinned. "You were wiggling all over the place you wanted it so much. I just want to make you happy."

"No. Thanks anyway." She was suddenly aware that her roots needed a touch-up.

"Okay for now," he said above the din, "but next time I ask, I expect you to say 'yes.'" He smiled and disappeared into the commotion.

Leela sat entranced by the intoxicating scene—there hadn't been such sensual psychedelia since the 60s. Sitting there on the bulkhead, drinking beer in the morning sun of India, Leela realized she was happy.

I N GOA, THEY HAVE FULL MOON RAVES ON THE beach," Richard had said back home.

"You're kidding, in India?" Leela had been shocked that holy India would host such a profane party atmosphere.

"Yeah, a whole rave scene with kids from all over the world, dancing high on Ecstasy all night long. There's even a distinct kind of music coming out of that scene, Goa Trance."

Leela contemplated this tidbit and wondered if Goa Trance sounded like that music she had heard at James's party, while Richard started blasting *The Greatest Hits of Classic Rock*. My god, she thought, this rusty old music, but she had been reading *The New Rules* so she kept quiet.

I N RETROSPECT, THE BEST THING SHE GOT OUT of that relationship, if that's what you could call it, was that it had something to do with why she had decided to go to India. When he had told her about the scene in Goa, she wanted to go. Go to Goa.

Goa. The Christian part of India, full of picturesque churches and roadside shrines. Leela had read in *The Lonely Planet* that St. Thomas, who doubted the divine until he could experience it sensually, is rumored to be buried there. Goa, cleaner than the rest of India, and more prosperous too. Then this other part of Goa, the traveler scene, world-renowned for its thumping techno beats, electronic riffs hurtling across the sky, smell of ganja, sweat, and sea air.

The rave scene was very much alive in Goa, a small state on the west coast of India, especially on the nights of the full moon. Travelers from all over the world trekked to these beaches to party until dawn, high on Ecstasy, music, and each other. She had traveled half her life to get here.

Suddenly as she scanned, Leela saw larger than life another woman her own age. She felt a shock of familiarity, of comfort and at-homeness. The other woman looked great: slim, tanned, showing off her cleavage in a push-up bra, high and happy.

She turned at that moment and looked directly at Leela. A moment passed, then she flashed a smile and gave a big thumbs up, lifting her *Kingfisher* into the air. Yeah! Leela gave her a big one back. She started picking her way through the crowd over to where she was. When she reached her, the woman was dancing and whooping into the scene.

"Hey, great party. You live here?"

"Yeah," the other woman said, yelling over the music, "a couple of years now." Her short brown hair was fried from the summer sun's attack.

"Cool. How is it?" The music was so loud each word seemed to stand alone.

"Having the time of my life," she shouted. "I ain't ever goin' back." She took a slug of beer and grinned. "Name's Angie," she said, holding out her hand. Her fingers were short and square, and she was wearing no rings.

"Leela. What goes on around here? I mean when the party's over and all."

"Are you kidding? In this place the party's never over!" They both laughed. Leela felt Angie looking her over, assessing her *True Religion* jeans and black T-shirt. Angie motioned behind her. "Look, I need to go get some water from my bike. Want to go with me? It's quiet out there, and we can talk on the way."

"Sure," Leela said, relieved for a break from the scene.

She followed Angie out through the boogying crowd behind the bar. The hallway opened onto a field with over a hundred motorbikes parked gleaming in the sun.

"What did you used to do before you came here?" Leela asked as they walked.

"Oh, I had the big successful career and all that doodah, but things in my life were about as linear as they could be. Can you believe it? I hadn't had a boyfriend in over three years." They turned down a center row between the bikes.

"Guess that's not a problem here," Leela said. "Tons of hot guys."

"My boyfriend and I have been together for a year and a half. Right now he's back in Israel for the summer to make some money. Says he'll be back in the fall."

"Sounds good," Leela said.

"He's very sweet and attentive. Chased me for a change, know what I mean? That never used to happen in the West."

They had arrived at an orange scooter with tarnished chrome. Angie unlocked the compartment and took out a fresh bottle of water. She leaned back against the bike while she took a sip and then offered it to Leela. "What about you?"

"Oh yeah, the career and all that; same story," Leela said. "Except I had boyfriends but, my god, one heartache after another. So much misery. I'm at this point where I feel like I don't know anything anymore." She glanced at Angie who was studying the ground. "It's like I'm back at square one, like I don't understand the first thing about love or anything."

Angie looked up and raised the water bottle to her lips. Leela noticed the scratches on her arm, and wondered. "That's a good place to be, actually," Angie said. "You can learn something from there."

"What do you mean? Can you teach me how to meet the right guy like you did?"

Angie scanned the field of bikes, then turned to Leela. "Look, it's not about 'meeting the right guy,'" she said, hoisting herself up to sit on the scooter seat. "Somebody told me once that midlife is when you discover that you've spent your whole life climbing up a ladder and you've gotten to the top, but it's the wrong wall."

"I'm definitely at the wrong wall," Leela said. "And now I'm getting too old to find love, the only thing I've ever wanted, really. I'm afraid of losing whatever attractiveness I may have had, not that I was ever a looker anyway."

"You're fine," Angie said. "It's not about looks or age anyway. You'll learn about that if you stay here. Most Westerners get all screwed up about it, especially Americans. With the constant media barrage, it's no wonder."

"Maybe I'll stay here and party for a while."

"The season's just about over in Goa, so it's not about staying here," Angie said. "Before long it'll be really hot, so everyone starts heading out. How long can you be away?"

"I don't have to go back at all if I don't want to," Leela said. "What's there to go back to? Lonely dinners of Lean Cuisine and excruciating first dates? If I really found something, I could go anywhere. With anyone."

Angie looked up at the sun, then back at the field of scooters. She looked at Leela. "Do you really want to learn the nature of love? Get to the bottom of it?"

"Is that possible?"

"There's an ashram up in Maharashtra. You'll learn everything you want to know there."

"Ashram? I thought ashrams were these gray places where celibate people sit around silent all the time. For excitement they put a little seaweed in their rice."

Angie laughed and nodded her head. "Most ashrams are like that, it's true, but this one is more like a resort. There's a swimming pool, sauna, dancing at night, cheap places to get a massage. There's this woman there, Mevlana, who teaches groups, a yearlong seminar. It's a scene; there are cool people from all over the world."

"Hmm."

"Of course if that's not your thing, you could venture out with the crowd that's going up to Manali to hang with this guru who's a big advocate of drugs, says they are 'on the path.' You can see how that would appeal to this crowd." Angie laughed. "He holds a summer camp in the Himalayas: DJs and parties interspersed with periods of meditation. So that's another option."

"You did the thing at the ashram?" Leela asked.

"I wouldn't have my relationship now if I hadn't learned what I did at the ashram," Angie said. "It's hard to explain. There's some kind of energy there—it changed my life. Want to start heading back?"

Leela followed Angie through the crowd to the railing where she had first spotted her. The dancers below were still at it full force, a carnival of light, rapture, and high times.

"You know I love Zach," Angie said, "but if by some chance he doesn't come back—" she shrugged and swept her hand over the scene— "it's not going to be the end of the world as it would be back home. That's just one of the many things I learned at the ashram."

They smiled and gazed out together at all that testosterone.

"I'm actually taking a bus up to the ashram tonight," Angie said, "so if you want to come, you're welcome to tag along. It's a sleeper bus. You go to sleep, bang, you wake up, you're there. That's assuming you can sleep on a rattly old Indian bus. You get your own private bunk; it's really clean and super cheap."

"Sounds tempting," Leela said, "but the next stop on my itinerary is the ruins at Hampi."

"That's a cool thing to do too," Angie said. "There's a hip scene there, whatever. You can check out the evidence of ancient aliens. But I'm just saying you'll find way more than you're looking for at the ashram, and it will be more healing than all the therapy in the world. But of course it's your call."

She knocked her fists on the railing. "Think it over: either you're at the bus stop tonight at six o'clock, or you're not. I need to go up there on some business and you're welcome to come along, that's all."

"Thanks," Leela said. "I really appreciate it. I'm going to go down and dance for a while and see what's up. You really think it's worth it?"

"You have to decide if you want to take the risk," Angie said. "At the very least, it'll be an adventure, yes? Now, back to the party—the boys are waiting."

Leela and Angie clinked imaginary beers as a toast. It was so right and yet disorienting because they were the only two. *A secret sisterhood, a camaraderie, a clue,* Leela thought, *about how to stay alive.*

Taking her place on the bulkhead once again, she smiled into the crowd. Her toes started to tap, and she dared to dance a little bit by herself. She felt her life force returning, pulsing in her veins. *The world has forgotten*, she thought, *the healing power of ecstasy, sex, body freedom. We have become totally out of touch with the Mystery, the Divine.* Here it was like those tie-dyed times all over again only sleek, up to date for the information age with machines pumping the beat. Maybe because of the natural setting, in spite of the drugs, or who knows, maybe because of them, it was one of the most life-affirming scenes Leela had ever encountered.

As she sat there luxuriating in the sun, she saw the *om*-shirted boy from before dancing by himself, twirling a little pirouette. He must have felt her looking at him, because he abruptly turned in her direction and caught her eye. He started walking toward her, his dark hair glinting, his chest held high and proud. Leela took a deep breath, and knew that all she needed to know right now, in this moment, was that a guy more than ten years younger than herself was going to ask her to dance, and she was going to say yes.

I cannot stand another minute of this boring just-sitting-there, Leela thought, digging her fists into her thighs. *I am going mad.* Through the mosquito-netted walls of the meditation hall, which was really a gigantic oval tent, she could see fifty or more people sitting in perfect silence. *What in the world had Angie been talking about, that you could learn the truth about relationships here?* Everyone she had encountered so far seemed aloof, averting their eyes if met, and refusing to indulge in small talk at the dining tables.

Three weeks at the ashram, and Leela was ready to go home—home, where things made sense. Oh, the ashram was beautiful all right, a virtual oasis in the midst of the confusing chaos outside. Covering a full city block, inside its eight-foot walls, banyan and arjuna trees provided shade and cleansed the air, white stone walkways led from one building to the next, and lush vegetation served as ground cover. There were small seating areas for meditation or rendezvous, ponds full of koi and swans. There was the Jade cafeteria, a coffee bar, and an Olympic-sized swimming pool nestled in a grove of trees. Zipping her jacket up tightly to the neck, she turned down the walkway in the direction of the cappuccino bar.

Here, she thought, *let's see what happens with this guy.* Approaching from the direction of the tennis courts was a tall and handsome man who obviously spent a lot of time at the gym. Everyone here, it appeared, was a hottie. It was as if all the good-looking people in the world had been given one-way tickets to this Third World paradise, but they were out of reach and you couldn't touch. *I'm going to try to at least get this guy to smile at me*, she thought, *Please, just a smile. Somebody here has to be friendly.* She looked up, hopeful, expectant, as he passed by without a glance.

"REMEMBER ONE THING," ANGIE HAD SAID. "Everyone you meet is your teacher. Even people you'd never suspect. And never pay full price. Everything, I mean each and every good and service, is to be haggled down to half the asking price."

"That hardly seems fair," Leela said. "Everyone's so poor here."

"You'll ruin it for everyone if you don't." Then Angie had picked up her bag, ducked into the waiting rickshaw, and sped off. "Don't forget to wear sunscreen," she yelled back, leaving Leela abandoned and alone at six in the morning at the Maharashtra bus stop.

Angie had pointed in the direction of the ashram and told her they'd help with the necessary logistics. Leela had taken the mandatory AIDS test required for ashram entrance, found an available flat on the bulletin board, and then needed to find out where to have a coffee and get something to eat.

"There's only one place to go, really," the man at the gate had said in impeccable English with a German accent. "All roads in the universe lead to the Mozart Café."

The first time through the Mozart she couldn't believe that anyone but criminals and lowlifes would frequent such a dark, drug-infested place. The café was L-shaped, and she could smell marijuana when she passed the denizens at the further end. They looked gnarly and unwashed, wearing faded Indian gauze tops and cargo pants, sitting slumped over tiny cups of espresso and plates with long-ago-eaten food that had cigarette butts put out in them. Leela took one look and exited to eat solitary meal at the China Gate Restaurant recommended by the rickshaw *wallah*.

LEELA CLIMBED THE STAIRS TO THE SHIVA Cybercafe where she had been spending an hour a day of late emailing people back home. Since she had little human contact among the hundreds of people she wanted to meet, this was the best solution she had come up with for nurturance and emotional food. Her friends back home were feeling much more intimate with her now that she was on the other side of the planet, and they chatted online with her every few days.

There always seemed to be a lot of colorful characters at the computers besides the hip Indian teens who ran the place. There were the slender girls baring their flat stomachs while writing emails home in Italian, stylish Aussie skinheads with goatees, and trustafarians on vacation from Vassar pretending to be poor. Everyone was adorned with traveler jewelry: conch shell anklets, bracelets made of guitar strings, and earrings from Tibet. Leela loved to eavesdrop and snoop over everyone's shoulder, rarely getting caught, looking away furtively when she did.

A redhead about her size and age behind her to her left was talking out loud to himself, not like a crazy person, more like airy and humorous and trying to lighten up his surroundings. She ignored him as she answered thirteen new emails, but he kept up his patter and it was hard to concentrate. She glanced over when he pointed at his screen and called out, "Hey, look at this."

She didn't see much to get excited about. It looked like a bunch of song lyrics arranged in the four corners of the page, which turned out to be exactly what it was. He was making a book with the words to the songs of his life entitled *Ian's Greatest Hits*, only he hadn't written any of them. He was using the cybercafe as his personal office for this mission rather than for communicating with the people back home like everyone else.

"You're an American," he said with a British accent, leaning back in his chair so far she thought he might tip over into her lap. His nose was peeling from sunburn. "Are you here for Mevlana's tantra group?"

"Tantra? No, I'm supposed to be here for some kind of group with Mevlana, but it isn't tantra," Leela said.

Ian was chuckling. "Tantra!" he said. "That's the only thing Mevlana teaches. By the looks of you, I might have well said it's a group practicing BDSM, or incest with little girls. Ha!"

Leela felt her cheeks redden. "Well, tantra is in about the same category. You know, ads in the back pages of the personals. I'm not into all that sleazy stuff. I'm pretty vanilla myself." *I can't believe I just said that to a total stranger*, she thought.

"Yes, that's the West's usual bastardization of what it doesn't understand," Ian said. "Tantra is really the name for the spiritual path where everything is considered sacred, everything, including sex. In other traditions, sex is considered a hindrance to spiritual growth, but it's the opposite in tantra. So Mevlana's groups are all about that, all things being spiritual, including sex and relationships."

"I don't know," Leela said. "That's quite different from what I was expecting."

"It will be so far beyond 'different from what you were expecting' as to completely blow your mind." He laughed. "Isn't that why you're here?"

She thought it over. What was she here for if it wasn't for her circuits to be blown? "I don't know," she said. "I'd have to know more about it."

"Well, it'll be cool. And I'll be in there. We can take it together," he said. He got up to leave. "We'll for sure be seeing each other around the ashram, maybe get together for dinner, and hopefully I'll see you in the tantra group." He then bent down and kissed her on the lips, sending an electric shock between their mouths that surprised her because she hadn't taken him seriously up to that point. Leela watched him as he decamped out the door, turned, and gave a little salute.

She focused her attention back to the email she had been writing, reviewed it, and hit *Send*. It was beautiful outside and life was happening. Maybe she'd give it another try. Things were definitely looking up.

"Hey, the American girl!" Leela recognized that voice. "The girl who's going to be my tantra partner."

She deposited her tray of empty lunch dishes onto the conveyor belt to the kitchen and turned around to see Ian standing there, not much taller than she, smiling as wide as the moon. He slipped his arm around her bare shoulder and started them walking.

Once again she was surprised by how his skin stimulated hers with its mere touch. She found herself snuggling into the hollow under his arm as if she'd been comforted there many times before. The joining of two puzzle pieces, that's how it felt. They stopped in front of a little alcove in the trees, wordlessly delighting in their connection. Ian and Leela embraced, and only later when she came up for air did she know what happened.

They must have just started kissing; they must have just started going at each other; it must have been a mad wild animal sort of thing. They must have lost all sense of where they were, or who they were; they must have just started removing each other's clothes. So much rubbing and slipping and stroking, so much blissed-out sunlight. *It wasn't that we actually did it*, Leela thought later when she was trying to figure it out, *but we did go further than anybody in their right mind would have gone.*

All she knew was that suddenly there was a white-haired elder looking disgusted and saying, "My god, will you two take this home? I can't believe you would be like this right in front of everyone, have you no shame?"

Leela had plenty of shame, thank you. It had just seemed to happen without any input from her. She and Ian walked back to the lunch area, and she could see he was feeling sheepish too. She felt like everyone at lunch had seen them, and all the people on the streets, and everyone she had ever known including her parents.

"Let's get out of here," Ian said, and Leela was relieved when he put her on the back of his motorcycle and took her home so they could continue what had started so hotly right there in front of everyone.

It turned out he had a beautiful scar right above his left cheek, right where it becomes the back, and sweet freckles dotting his chest and arms. It was surprising how their spontaneous sport seemed so open-hearted, open-eyed, close not closed. He took her out to dinner afterward at his favorite place for Malaysian food and fried bananas with strawberry sauce. "You know more than me," he said smiling, referring she guessed, to a few tricks she had picked up here and there. Then they went back and did it some more, not coming out again until late next morning.

The walls of his room were decorated with snapshots of all the places he had traveled, and he had traveled a lot. Aligned in a four-corner grid on each wall were pictures of Amazon Indians, enlightened beings, and friends and lovers including pictures of girls he was in bed with. He apparently knew how to find someone to be with wherever he was, someone to hold him and be close with and come with. Countless CDs were stacked neatly on shelves under the pictures, the disks that held the lyrics to his songbook. That night he sat and softly strummed the guitar, singing her songs from his collection. It was cool and intimate and easy, and it seemed like something good was starting to happen. Leela heard a voice in her head telling her she wouldn't be back, but everything was so sweet and wonderful between them she chose to ignore it. *After all, he had shown her how to put up the mosquito net, which is not something you do if the person is not coming back, right?*

3

THE NOISE EXPLODED AS LEELA WALKED OUT the gate. Three-wheeled rickshaws idled noisily waiting for passengers. A group of four men stood arguing loudly in Hindi. Motorcycles and cars careened to avoid collision. Tinny Indian pop music screeched out the window in the apartment building across the street. Not wanting to go back to her isolated flat all alone, and since she had no idea where Ian was or how to contact him, Leela began wandering down Laxmi Road with no destination other than away.

Leela had not gotten used to the sheer volume of people, the mass of conflicting colors, smells, and sounds. The air was rank, filled with soot and leaded exhaust. Little businesses had grown up in the enclave around the ashram trying to sell what Westerners missed from back home. There were restaurants serving every type of food: Italian, Indonesian, Oriental, and of course, Indian. The street was lined with carts selling fruit, tie-dyed clothing, and fried Indian pastries only the natives would eat. As she walked,

Leela passed hand-lettered signs advertising Tibetan massage, healing Reiki, Ayurvedic medicine, and Amara's Used Books. Hanging from a tree was a crudely rendered likeness of Sai Baba, a guru from the south of India. She walked past a dog lying by the side of the road that she was sure was dead, but when she stopped and saw its shallow breath, realized was just malnourished and taking a nap. She passed the men taking up the sidewalk with oily cogs and bolts and spokes that was the village bicycle repair shop, and past the vendors selling brass statues of Vishnu and Ganesh. As she got to the bridge, Leela steeled herself not to look down at the horrendous garbage littering the stream and banks, knowing she would gag if she did.

Across the bridge she saw a sign: *Gauri's Beauty Salon, For all your Needs. When all else fails*, Leela laughed to herself, *get your nails done*.

She turned down an unpaved lane. It was quieter off the main road, although a rickety rickshaw shot by, expelling smoke and fumes. As she neared the end, one of the houses held a small sign in the window identifying itself as *Gauri's*. She slid the steel bar that opened the gate, and entered through the door that was slightly ajar.

Inside was serene, and the tile floors were cool beneath her feet as she slipped her shoes onto the rack. No one came to greet her, so she climbed the stairs to the second floor. There in the middle of the room sat a blonde reading an Indian fashion magazine with her feet in a tub of water. Two skinny Indian girls in saris knelt at her feet. The only light was from the windows, and the walls were bare except for a fish-shaped clock that was stopped at 4:35. A plump Indian woman in *punjabi* dress approached smiling. The gold braid on her tunic matched that around the hem of the trousers, and her shiny black hair fanned out over her shoulders.

"Hello, madam," she said. "I am Gauri. How may I be of service?"

Leela pondered the list on the wall. Haircuts, color, leg waxing; everything was available, including a ten-dollar full-hour massage. She studied the offerings, hesitating.

"I would definitely recommend the pedicure," the blonde said, looked up from her reading. "I treat myself once a week." The kneeling girls were using tiny razors to scrape the calluses off the soles of her feet, and the woman winced as she spoke. "It's impossible to keep nice feet here. They can massage in all the rich creams in the world, and still they never get as clean or soft as they were back home."

Leela appraised the woman in front of her. She was a few years older, small-boned and slim, with carefully applied makeup and well-cared-for skin—quite beautiful, in fact. She was dressed like most Westerners in a *kurta* and draw-string pants, but somehow on her, they looked soft and elegant. Her hair was limp and thin. At least she's not perfect, Leela noticed with relief.

Gauri gave instruction in Hindi, and the two girls got up. One returned with a plastic chair for Leela; the other with a steaming tub. As Leela slipped her feet into the hot water, she felt the warmth travel up her body, branching up and spreading until she let out a sigh of contentment in spite of herself. One of the girls started massaging her neck, and Gauri walked over and added a drop of sandalwood oil to the water.

"Ah, now this is great," Leela said, relaxing back into her chair. She smiled at Gauri and looked back at the other woman. "Unless I'm imagining things, you seem like you've figured out how to make it work here."

"I've figured out a few things."

"I'm not sure I like it here," Leela blurted out. "I keep feeling overwhelmed, like I want to go home. Everything's so dirty, so strange—even bizarre!"

"The bizarreness never goes away, and that's the good news!" The blonde smiled at Leela. "Yeah, I get that feeling that I can't take another minute sometimes. By the way, my name's Kate." They exchanged nods. "It is distressing at times—the culture shock and all."

"I mean, there's lots of cool stuff here, and the ashram is beautiful and all, but—" Leela paused, self-conscious for a moment. "People aren't friendly or something. I finally met a guy yesterday, but before that it was three weeks without anyone barely even saying 'hi!' You're the first person I've met who's been open. Maybe it's me."

"Nah," Kate said. "It's not you. It's very hard to adjust. I've been here for almost a year and that feeling that it's too weird has never completely gone away." The girl at her feet was applying a pearled rose polish. "But you get into a groove, you know, find the things that you like to do, that remind you who you are. Like coming here to Gauri's. I'm not one of these backpacking hippies who are checking out all the ashrams on a grand tour after college. Even here in Spiritual Land I need to do the things that make me me. And thank god that at this ashram, what makes you you is permitted, within limits of course."

Leela closed her eyes as the girl massaged her legs and feet. She took in a deep draft of the sandalwood, and relaxed into the warmth, the pampering, and the girlfriend-ness of it all.

"You know what I do when I get that overpowering urge to go home?" Kate asked. "When I can't stand it another minute? I go for an hour-and-a-half mini-vacation in the West. The best thing is, it's only a five-minute ride from here. Would you like to come with me when we're done?"

THE TAXI DEPOSITED THEM AT THE HOLIDAY Inn. Two footmen in ceremonial dress and turbans opened the car doors and escorted the women into the hotel lobby. It was the first time Leela had felt refrigerated air since she had been in India. The bar's wood-paneled walls and tiled floors were soothing, affluent, designed for Western executives on expense accounts. As with hotel bars in the Midwest, there was a tiny dance floor encircled with disco lights. The TV above the bar was showing sports, only this being India, the game was cricket. It was immaculate and civilized, a holdout from the days of the British Raj.

A formal waiter wearing a starched white shirt and black tie appeared to take their order.

"*Kingfisher,* please."

"A martini," Kate said, lighting a cigarette. "Straight up."

"Certainly, madam," the waiter said, setting down tiny silver pots of peanuts and homemade potato chips, minuscule by American standards. "Would madam like that with or without ginger ale?"

"Never mind," Kate said. "Bring me a double *Bombay* on the rocks." She turned to Leela. "Now, tell me about the overwhelm."

"I don't know," Leela began. "From what I heard in Goa, I don't know if I thought all the men would be lined up to meet me or what." She drummed her fingers on the table. "I mean, I can be sitting at a table eating lunch, and someone will sit down and not even nod their head in greeting. All the guys I've seen here seem intelligent, gorgeous, affluent enough for foreign travel, and obviously they're on some kind of spiritual path; just my type, every single one of them. Which seems to intensify my depression; I feel like I'm holding on to hope like a bitch who won't let go of a bone."

"I hope you're at least somewhat of a bitch," Kate said, "because if you are, we have the potential to be friends." Leela was liking her more and more. "It's not you. You're not the first person to say that when they got here this ashram was the loneliest place on earth. After all they've heard, it's a colossal letdown." She let out a long measured exhale of smoke. "First of all, there's an expectation at the ashram to not interfere.

What you've experienced is it coming across as cold, but what it really is is people respecting each other's space. Like some people are here to go inside and be silent and meditate, and everyone respects and makes a space for that.

"Plus, everything's magnified here. Because it's an 'energy center,' a higher frequency or whatever, everything's more intense—your insecurities, your patterns, your fantasies and how much they differ from reality. All these people working on themselves attempting to grow, well, it creates a whirlpool, sucking everybody in. Or so they say. I'm not really into it myself."

"Yes! That's it! That's what I've felt." Leela felt a sense of well-being swell through her body. "It's really great running into you," she said. "There should be a welcome committee like you explaining things to new arrivals."

"Most people are met by a welcoming committee of another sort," Kate said. "So tell me your story. Where are you from?"

"Portland," Leela said, taking a sip of her *Kingfisher*. "I've been in this career for years working in HR. 'Human Relations' sounds people oriented, but it's really about making sure employees do what management wants and getting rid of those who don't. The company I'd been working at for ten years was sold, and when I was given the option to leave with a healthy severance package, I jumped at the chance." She poured more beer into her glass. "But then I had time to take stock: Here I was halfway through my life without a job or my Perfect Beloved or anything I thought I'd have by now, you know what I mean? Pretty bleak. So I decided to travel a bit and try to figure things out before I settle into the next thing. How about you?"

"Let's just say the divorce settlement was rather profitable. And his mom is keeping the kids while I figure out my next step." Leela watched as Kate's slender hand reached out and fished a single peanut from the bowl. "You know how it is those last years of marriage—hadn't had sex in years, and when we did it was dead. I heard about this place when I took a tantra weekend up in Marin County. I'm not interested in tantra per se; I just like being where there are trained men. Better in bed. Anyway, here at the ashram I'm taking dance classes and painting--when I'm not vegging. I guess I've stayed because the men are so good-looking."

"Yeah, what's up with that?" Leela said. "It's like they put out a net and only the 'tens' are allowed within a two mile radius. It's like rubbing sand in a reopened scar seeing so many gorgeous guys every day."

"Had a bit of man trouble?" Kate asked.

"Who hasn't?" Leela said. "I was married once but that was a long time ago. Since then it's been one dysfunctional thing after another. I just don't seem to know how to find or keep a decent relationship. Plus, I keep freaking out about how hard it is to attract someone now that we're older, and what that means about the future. I just can't go there. It's too upsetting."

"There are so many guys here who cares? It's about developing a place inside where you know who you are, and you can get who you want. You'll learn about that and a lot of other things here," Kate said. "This place can be a gas—just give it time to snap into gear." She took another sip of her cocktail and lit a cigarette. "Have you been to the Mozart Café yet? That's where all the action is."

"That place?" Leela said. "I stuck my head in once, but it seemed so sleazy I left."

"That's what I thought at first too," Kate said. "All those hippies selling drugs at the one end. But it really is the center of the known universe. Everybody on earth ends up there sooner or later. If not in this life, in another one."

"If you say so."

"We'll go there sometime. You'll see. It's one of the best ways to meet people." Kate said, "Ah, it's such a relief to talk with another American. This struggle of having to translate and say everything twice, it makes me exhausted. You haven't experienced that yet? You'll see, most of the people here have surprisingly good English, yet it's still tiring. With a native speaker, one can relax." She flicked a stray peanut off the table.

Leela looked around the bar. Two American men with beer bellies bursting against their Oxford shirts had come in, changed the channel, and were high-fiving a soccer goal on the TV. She noticed six waiters standing at attention for the pleasure of the four patrons in the bar. It was so clean, so civilized, so different from the cacophonous mess outside. "Okay," she said. "I think I can stand it if I can get away to this place every now and then."

"You should go to the dance at the ashram tonight," Kate said. "They're usually a blast. We can meet for lunch tomorrow, and you can tell me all about it."

"You're not going?"

"No, I have a date with this hot French guy. *Ooh la la*. But you go. Maybe you'll see your new fling there."

The waiter was standing in front of them. His pitch-black hair was slicked to one side, his manner obsequious to the point of cartoon. "Madams," he said, clicking his heels, "May I get you anything else?" When they said no, he stiffened his spine like that of a palace guard, bowed as though they were baronesses of the empire, spun around and headed off.

Kate lifted her eyebrow at Leela, and they collapsed on the banquette in peals of laughter. Leela tried to duck under the table so the waiter wouldn't see her, but gave it up as a lost cause. This full belly laugh was the first she had had since leaving home.

LEELA FLUNG HER ARMS TO THE RIGHT, THEN
to the left. She dropped to a squat and rocked her knees
from side to side. *Djembe* drums pounded while the singer's feverish voice inspired all kinds of arcane movements.
Around the meditation hall, dancers were lost in their own
worlds, ardently responding to sounds they had never
heard before.

The ashram sponsored a nightly world-beat danceathon,
or a trance party, or eclectic nights with rock or rap thrown
in for seasoning. Leela looked to her left and observed a tall
angular man whose long hair was piled on top of his head,
whirling nonstop. As she watched, his arms moved rhythmi-
cally out and then back in, almost embracing himself. *How
does he do that?* she wondered. Next in her line of vision was
a Black woman wearing a huge headwrap standing alongside
the edge of the dancers, bobbing her head with the beat. A
couple was incongruously performing the Lindy hop. There
were so many interesting-looking individuals, and no one

but the couple seemed to be interacting; everyone was creating their own individual dance world.

The music shifted to an Arabic belly-dance number, and Leela decided to more fully check out the room. She began to maneuver her way around the hall, scanning to see if Ian was there. She sashayed closer to the door that led to the coffee bar, then circled by the one that opened out onto the walkway. There were lots of good-looking men, but no Ian, and no one else who particularly caught her fancy.

She moved closer to the center of the room and there at its heart a man appeared spotlighted in her vision. He was moving gracefully in his mapped-out private dance floor, and he radiated a glowing vitality. He had no body fat, and his toned arms were defined and buff. His hair was on the long side which added to its sensuality.

As she got closer she could see a mustache that was not noticeable from far away because it was light and because he would have looked better without it. Actually, without it his face might have been too feminine, he was that pretty. Up close she could also see that his skin had seen too much sun so was a little coarse, but at a distance it was tanned and lovely.

She watched his feline grace and how at home he appeared to be in his body. True, he was handsome, but it wasn't only that, there was a raw sexiness that crept out of his pores. *The most attractive person on the planet*, she thought, *is an older person who has maintained their looks and vitality, coupled with increased self-knowledge and power. He looks like he might be the Perfect Beloved,* Leela thought.

He suddenly looked up and their eyes met. Leela stared back, transfixed. Holding her gaze, he smiled, then winked. Leela felt shy and dropped her eyes. *Was it happening? Love at first sight?* She looked back, but no, he had danced on.

EELA AND KATE SAT HAVING LUNCH AT THE ashram's Jade cafeteria. Blue umbrellas covered the tables on the leafy terrace, sheltering the diners from the sun. The ice had melted in their glasses almost as soon as they sat down, and there was very little breeze. Leela picked at her tofu lasagna that was a bit dry, while Kate ate the cheese version with a side dish of spiced lentils.

"*Ooh la la,*" Kate said. "Pierre was all I hoped he'd be. *Très magnifique!* I hope your new friend Ian is half as wonderful as he. By the way, did you see Mevlana's husband last night at the dance?"

"Husband?" Leela pushed the lasagna away. She had no appetite for food in this heat. "I didn't know she was married."

"Yeah, he's a dancer, that's why I thought you might have seen him. And a musician, guitar, I think. He's so . . . oh look, there's Her Royal Highness."

Leela followed Kate's finger to a woman surrounded by an entourage of admirers. The circle around her was a hive of activity, people vibrating like glass panes in an earthquake as they came and left. The woman herself was at least six feet tall. Her blue-black hair curled back from her pale white cheeks in little wings, and even from a distance, one could see that her pointy face was lined and no longer taut. Her body was pudgy in the middle though her limbs were thin.

"That's her?" Leela asked, watching as yet another man came up to greet Mevlana. The two embraced with a hoot of mutual recognition.

"Yeah, it was a shock to me too when I first saw her," Kate said. "My god, that Jennifer Aniston hairdo was out of date twenty years ago, let alone now." She brushed her own hair away from her face where it stuck from sweat. "And her hair color, so obviously dyed. No one who's over fifty has hair that color, give me a break." She reached for a cigarette. "Why doesn't she get some work done, a little tuck here, a nip there? She's got a public to think about." They watched as Mevlana began walking toward an empty table, people moving out of her path like from the wake of a boat. "Like she's royalty or something," Kate sniffed, exhaling smoke.

Leela had to admit that observing Mevlana in person, she seemed not at all what she had imagined a famous tantra teacher would look like. Despite the throng around her, she seemed too old and out of it. "I don't know," Leela said. "I'm not sure I want to attend a group with her as the leader, despite all the buzz."

"HERE YOU ARE," IAN SAID, AS HE APPROACHED her in the walkway. "I was afraid we'd lost each other." He slipped his arm around her waist, and Leela felt the heat of their connection warm her body. "I want to invite you to come to the swimming pool this afternoon. A bunch of us are getting together, and it'll be fun," he said, stroking her arm softly.

Hanging out at swimming pools was something Leela regularly avoided, as she disliked exposing her less-than-perfect body to the critical eye of strangers. "Thanks, but how about something else? I don't really like lying in the sun, skin cancer and all that. I don't like the scene there."

Ian was staring at her. "How do you know you don't like it if you've never been there with me?"

He had a point, so she ran around all morning to the little Indian boutiques surrounding the ashram trying to find a bathing suit that was halfway flattering. When she got to the pool, Ian was poured into a chaise lounge, his skin rosier than it had been the night before. Accompanying him was the beautiful girl from Goa who was apparently named Nicole, a very large guy in all respects who introduced himself as Brandon, and Ethan, wearing black shorts and appearing hungover.

The pool was a colossal kidney bean landscaped with sweeping date palms and jacarandas. Thirty or so people were lounging in white deck chairs or lying on mats, lazing away the afternoon. A few were swimming quietly, backstroking or dawdling on air mattresses.

"Dieter's party got busted last night," Brandon said. He picked up a booklet and began fanning his face. "I wasn't there but I heard they confiscated his equipment."

"Jeez, another one bites the dust," Ian said. Leela noticed that Ethan had angled his chair away from them and disappeared behind his shades.

Nicole was applying sunscreen lavishly to her legs and feet. "Hey, has Andrew gotten back from Goa?" she asked.

"Haven't seen him yet. But that doesn't necessarily mean anything. You know how he disappears from time to time."

"Who's Andrew?" Leela asked.

"Never mind," Ian said. "You don't need to know."

"Ian!" Nicole exclaimed. "You can be so possessive. She gets to know who he is. She'll probably meet him anyway. Andrew's the one all the girls want to be with."

"And all the guys want to be," Brandon said.

"Oh, *that* guy," Leela said. "But who is he?"

"Rumor has it that he and Mevlana were a tantric couple once. She went on to teach groups, and now he teaches individually. Or so people say. Nobody knows really. It's all very mysterious."

"Don't you worry about it," Ian said. "We're having our own little tantra group right here by the pool today." He leaned back in his chair and closed his eyes.

The afternoon ambled on for a while, too long for Leela's taste, and finally when the sun's angle had shaded their area, it was time to move on.

"After we clean up, we'll go for dinner," Ian said, veering

off toward the men's shower. Leela entered the women's, bracing herself against the mildewed scent of matted hairs in the drain plus Lysol. She looked into her bag and realized she had forgotten her shampoo. *I'll try to catch Ian before he's all soapy and wet,* she thought. Turning the corner, she started to call his name but stopped dead in her tracks.

There stood Ian not showering but talking to a magazine-perfect Barbie girl, a flawless Swedish fantasy figure. He was obviously into her, what man wouldn't be? Leela watched as Ian reached out and touched the goddess's wrist, while her eyes widened and her chin tilted coyly to one side. She was obviously into him too. The sparks that were flying between them, if it were night, would have lit up the whole sky.

The real issue, though, was that the way he was flirting with the perfect Swede was exactly the same way he had flirted with her, like a practiced art, something he was obviously very good at. A spasm cut deeply into Leela's solar plexus, and she turned around without the shampoo not saying anything at all.

"WHAT'S WRONG?" IAN WAS TRYING TO LOOK into her eyes.

"Nothing."

The cucumber *raita* that accompanied the curry was not any thicker than the silence between them. Leela was aware that her unspoken jealousy and anger were totally screwing up dinner. *It was none of her business who a man she barely knew talked to, it had just seemed like he wouldn't want to get it on with someone else because they had something going. But did they really have something going? How could they when he might be off to China or Thailand or Jakarta in three or five or ten weeks?* She knew that once again she had set herself up again for a heartbreak based on ephemera.

Still, she didn't say anything. *You might lose the guy if you do.*

After dinner, he headed the bike to her place, not his, then idled outside her door waiting for her to dismount. "I need some space," he said. And he was gone.

LEELA ENTERED THE WALKWAY OUTSIDE THE morning meditation scouting for one of the rare chairs. Oh my god, she saw him—there he was, the Perfect Guy. The one she had seen at the dance, that most beautiful perfect guy, sitting there with an empty chair beside him. *Do I have the nerve to go up and ask him if I can sit there?* Leela wondered. While she stood hesitating, Mevlana walked up, kissed Mr. Perfect on the lips, and took the seat herself. *Damn her*, thought Leela, *damn*.

"Hey girl," she heard Kate call out in a mock whisper. "Over here." Looking around, she saw Kate sitting under a palm frond the size of Ethiopia. She made her way over as

Kate was finishing the last of her banana and peanut butter on toast.

"Hey, can I talk to you?" Leela asked. "Something's happened with this guy I'm seeing that I don't understand how to handle."

"Okay if it's later?" Kate answered. "I'm already late for class. Here, quick, before I go, feast your eyes on a rare specimen of male beauty--right over there. I have to say that Bashir makes up in looks for whatever Mevlana lacks."

She was pointing to The Perfect Guy. "That's Mevlana's husband?" Leela said. Envy moved through her like quicksilver. "But he's so much younger than she is, so much prettier. How does she do that?"

Kate shrugged. "Leave it to Mevlana to have snagged the hottest man on the planet. Look, I'm leaving. Take my chair." She stood up. "We'll meet up at the Mozart later, okay? I'll turn you on to its charms." Leela nodded and sat down, as Kate tripped off to her dance class.

What does Mevlana have anyway? Leela wondered, staring at the couple. They were sitting so close their heads were almost touching. Leela watched Mevlana take a spoonful of food and flirtatiously slip it into Bashir's mouth, slowly licking her lips. He began to chew as if he had never tasted anything so sweet, his eyes never leaving hers. They were all smiles, and Leela saw the lines in Mevlana's face soften and blur. Bashir slid his spoon into the grinning half-moon of papaya, its orange flesh standing stark against the shiny black seeds. Her mouth received the morsel; juice dribbled down her chin. He reached over and licked the juice off her face, then moved his tongue to her lips where they engaged in a long tropical kiss. Leela dropped her fork. It was somehow the sweetest, most innocently open thing she had ever seen, the way they were just eating each other up.

That's an intimacy I've never seen between a man and a woman before, she thought. *Not with any of my previous lovers, not with my husband, not between any of my friends, and certainly not when I was growing up.* It was sweet and innocent, but also knowing and mature, neither of them hiding or afraid or power tripping, but out there and risking and present. *That's what I want,* Leela thought, *what Mevlana has.* She suddenly wanted it like she'd never wanted anything before. *I want to learn whatever she has to teach; I am willing to sit at her feet.* She could hardly believe what she was hearing: it was almost as if the words were speaking themselves.

She looked back at the lovers. They had forgotten their food and were giggling like children who had pulled a secret prank. The sun shone through the bamboo throwing a spotlight onto their space. They had stopped and were breathing deeply, holding and caressing the unblinking gaze between them. It stopped Leela's breath seeing them like this, sitting together in such a silent intimacy. Bashir looked at Mevlana like she was the most beautiful woman on earth, and for an instant, Leela could see that she was.

A WHISPER OF SMOKE CURLED UP FROM THE remains of the funeral pyre. Black chunks of wood, or were they charred bones, lay scattered among the ash, burned down level with the sides of the pit. A slight wind blew a curtain of soot in the direction of the building on the left, its wall emblazoned with a large red swastika.

Although Leela had been told that the Nazis had inverted the Indian image for their own uses, and that the Hindi sign symbolized the turning of the wheel of life, still, a spasm of shock registered whenever the broken cross announced itself so boldly.

She turned her head to her right. Three more pits had been dug into the stone flooring, spaced in a perfect line. None of them hinted of recent activity. Behind lay a grassy slope rising up to the road above obscured by bottle palms and eucalyptus trees.

In front of her, Leela observed the panoramic view of the river flowing downstream toward the ocean as it had for

millennia. The view from her bench was pastoral: the washerwomen toiling in their brightly colored saris, the cowherds
and their charges along the banks. A few lazy clouds drifted
in the lapis-blue sky.

How calming to sit in this place where death was accepted as part of life, not a shocking intrusion as it would have
been in the West, rather, it was a mesmerizing reminder that
everyone would someday turn to ash, everyone, including
herself and all she loved and all she had ever loved in her life.
Here in India, everyone's body met its end as cinders in a pit
at the burning *ghats,* an integral part of village life.

Leela looked down at the dog that had parked itself beside
her. It hadn't stopped scratching the entire time she had been
sitting here. As skinny as all the other dogs that appeared dead
by the side of Laxmi Road, its white and orange fur was muted
by layers of dust. On the flank where the incessant scratching
was taking place, all its hair and some of the flesh were gone. It
was so dirty and mangy and the open sore so raw there was no
way any human being other than Saint Francis would touch it.
Despite this, the animal kept a perfect dog smile on its face, as
if it hadn't given up on the possibility of human affection. Still
hoping for a miracle, it just kept scratching and scratching.

Love has failed me in this life, Leela thought. *Or, the real
truth about it is, I have failed at love.* Richard, Tom, and the
others lay strung out like a broken strand of ersatz pearls
stretching all the way back to her teens. All had started out
with such promise; all had ended so fruitlessly. She had never been able to get it right, not even close.

Leela ran her hand up her thigh, where it came to rest on her abdomen. *So many years of trying to get it right*, she thought. All the women's magazines promising that if you got thin enough, that if you bought the right clothes, or had glowing enough skin or shiny hair, or were young enough, love would find you. She had tried to fix her body, her looks, get in shape, and it had helped, but it hadn't worked. She thought of all the therapy she had sat in for countless hours, analyzing her relationship with her father, her mother, her fear of men, watching her patterns. In the seventies it was demanded that one be promiscuous and "unattached," then in the eighties she had gotten married, each partner bound to their own career. There were the foot-long shelves of self-help books promising that if you learned to become totally independent, then you would be worthy of being in a relationship. *Wasn't that a contradiction? How did learning to be alone give one the skills for intimacy?*

The loss of her job? Essentially, it didn't matter. She had thought the promise had been that if she got a cool career and made more money, she would attract better men. Oh, there had been certain satisfactions in molding herself into a person capable of a successful career, able to make more money than most, and it had been fun buying Dolce & Gabbana. But the "better men" had not materialized. It was all torn wallpaper on the walls of the house she had been longing to live in all her life, the house of love.

Every single thing she had ever done had been in an attempt to attract the Perfect Beloved. And here, halfway through her life, his presence was as illusory as it had ever been.

Why had she been brought here? How was it that her life had led her to this most unlikely of places? Here where it seemed she was suddenly back at the beginning, not even knowing the basics of how to connect. Here at the ashram, despite that the men were all handsome and affluent and on some sort of path, further learning was required to understand even the most rudimentary social skills.

This is the time, she decided. *This is the place. I am going to go for it totally. I am going to heal myself of whatever is in the way of my learning to love someone, of whatever it is in me that I haven't been able to attract the Perfect Beloved.* A tear started its slide down her face. *No matter what, I will go for it. Whatever it takes. I believe in what Mevlana has to impart. I surrender to the higher wisdom of this place, to this teaching, to the ancient secrets in modern-day form. Whoever is sent to me, I will do my best to love. If pain is required, I am not afraid. I will learn and be fearless and go for it all the way until I am finished, until I learn what it is that I need to know.*

No, she thought, *this is crazy. What am I thinking? I've got to get out of here, and fast.* First she would finish touring all the celebrated Indian tourist spots: the Taj Mahal, Rajasthan, Varnasi, and then go home. Leela circled her belly with her hand while an image appeared of a long expanse of a solitary evening, another glass of wine being poured, a double feature on Netflix. *Go back home to what?* Her empty apartment? To another job she hated in a field she had no respect for? She thought of Sara and Mark and Jillian; they were worth going back for. But as supportive friends as they were, they had their own lives and couldn't fix what was wrong with hers.

Other images arose: Bashir dancing with his sinuous movements, his lithe grace. The beauty of the early morning dew on the palm fronds outside the meditation hall. Mevlana's face in the presence of Love. Leela suddenly sensed the smell of papaya and of mint, and felt the humidity of the air against her skin.

She looked up at the burning sun. The surrounding aureole seemed to be vibrating with passion and life force. It would blaze on forever no matter what happened to her, whether she ever found love or not. But with her own life half over, and with the complete insignificance of it to anyone but herself, Leela knew that her life would not be worth living if she did not go for this totally.

To her left some of the ashes were still smoking. Someone's body had been burned the night before. Someone's life had ended, and their family and the village had honored their passing. *All as it was, all as it ever would be.* As would someday soon enough be her time.

The dog was still scratching. A trio of bats passed through her line of vision as she gazed out at the river. Bats didn't usually come out much in the day, but there they were. The sun nodded. It had heard her resolve, her yearning. Leela stood up. She would do it. She began the walk back to the registration center to put down her money for Mevlana's yearlong tantra seminar.

tHE SKY HAD REACHED THE MOMENT OF DUSK when the evening lamps snapped on. In the meditation hall as she passed, Leela could hear a DJ practicing for tonight's dance. She turned a bend in the walkway and there was Ian standing right in front of her.

"I want to talk to you before the group begins," he said. He motioned her to sit on a bench by a grove of bamboo. Leela wished he would put his arm around her so she could feel how perfectly she fit underneath it, but he did not. "Even though we have a little upset right now, we have a good connection, you and I," he began. "Who knows what will happen?" His eyes were soft-focused yet direct. "I want to make sure there is no misunderstanding between us. We are not going to be partners for the group. We are both free to be with other people."

"Okay." Leela's eyes widened as the bleached-blonde Japanese girl sauntered by.

"Okay, good then. I'll see you tomorrow in group." He got up to walk away.

Something suddenly occurred to Leela that was totally new—instead of sitting around trying to figure out everything by herself or with her girlfriends, she would ask Ian to help her, even if it upset him or made him mad, or if it made her not a cool chick or whatever the consequences. She wanted to learn whatever the cost. So she stood up and asked him to talk with her, there in the shaded grove under the moon.

"Ian," Leela said. "I want to learn to do it more like you do."

He didn't say anything, but she had definitely succeeded in getting his attention.

"I don't know how to do this in-the-moment kind of thing. I know we haven't been together that long, but it's been good, and I don't know how to not want that to continue. I mean, I get that we're not going to be together for the long term, but I don't know how to not want that."

She could barely see his face in the darkness, but his voice was tender as he spoke. "You have to be in the moment. That's how it was then, and that's not how it is now. Right now things are not good between us, so I don't want it in my life. If things get good again, we'll see what happens. Besides, you have to remember that all relationships end. It's just a matter of time."

"What do you mean?"

"They all end. One person moves on, or the other one does. Even if they last more than fifty years, one of the people dies."

"So how do I learn to do it more like you do?"

"You have to know that you can't make anything happen. If someone wants to be with you, they do; if they don't, there's nothing you can do about it. You can't make anything happen—I know that. That's the difference between you and me."

The air was chill and she wished she had her jacket. In the heat of the day it had seemed like it would never grow cold again. She heard the music from the dance starting up in the background, but it didn't move her. "There must be some people you want more than others. The ones who break your heart." She was imagining him with some girl he had left in Germany or Japan, imagining him still pining for her, *though not for me*, she thought.

"Of course there are," he said, "but even then I can't make anything happen."

She thought of the men she had known. The difference with Ian was, although he obviously knew the techniques of an accomplished womanizer, his heart was amazingly open to the moment, and he was available for this fragile emotional healing. It was safe to be vulnerable with him and tell him the truth about where she really was.

"Then how do you stay in the moment with what's happening and not project out into the future or the past?"

"You watch your breath and center yourself, breathe. That's why we've been doing all this meditating."

He was regarding her with real affection which made her look away, more embarrassed than if he had been rejecting and cold. It was he who knew more than her, despite her grab bag of sexual tricks. He knew about love and intimacy existing in the moment, not in some mental fantasy life. She could feel herself becoming somebody else; her arms being torn from her body, her heart ripped open, parts of herself that had needed to die for a long time facing their own demise. She was participating in an amputation, and although it was cold and clinical and harsh, it was exactly what needed to happen.

"I feel like I'm about to jump off a big cliff, and I'm scared. I need some help."

He looked at her kindly but wasn't going to take the bait. "Maybe you'll find out it's only a one-foot drop."

She had to admit this idea was pretty intoxicating. What if she was only manufacturing drama? "What do you mean by that?"

"You think it's a big cliff, but it's only a one-foot drop." He paused and looked over at the road. "Anything else? Do you feel complete? Because I'm going to get going."

As she watched him leave, she again felt the longing for home where things were familiar, where she could just relax with all her familiar dramas, and her friends would console her by saying this guy was just another asshole, and she could go on as usual believing that there was no love out there for her. But no, she had made a commitment to stay and heal herself of this, and this was where she was going to be until it was finished.

OUTSIDE UNDER THE TREES STOOD A LONG
line of aspirants, fifty in all. Small pods of outgo-
ing types were murmuring among themselves, but mostly
people stood nervously, awkward in their aloneness. It was
twenty minutes past the starting time of ten o'clock and the
tension buzzed loudly in Leela's ear.

At last the line began to move and one by one, they
entered through an archway flanked by a man and woman
in white kimonos. As it was her turn to be greeted, Leela
met the man's eyes which burned a deep chestnut brown,
matching his tousled hair and sideburns. He winked and
squeezed her arm as she passed, while she checked out his
nametag: "Travis." *Hot*, she thought, returning his smile. *If
he's part of this group, good chance it'll rock.*

She left her shoes and bag in the rack in the corridor,
then entered a spacious room painted a soft petal pink.
Downy pillows lined the walls and a pile of foam mattresses
was stacked in one corner. Two granite lovers carved into

a perpetual embrace stood at one end, and at the other Mevlana and Bashir sat on a raised dais on brocade cushions, flowers and bowls of fruit on small tables beside them. To their right was a table holding an elaborate sound system and a mélange of instruments: congas, various rhythm makers, a saxophone, and guitars. Other men and women in white kimonos were offering each participant a jasmine flower which Leela held up to her nose with a deep inhale.

They were all in the room now. Leela scrutinized the group, which appeared to be half men and half women. She saw Ian next to the perfect Swede, and her stomach clenched. There were Brandon and Nicole from the pool, and the bleached-blonde Japanese girl next to the dark-haired boy Leela had danced with in Goa. He was staring straight at her, but Leela quickly diverted her gaze, pretending she hadn't seen. She preferred to admire the stocky man with short-cropped hair, and the slender one whose hair was wispy and shoulder-length. The handsome, unfriendly gym rat who had ignored her in the walkway sat right up front. Several heads in the room were silver, and one man was obese.

Bashir waved his hand, the musicians stopped, and a track of irrepressible African highlife began. Mevlana stood up and the men and women in kimonos began encouraging everyone to dance. *How embarrassing*, Leela thought. She forced out a little side-to-side movement but it didn't take hold, and from the looks of people in the room, they weren't feeling it either. Everyone kept to themselves, not looking around, although as in every crowd, a few gregarious sorts were performing exhibitionistically up front.

Bashir stepped off the dais and began to dance. When his energy entered the mix, everything transformed. The way he so fully inhabited his body was infectious, and participants loosened up and started going for it. The men began to relax, the women to feel more flirtatious, everyone feeling less competitive, less needing to prove anything, more feminine in his presence. Leela began to find her groove. Beads of sweat became visible on faces; a light smell of perspiration and grunts of pleasure filled the room. The statue of the lovers was the only still point amidst the swirling action.

Abruptly the music stopped. There was silence. The participants took their places around the room in a circle with Mevlana and Bashir at the head.

"Welcome," Mevlana said, looking regal in her chandelier earrings and glass-beaded tunic. "Welcome to the yearlong seminar. You are brave souls, and I salute your search and what it took for you to arrive at this place." She raised her hands in the folded position of *namaste* and scanned the circle slowly, greeting each one in the room.

"All of us in this group are here to learn the art of opening more fully to love. I realize some of you are here because you've heard tantra is about sex, and if that is why you're here, perhaps this news brings a little disappointment?" Nervous snickers erupted around the room. "Tantra includes sex," Mevlana continued, "but it is really about love. In the West there are abundant tantra classes that will teach you positions and how to have bigger orgasms, and you will probably achieve that as part of this group, but that is not our purpose. True tantra is about the transcendence of sex, to evolve beyond, not staying in it. Our work is to so enliven ourselves that we open to divine ecstasy, so that we may become blissful bodies of light."

Sounds good, Leela thought. She crossed her legs in the other direction. *I wish there weren't so many pretty young girls in this group. How can I compete?*

"The group will take place in ten-day intensives," Mevlana went on, "and you will go out and live your lives in between. In this case, however, it won't be the same as normal life, because you are still enrolled in the group and you are still here at the ashram which is an energy vortex. As in all of life, the energy will follow your commitment, and as you encounter others, everything that happens to you is part of your learning. Don't think anything is different, or not included, or extracurricular. It's all part of the same whole. Your learning experience. Your tantra group. Your life. You may have noticed something of the fine caliber of people who come here; this *sangha* or spiritual community is here to support your growth.

"Enough sitting!" She glanced at Bashir who stood up without a word and walked over to the music player. "Let us begin this time together with something you will practice each day for the next year, Kundalini Meditation. This is a beautiful way to loosen the body, to shake off tension, and to increase your aliveness." Mevlana stood and smoothed down the folds of her *kurta.* "It is said that for a woman who has trouble with the orgasm, if she does the Kundalini Meditation every day for a month—" Mevlana smiled. "There will be no more problem."

The group digested this information. "There are four parts to the meditation, each fifteen minutes long," Mevlana continued. "First the shaking." She anchored her feet firmly on the ground. "Allow your feet to feel the energy that comes up from the earth, which then rises and shakes the pelvis. The rest of the body follows. This is wild abandon shaking; be free with it; shake everything out.

"The music will then change to signify the second part, which is to dance. Always, in tantra, we dance! The music will change again for the third part, sitting. This is a beautiful opportunity to be with what is, and feel the perfection of the present moment. The music will stop and for the final part, the sitting will continue in silence.

"It is best to do the meditation with eyes closed, and if it is too difficult not to spy on your neighbor, you may take a blindfold from one of the assistants." The people in white were standing with blindfolds in their hands. *That is way too kinky*, Leela decided. *I want to retain the option to look at people if I want.* "Now," Mevlana said, "no more words, let us stand up and help nudge the kundalini awake."

Bashir flipped the music on and came to the front of the room. Unseen hands were striking the keys of a xylophone, back and forth, back and forth, back and forth. Leela experienced the movement travel up through her legs, but she felt stiff and awkward. Peering out from under her eyelids, she looked around the room and saw that other people were moving artlessly as well. "Don't do the shaking," Mevlana called out, walking among the gesticulating people with a microphone. "Let the shaking 'do' you. Feel the energy come up from the earth and move your body. All you need to do is let go." *I can see how this could wake up the pelvis*, Leela thought, feeling how tight her own was.

The music changed to drumming and maracas backed by a haunting woodwind. Leela found herself dancing freely, without restraint, and was surprised when she opened her eyes a crack to witness that some people were barely moving. "Keep your eyes closed," Mevlana directed. "Stay inside with your own process." *It is easier*, Leela thought, *when no one can see you.*

Tibetan bells and gongs reverberated out into the silence. The group sat down as one to listen to the music. One bell rang out, then another, overlapping. Then came a harmonium, a harp being strummed, a flute coming in at the most exquisite moment, sounding like the first sound in a clear morning. Leela felt the corners of her eyes moisten.

Then the music stopped and all was silent. "Listen," Mevlana whispered. "This is the silence behind the sound in every moment."

When the meditation was over, the assistants helped the participants rearrange themselves back into the big circle. Leela noticed that faces were flushed, and that she was finding the people in the group more attractive.

"All right," Mevlana said. "This Kundalini Meditation is helpful for everyone; it shakes things up. You feel more alive now than when you came in, yes? Very good. Now. One more thing we must attend to, and then we will break for lunch." She paused and scrutinized the room. It fell silent, as quiet as the darkest of outer space.

"There are many things that will happen in this group that you will be sworn never to tell. The exercises you will practice are powerful, and after you experience them, you will see that it is important for all future students to be able to approach the technique with a fresh mind. You are free to tell people about your process—about what happens for you—but one of the requirements for participating in this group is that there will be things you will be asked never to reveal to any living soul." Leela felt a cold draft graze her cheek as she looked at Mevlana and Bashir sitting in front of them, the keepers of the mysteries.

"You may not feel that you can keep this promise," Mevlana continued. "That is okay. You are free to leave now with a full refund, no questions asked. Anyone who wants to go can do so. There are other ways you can learn tantra, but not here with me."

No one got up. It seemed to Leela that the room was holding its breath.

Mevlana said, "I will go around the room now and check with each of you if you are willing to swear the oath of secrecy."

The first one on her right was a slender Asian man and she looked deeply into his eyes. "Are you willing to forever until your death keep secret the teachings in this group? Share only your own growth experiences but not how you got them?" Her gaze penetrated deep into the man's soul, searching for his character and his truth.

He looked back and solemnly said, "I will." It was almost a marriage vow.

Mevlana went around the room to each one, Ian, the blonde Japanese girl, the boy Leela had danced with, all the others, one by one. Leela looked at each participant, wondering, while she awaited her turn.

Mevlana got to her. "And you, do you swear?"

Leela took a deep gulp of air. Her resolve was firm. She was willing to do whatever it took to learn the secrets Mevlana knew. She swore never to tell.

LEELA HAD TO SPEND THE REST OF THE DAY watching Ian with the perfect Swede doing all kinds of affectionate things. She began to cry, right in front of everyone, and just kept sobbing as if it would never stop, letting it all come out, all the heartbreaks of her life running out of her like the blood draining from a gangster who had been shot. All she could do was just keep breathing, let it run its course; try not to stop the flow. It nearly broke her heart, *but,* she thought, *that's the point, isn't it? Why should my heart get broken over a guy I just met? I don't care how strong the connection was.* All her life she had been protecting herself from this very thing, and the toughest part was that he still liked her, and she still liked him. In the West, all this would be hidden, taking place behind your back, and you would have to be really angry and make the guy out to be wrong. But here it was just a guy you liked who liked you who had met someone else he liked more. A simple story.

LEELA ENTERED THE MOZART FOR HER PRE-appointed meeting with Kate. Could this be the same café she had ruled out previously? The place was jamming, the noise an uproar, cigarette smoke hazing the air. Every seat was taken, and by the most bohemian crowd she had seen since Goa. Skin was showing everywhere: boys' biceps, girls' cleavages. There was the clatter of coffee cups and the sound of laughter, and the standing-room-onlies prowling the aisles. Leela scanned and finally found Kate in a huddle with two matching men.

"Hey, Kate," Leela said, feeling extraneous as she stood there, an interruption at their little *ménage à trois*.

Kate looked up. "Hey!" She smiled as she blew smoke out the side of her mouth and waved her hand to join them. "Leela here is from Mevlana's group," she said to the young skinhead beside her.

"Always room for another tantra girl," he said, squeezing out a tiny space beside him. "Sit yourself down right next to me."

"Are you guys twins?" Leela asked. They were identical with their nearly bald heads, their one-day's-growth beards, and the shrunken T-shirts clinging to their concave chests.

"Equally adorable," Kate said, reaching out and patting the thigh of the one next to her. "Which one should I choose?"

"Don't make me jealous," the other said. Someone from another table let out a war whoop and laughter exploded.

Leela examined the finished plates of food on the table and realized she hadn't had lunch. "I'm going to grab something to eat before I join you," she said. "Anybody want anything while I'm up?"

She made her way through the motley crowd to the counter. The handwritten menu above the pastry case was composed of items one would find at any gourmet health food establishment back home, almost. There were seven choices of types of veggie burger served with salad, sprouts, and grated carrot, vegetarian lasagna, pizza, and all manner of egg dishes. There were freshly squeezed juices including shots of wheatgrass, hot ginger tea, and multiple varieties of coffee. On the counter were rows of hand-wrapped packages of supplements: spirulina, flaxseeds, and honey from exotic places like Bhutan. They really have it down what Western travelers like, Leela thought to herself. She diverted her eyes from the pastry case filled with European delicacies: croissants, strudels, cheesecakes, barley cookies dipped in chocolate. She didn't want to be tempted.

While waiting for her espresso to brew, Leela looked at

the hand-painted advertisements for various entrepreneurs that lined the walls of the café. There was the Seven-Day Colon Cleansing Program, Dr. Tsenpo's Tibetan Acupuncture Clinic, a craniosacral massage school, and the Izizi Boutique. When she was handed her coffee she picked her way back to Kate's little clique.

"See, I told you," Kate said. The two men looked at her expectantly, hanging on her every word. "This place is very sex, drugs, and rock'n'roll, isn't it?"

Leela grinned. "It's growing on me," she said. "I can see how someone could come to love it. There's a certain . . . aphrodisiac quality."

"Yes!" Kate said. "You can come here any time, day or night, and find a flirtation, a raisin crumb cake, or if you are of that persuasion, drugs of any flavor. Everybody's here—it's where we all hang out. Tantra people like you, adventurous people like me –"

"Let's hear it for adventure," one of the twins said, leaning in close.

"There's the yoga crowd as well," Kate went on. "This town is also the home of the famous Saraswati Yoga Institute which is more your traditional ashram. When the students there get tired of the mediocrity, they come here to spice things up. See those two over there?" Leela followed her finger to a couple hunkered together, looking pale and lost as if they had stumbled into the wrong party.

"Yeah, the 'real meditators,'" the boy said. "The ones who don't come here for the sex."

Kate elbowed him in the ribs. "You young guys are so endlessly horny," she said. "And we love it." She turned back to Leela. "Sometimes over the course of their stay these people get laid and loosen up, but most of the time they just return to their 'real' ashram where celibacy is considered a virtue."

"I volunteer to help convince the next lost yoga girl to stay and join us," said the man next to Leela. She had noticed finally that he had an earring while his brother did not. "And, I'm still working on my strategy to do Mevlana."

"Do? As in fuck?"

"The ultimate fuck," the young man said.

"The penultimate notch in your belt," Kate said. "That's what you're after."

"As in trophy?" Leela had never considered such a thing. "I didn't know older women could be rock stars you would want to 'do.'"

"Are you kidding? I'd do her or any of the other gorgeous older babes around here. They're so hot. My dream is to be with all of them." He grinned. "All of *you*."

Leela tried to digest this information as the waiter delivered her veggie burger. "Help yourself to these fries," Leela said. "I'm not going to eat them. Too fattening."

The twin with the earring grabbed a fry. "Not to change the subject, but has anybody told you the story about these guys who work here? They've all immigrated from Nepal. Rumor has it they're all in one flat—all these gay boys sleeping together in one room."

"Very cozy, I'm sure."

No-Earring looked at his watch and started to get up. "As much as we'd like to stay, we better go if we don't want to be late." He explained to Leela, "Aikido class. At the ashram *dojo*."

Earring gave Kate a squeeze and stood up to join his brother, and they exited out the side door.

"How's it going with that guy you met?" Kate asked, lighting another cigarette. "What was his name, Igor?"

"Ian. He met somebody else. I thought he might be the one, but I guess around here it's 'easy come, easy go'." She looked at Kate to see if that was the right attitude.

"Bummer." Kate signaled to the Nepalese boy to bring her another coffee. "Don't worry about it; there'll be someone else along shortly. In fact, how about him?" She pointed to a slender man with wispy shoulder-length hair who was passing in the aisle.

"Hey," Leela called out. "You! From the tantra group."

The man swiveled his head and his face lit up. "*Ciao, bella,*" he said, bending over Leela and giving her a hug. "So good to meet you in the real world."

Leela could see out of the corner of her eye that Kate was raising her eyebrows and mouthing "CYU-OOT!" She was also shaking her hand as if it was on fire.

Leela ignored her, although she agreed. "How do you find the group so far?" she asked Stefano.

"It gets off to a good start," he said. "I meet many, many good people, and many beautiful women. I carry good hopes for this group."

"Me too," Leela said. "Would you care to join us?"

"This I would love but I take quick sandwich back to my flat. I must sleep before the afternoon's group." He leaned down and bussed her cheek. "Until then, *bella*," he said, heading off to the order counter, becoming lost in the crowd.

"Now that's my idea of what the perfect guy for you looks like," Kate said.

"You think so?" Leela said. "Hmm . . . I could see that." *Maybe he's the one.*

A

LL FIFTY OF THEM WERE ARRANGED INTO two rings in the middle of the room, the men on the outside facing the women's inner circle. Bashir and the musicians were fiddling with the sound equipment over on the Persian rug by the left wall. Some visiting Sufi musicians from Iran were tuning up on the *qanoon* and the *ud*. Leela immediately felt an affinity with the old gentleman with the curly white hair, and the woman beside him wearing gilt sandals.

"Today, the Heart Dance," Mevlana said. She walked over close to Bashir and they exchanged a smile. "Begin by looking into the eyes of the man or woman in front of you. This will be your partner for the first segment of the dance." Some of the women had to turn to face the men in the outer row. Leela found herself paired with Rolf, a man in his mid-sixties with very little hair and his beard clipped short. His blue eyes were kind, and Leela felt relieved to be with him.

"*Namaste* your partner," Mevlana said. "Salute the divine god or goddess within." They all raised their hands in front of their hearts, and bowed slightly while keeping eye contact. It was a very intimate gesture, and Leela couldn't help giving Rolf a big smile.

"When the music starts, you will each raise your right hands up to touch in the air. Holding your arms like this, circle around, like so." Mevlana demonstrated the move with one of the assistants. "Then change hands and circle in the other direction, keeping eye contact at all times. When the music changes, circle alone, then move on to the next partner who is waiting for you."

As Mevlana demonstrated, the musicians started up, and the group practiced one round. This time Leela ended up with a very young and skinny boy she hadn't noticed before. He was so timid he must have been keeping in the shadows. He looked shyly away, finding it hard to keep eye contact with her.

"Keep honoring your partner, for this is a chance to open your heart to the other. Look deeply into his or her eyes; discover their treasures. Savor the few moments you have with this unique being, before the dance moves you onward."

Each new partner was a mystery, a completely unique experience. Leela felt her heart warm and expanding. As they whirled around each other she thought, *When they say 'I am opening,' it is quite literal.*

The music continued for a few more rounds, until the door opened and the stocky man with close-cropped hair hustled in, breathless. *There's that guy again*, Leela thought. *Very intriguing.*

"I'm sorry to be late," he said. "This girl fell off the back of my scooter and I had to take her to the hospital. But you can carry on now; I'm here."

"Join the circle," Mevlana said. "Take your place."

"But now there will be an uneven number," someone said, obviously a mathematician. "Each round, someone will be without a partner." Everyone contemplated the equation. Leela hoped it wouldn't be her.

"But that's just how love is, isn't it," Mevlana said merrily. "Sometimes it's there and sometimes it's not. Don't take it personally."

The musicians struck up again, and the dance continued, each participant pairing or being alone as the dance demanded.

ETHAN WAS GRUMPY, AND LEELA FELT RIPPED off having him as a partner. It was certainly bad luck, because neither one of them would have chosen the other. It didn't matter how lovely the weeping willow tree or the pond were, it was just not enough fun. Neither of them had written a word.

When Mevlana had instructed everyone to find a partner, some group members had paired up immediately. Others, including Leela and Ethan, had lingered, unable to choose. They hesitated, wandering around, not really looking at the other unpartnered folk. The choice seemed too important. They strained with the possibility of mistakes being made.

"Stop thinking and choose someone," Mevlana had finally said, exasperated. "You don't need to make a commitment to marry this person. If most of you would stop focusing so much on looks, you would probably have a lover by now, and not have to be here working so hard to open up."

People who refused to choose were put into pairs by the assistants. Upon seeing it was Ethan, Leela had felt a twinge of interest, until she discerned his coldness and disregard. Instructions came to sit down in pairs and get to know each other for five minutes each. They were to share where they were from, how the group was going for them, and something they liked to do for fun.

The room had filled with the murmur of fifty voices, punctuated at times by laughter. Leela told Ethan about her trip from the West, how she loved the ashram, and that this exercise scared her because she didn't know what was coming, and everything in this group was so intense. The bell rang and they switched. Ethan said that he came from Melbourne, that he might drop out of the group any minute, and that for fun, he tortured small animals.

"Do you feel better about your partner now after sharing? Of course you do," Mevlana said. Leela raised her eyebrows. "Those of you who had trouble choosing a partner may find this exercise most insightful." The assistants handed out notepads and pens.

So there they sat, Leela and Ethan, on benches near the shady tree, mostly not trying to compose love poems to each other. Leela reflected on Mevlana's words that they could "let themselves go," "honor this wonderful human being who is your partner," "make it poetic, make it grand, and make it reflect your partner's beauty." How embarrassing it was to write a love poem to a stranger, let alone write one at all. She looked up at the willow and wondered if this was why it was weeping. As she looked at Ethan, he scowled. There was nothing written on his page.

Nothing written on hers either, for that matter. Leela tried hard to think what was lovable about him. What would his mother say, or his last girlfriend, if he'd ever had one? How would he have felt to her when she was in his arms? Who was he deep down in his soul? How might he be if he weren't so morose? All these answers she jotted down, and then with a flourish she added a flowery word, a bit of sex, and allowed for a little gushing. She tried to remember phrases from the Song of Solomon, or Elizabeth Barrett Browning's letters. After all, she was the writer of this love letter, and this was her appreciation for love itself.

It had absolutely nothing to do with him.

She was the lover, the one who spoke of love. She offered up words of kindness and adoration, of praise and attraction. She opened her heart to how she imagined he might like to be spoken of, and gave him those gifts and more. Her paper had many black scratched-out words, but more kept flowing from her pen, so many words of love dammed up for so long.

Travis, one of the assistants of the group, came by and told them time was up. *That chestnut hair and those eyes are driving me mad*, Leela thought. *Wish I'd been doing this exercise with him.* She finished her last line, and then laid down her notebook. "Okay," Travis said. He offered a sly smile that barely moved his face. "Now deliver your poem to your partner with as much gusto and love and tenderness as you can muster. Be dramatic if you wish; go ahead and get down on your knees!"

Leela swallowed her embarrassment. *Share this, what she had written in a moment of passion?* Travis wouldn't leave until one of them started, so haltingly she began telling Ethan how his lips excited her, how he was a man of truth and wisdom, and how she admired his strength of character in moments it was put to the test. She paid homage to their lovemaking in all its forms. She told him she would never leave him, he was her man forever, and she loved him beyond measure, through this life and into the next.

"Okay, your turn," she said. It had actually been liberating to speak and hear such words come out of her mouth. She was a lover who could articulate the words of love.

Ethan sat there, sullen. He refused to participate. Leela looked at him expectantly. She wanted to hear some exalting words back. It would be so delightful, and so much fun. He didn't realize it didn't mean anything to her; she just wanted to hear a man say those words.

"Look," he finally said. "You're okay-looking, and probably a nice person, but you're not my type."

This is really breathtaking, Leela thought, just as Mevlana said it would be. *The quality of writing a love letter or of being a lover is completely within the one writing or doing the loving. We mistakenly think it has all to do with the other, but it has little to nothing to do with them at all. We are the ones who either choose to shower our beloved with love, or decide rather to be stingy with our adoration or eloquence.*

Ethan sat glowering at the grass. "This whole exercise was stupid," he said. "I'm going to ask for my money back." He stood up. "I'm taking off; maybe you'll see me around sometime. This really sucked."

"Before you go I want to thank you," Leela said. She felt powerful knowing that his rudeness had nothing to do with her, and everything to do with him. Smiling sweetly she said, "If you hadn't been such an asshole, I'd never have gotten the lesson at all."

ola, señora," RAÚL SAID, NODDING TO LEELA as he passed. An earring made of bone lay neatly tangled in his acorn-colored hair.

Leela stopped dead in her tracks. *Wasn't "señora" a term for women of a certain age?* She had been feeling particularly frisky this afternoon but suddenly she doubted whether she could attract a bumblebee.

Raúl had made quite a splash when he arrived a few days ago at the ashram, the ripples fanning out to tantalize women and men of every persuasion. Tall, slender, gypsy-looking, his wrists were adorned with bracelets, and amulets hung round his neck. Despite these feminine accents, there was no mistaking his heterosexual, Latin allure. Raúl was thus far to be found surrounded by an entourage of women each hoping she might be the one special enough to snag his heart.

Leela was not impervious to his allure as a universal

object of desire. She had wanted his acknowledgment as much as anyone else. *And his response to her level of magnetism was to call her señora?* She pondered his sexy swagger, and how he had seemed to nod at her with respect rather than flirtatiousness. *How ill-mannered. How upsetting.*

Proceeding with her head down, she steered toward the coffee bar on autopilot. The kids from Goa passed in silence. There under a tree nursing a latte sat Paloma, an older woman who lived next to her flat, plump, sedentary, nurturing, and safe. She motioned for Leela to join her. *What a waste that she lives in Ibiza, the party capital of the world*, Leela thought, since Paloma had told her she was completely finished with men.

"*Hola, dulce*," Paloma said. Her hair was unbecomingly short and she did not bother to color her gray. "You look like something has upset you."

"Well maybe, yes," Leela said, sitting down. She decided it was too late in the day to get a coffee. "You know that really hot new guy that arrived? I saw you speaking Spanish with him in the Mozart the other day."

"Raúl," Paloma said. "The one from Argentina. The chiropractor."

"Chiropractor?" Leela said. "He has a real job? He looks like a gigolo."

"Yes," Paloma said. Her mottled hands caressed her cup. "As soon as he got here he joined the ashram *clinica* and began giving sessions. He donates his time to keep *la gente* healthy." She took a bite of one of the several cookies on her plate, offering one to Leela who shook her head no. "He's quite a wonderful, generous person, despite how he looks like a party boy."

"I have to ask you something," Leela said. "What does '*señora*' mean? Isn't it a form of address for an older woman? I know it's for those who are married, but otherwise, isn't it somebody sexless and not available?"

Paloma was looking at her quizzically. "That's mostly true," she agreed.

"Damn." Leela's chin fell lower toward her chest. "Here I was hoping I looked particularly attractive to him, and instead I was looking like a *señora*."

Paloma didn't seem to grasp the gravity of the situation. She was through with men and thought everyone else should be too. "This is how it is to be older," she said. "And who cares? There's plenty in life without men. My relationships with *mi amigas* are more satisfying than men ever were. And I can spend my time painting and doing what I like without interference."

God spare me, Leela thought. *If this is what I have to look forward to getting older, I might as well end it now.*

At home she crawled under the covers even though the midday heat was melting the candles on the trunk. The full weight of the Western media's opinion of middle-aged women moved through her mind like a fungus. She knew with sudden certainty she was too old and doomed to a future of no men, no love, and no sex. It was more likely she would be killed in a terrorist attack than get married again. Attractive men would recoil, she would be laughed at by younger women, and she would end up as one of those lonely women with cats. Frumpy, frizzy grey hair, baggy clothes hiding her body, despised, impoverished, unwanted, and bravely putting on a front that this was all right. At one with Paloma and her cohorts.

Down she went. Down, down. The lack of a lover and the impending loss of sexual attractiveness weighed as the heaviest burden on the planet. This was the end. She had lost her appeal. She would have to reconcile to a life without sexual love, find what meaning there was to be had through work and service to others. That's what life was all about anyway, according to all she had been taught by spiritual teachers before Mevlana. She felt her aloneness in a way that was agonizing.

Tears started. The room darkened until only the light shining in from the window let her guess how much time had passed. In this most hopeless of states of mind, at last she was able to swim off to sleep.

TEELA WOKE UP THE NEXT MORNING IN A hangover of emotion. Where had she been? *Oh, the thing with Raúl.* She got up, dressed, and decided to go looking for him. She would ask him exactly what he meant.

She peeped into the clearing by the sauna that held the jacuzzi. Steam from the pool rose like morning mist in the empty spaces between the foliage and palms. Sure enough,

Raúl was in the bath with four beautiful women, a contented smile floating on his lips. Leela watched as one of the goddesses picked up a soggy porous sponge and soaped Raúl's back. Leela certainly couldn't talk with him now. She turned and headed to the Mozart for breakfast.

Walking back toward the meditation hall along the walkway afterward, Leela saw Raúl approaching, his wet towel slung like a horseshoe around his neck. He wore a sarong tied at the waist, and his body was slender and graceful. He nodded absent-mindedly as he neared, sharing a faint but friendly smile.

Leela blurted out, "What did you mean by calling me '*señora*?'"

"What?" Raúl had stopped in front of her now, a stunned look on his face.

"When you called me *señora* the other day. Did you mean that I look old to you, or what?" She sounded pathetic even to herself, but she had to know. She would never see him again after she left here. His silence made her realize she had made some huge mistake.

He reached out and took her wrist, guiding her to sit down on the stone wall that edged the walkway. As they sat side by side, he measured her pulse. He was looking into her eyes, but she could not meet them. It mattered too much. When she finally hazarded a glance, his eyes were soft and kind with full attention on her mind and body. Up close, the energy radiating from him was not so much of a sexual nature, as it was of extreme health and well-being.

"You are freaking out," he said, looking at her with his doctor's studied eye. "You are not getting any pleasure, that's what it is. You have to go into the body."

Leela felt relief to be seen, naked, although she had no idea what he was talking about. "What do you mean, into the body?"

"You are totally cut off from your own aliveness, your juice, your pleasure. The way in is through the body." He looked a bit bewildered that anyone could be so off base. "Hang out at the jacuzzi," he said. "Get a massage. Dance, the sauna, you need touch, awareness." He scratched his head and shooed her off dismissively. "Now go, give yourself some attention."

tURN INTO THE STAIRWELL RIGHT BEYOND the Muslim clothes shop"—that was the only direction she had been given. Up she climbed, past a cybercafe she had never used, past a store selling eyeglasses, and then a tiny travel agency. One flight above that, an unmarked entryway loomed with a rippling piece of white muslin serving as the door. As there was nowhere to knock, she walked right in. "Hellooo," Leela called. The room blazed with sunlight and was bereft of furniture.

Out came a smiling woman less than five feet tall holding a baby. Her black braids curled into snails atop her head, and her belted rainbow apron and the coral and turquoise charms around her neck and waist identified her as Tibetan.

"Is this the place to get a massage?" Leela asked.

A man came out from the hallway and stood beside his family. He had the same black hair and eyes as the Indians but his face was broader and his body more stocky. "I give you very good massage," he said, bowing slightly from the waist.

"Your baby is beautiful." The child's eyes were tiny slits and his grin was as big as his mother's. He looked like the laughing Hotei. The proud parents bowed again.

Leela followed the man back to a room with a simple massage table covered with a starched white sheet. There was a small pane-less window, and on the walls a poster of the acupuncture meridians, a map of Tibet, and a few hooks to hang one's clothes.

"There's a Tibetan doctor who advertises at the Mozart Café," Leela said. "Do you know him?"

"Dr. Tsenpo, he cousin." The man pointed to the hooks. "Please hang clothes. I come back when you ready."

"Wait, what's your name?"

"Gyeltsen. Thank you," he said, leaving her alone in the room.

While undressing, she examined the map of Tibet with its cartoon-like drawings of the main attractions: the Potala Palace in Lhasa, the monasteries Mindroling, Samye, and Trandruk, the Graveyard of Tibetan Kings, and Yamdrok Yumtso, one of the holy lakes of Tibet. The entire Tibetan culture had been dedicated to spirituality. Its cumulative wisdom was of such attainment the West could only speculate and romanticize it. And now in the current day, its secrets were being methodically and ruthlessly destroyed by the Chinese government.

I wonder if he's going to be as weird about female nudity as the other men here, Leela thought, hanging her clothes on the pegs. The guidebooks warned Western women not to expose any body parts when traveling in Asia, not even legs or arms. At the last minute, she decided to leave on her panties, and she quickly lay face-down on the table.

Gyeltsen entered without a sound. As he applied the oil and began running slow masterful strokes down her back, Leela found herself totally letting go.

That was the best massage I've ever had, she thought afterward as she descended the stairs. I feel so relaxed, so tingly alive in my body. It had lasted an hour and a half, and cost four American dollars. *It's amazing they charge so little—I could afford to come here every day if I wanted. I'm going to get a massage from Gyelsten as often as I can.*

I T LOOKS LIKE EVERYONE HERE IS DOING COKE."

"Coke? What do you mean? As in cocaine?"

Leela nudged her shoulder toward a man who was opening a tiny white envelope and sprinkling the contents over his food. He mixed it in and took a bite.

Kate started laughing and shook a cigarette out of the pack. "Fabian, from Austria. That's so funny to think of him as a cokehead. Ha! He's one of the people who's seriously here for meditation. The last guy you'd find doing drugs of any kind."

"I'm just saying that because everyone has those little envelopes, you know, like the ones people carry cocaine in. Or used to. Not that I know anything about it." Leela took a drink of water. "All right, maybe I did a little back when I was a waitress. But I was never really that into it."

"Sure, you weren't."

"I wasn't, really. Too expensive. And it's not my type of drug anyway—the big ego that comes from it is not my thing. All right, I know it's not cocaine because everyone dumps it into their food. But what are they doing?"

"Those are Ayurvedic herbs. You know how everybody's always sick here? If it's not diarrhea, it's the opposite. Always intestinal distress. Our bodies are attempting to adjust to the microbes of India, the different food and water, how dirty everything is, and the constant assault of pollution. So everyone is forever trying something: Ayurveda, acupuncture, eating plans. It becomes everyone's hobby, curing their digestion."

A hush fell over the dining area as a peacock strutted into the empty space next to the fountain. His head and body were electric royal blue, and his feathers lay lankly behind him, bobbing up and down with his languid walk. When the bird knew it had everyone's attention, he pivoted, shuffled his feathers, let out a call, and spread his magnificent tail. A hundred blue and green eyes opened, spread among the feathery spines, eyes that were so vivid and aglow they brought tears to Leela's own.

"This place is so amazing," she said. "Imagine that a peacock just comes in while you're eating lunch, and it's not that big a deal. Everyone just goes right on with their business."

"That bird is an example of pure narcissism," Kate said.

"Just like you, ha ha."

"Whatever," Kate sniffed. "Do you mind if I go on?"

"Just as I was saying. Sure, go on. Tell me about the cocaine."

"So," Kate continued, "people are always on these different diets prescribed by their doctors. One minute you're supposed to drink coconut milk and eat white rice instead of brown, the next it's brown rice with spices and plenty of pineapple. Go figure. It's all based on some intricate personality system. As far as I can tell, none of it makes any difference. We're doomed to be in poor health as long as we're in India.

"But of course, being Westerners, we believe there's something to do, so we keep trying to find the answer. We're seekers who come here, after all, and we're all so body-focused," Kate said. "Not to mention how it interferes with your sex life."

"Well, I could use a little help lately," Leela said. "I need to devote more attention to my body, so I'm told."

"I'll take you to Dr. Tsenpo's. He's this Tibetan acupuncturist everyone goes to." Kate put her unlit cigarette back in the pack. "You done with lunch? Let's go over there now."

As they exited the gate, a beggar woman in a soiled sari was accosting Westerners for help. "What's going on here?" Kate asked. "Usually the ashram guards keep these people from bothering us." She looked around. "No one's here, unfortunately. Have to do it myself. *Chalo!*" she shouted at the woman, brushing her away. "*Chalo!*"

The woman immediately winced and shrunk off. "What was that you said?" Leela asked. "It worked like a charm."

"*Chalo*. It's Hindi for 'fuck off.'"

"What? I can't believe you would say such a thing. To such an unfortunate person as that?"

"Look," Kate said. "This is another of those things that are cultural that don't necessarily translate. Everybody says it—it's the only thing that works. *Chalo*. Remember that word. It'll come in handy."

I'd never treat another human being that way, Leela murmured under her breath. *No matter what you say.*

THE WAITING ROOM AT DR. TSENPO'S WAS full of people Leela had seen around the ashram though no one she knew by name. As she checked in with the receptionist, two of the patients were called to go back for their treatments. The other people in the room were browsing through well-worn magazines and gossiping noisily, chatting with friends across the room.

"This place is a real social event," Leela said to Kate.

"Yeah, people keep getting sick so they keep coming back," Kate said, picking up an ancient *Glamour* magazine. "Dr. Tsenpo makes a fortune off the expatriate digestive system."

The room was sunny and bright, the light reflecting off the whitewashed walls. Next to the curtained doorway to the treatment area stood a shrine holding a photo of the Dalai Lama. The place was antiseptic and clean, immaculately ordered and maintained.

Dr. Tsenpo poked his head out from behind the curtain and motioned two more patients to come back. His slight frame was hidden behind his white lab coat, and his black hair was severely slicked back.

"That's four people we've seen go in and none come out," Leela said. "How many people does he see at one time?"

"Six. He's got a virtual assembly line going."

"I guess he's a miracle worker at making money too."

"That he is," Kate said. "Once he had me go over to his house at night to receive a special part of my treatment, and you wouldn't believe how posh it was, like some kind of sultan's palace. His ten-month-old baby had all these expensive Disney toys, and the TV was tuned to Star Cable which provides Western programming as well as stuff from all over Asia."

"Do you know his cousin, Gyeltsen?" Leela asked. "I'm seeing him for massage. He's quite a bit more low-tech. By the way, has anyone ever referred to you as *señora*?"

"My god," Kate said. "I cringe at the thought. Why, did someone call you that?"

"Yes, it was horrifying. I mean, I was feeling like I was looking good that day. Until I heard that."

"You look great," Kate said. "Don't worry about it. He must be blind."

"I've got to get some fresh air," Leela said. "I saw a

garden by the side of the building when I came in—looks cute. Make sure they come get me for my appointment?"

"Ha ha now that's a new one," Kate answered. "In India, going outside for fresh air. Ha ha ha."

Outside Leela encountered Paloma sitting under a spreading banyan tree. As she turned to face her, Leela observed the deeply etched lines around on Paloma's face and considered how she had been taught to find this unattractive and how instead, she found it reassuring and trustworthy.

"Paloma," Leela said. "I'm still upset about the whole *señora* scenario. Can you help me?"

Paloma chuckled. She smoothed her dress down her lap. "*Dulce*, sweetheart, don't you see? The whole aging phobia is a bunch of media *mierde*, capitalist conditioning perpetuated to make us buy things."

"What!?"

"Think about it: if we all freak out about getting older, we'll spend enormous mountains of *pesos* on creams and vitamins and plastics and Botox."

"Which Kate calls one of the Seven Wonders of the Modern World," Leela said, laughing weakly.

"Yes, the West is always trying to convince you that if you fix yourself, you'll be loveable. But, it's more than that," Paloma went on, facing her straight on. "The whole antiaging thing is fear of women, of women being powerful. Just as we start getting to the time of life when we're our most dynamic, we get hit with this obsession about our wrinkles. It keeps our attention self-absorbed instead of outwardly focused."

Yes, Leela breathed. *That's it.*

Paloma leaned in conspiratorially. "Also, another component is that when we hit maturity, we start to be the age of the mothers of the men in their prime, activating the incest taboo. They don't want to admit they are attracted to us, just as they didn't want to admit they were attracted to their own mothers—thank you, *Señor* Freud."

"Wow," Leela said. She glanced as a group of energetic twenty-somethings passed outside on the sidewalk. "You are amazingly calm about all this. I'm practically insane about the prospect of losing whatever sexual attractiveness I have. I can go into a panic attack at the mere mention of the word 'menopause.' The horror of the possibility of no more romance, and ending up all alone with hair on your chin."

"Yes," Paloma said, settling back in her chair. "They want you to be afraid. My deep acceptance has everything to do with living here for years and all the work I did with Mevlana. Back home you're considered all washed up, right? America has that insane prejudice about youth that doesn't exist anywhere else. The guys who come here are not operating from that mindset. Here it's more the European attitude that there are sexy, attractive women at every age.

"In the West it is believed that men hold the sexual power, that they get to assess women's value and choose who they want. Often they think they want younger women so they can hold rank over their partner. You and other women go along with this belief because you've been brainwashed since birth that this is how it is. In tantra, however, the sexually mature women have the power and carry the lineage. Younger women don't and can't have power of this kind—it takes life experience, failing, succeeding."

Dr. Tsenpo's nurse peeked her head out and motioned, and Leela stood up to go. "What else?" she asked. "Please give me a little more."

"Mevlana really sets the standard for the idea that women of experience are alluring and desirable. She's what? Late fifties? Early sixties? And yet every guy here would like to have sex with her. That completely burns people's out-of-date realities, wouldn't you say?"

I'd say, Leela thought as she disappeared into the waiting room. *Maybe even mine.*

THE MOZART WAS A WARM HAVEN AGAINST the drizzling downpour outside. A rooster crowed its morning wake-up call. Leela peered through the dark at the slender figure making its way down the aisle.

"*Bella!*" Stefano called out as he reached her table. "My favorite person!" He bent over and kissed her, his wispy hair tickling her face. "I love this together with you so many early *caffès.*"

Leela calculated that this was their fourth or fifth meeting this week. Sitting so close, whispering about the group, he would often put his arm around her and pull her close.

"I go," he said, pointing to the counter. "I buy you one more?"

His enthusiasm is certainly genuine, Leela thought as she watched him walk away. These morning encounters were certainly becoming intimate, but it hadn't gone beyond that. *Careful, girl*, Leela cautioned herself. *You can't make anything happen*—she knew that now. Still, she could hope.

EELA WALKED THROUGH THE MOZART LOOK-
ing for Kate. A distinctly herbal aroma emanated as she
passed the druggie corner. Moving down the middle row,
she saw Jack, the stocky man with the close-cropped hair
who'd had the accident with his bike, sitting at one of the
tables, silent while all around him chatted away. He was
facing out, scrutinizing all who passed, and when his eyes
met Leela's, he hastily looked away.

Leela found Kate next to the nonsmoking section,
looking lovely in her green tie-dyed T-shirt with a Buddha
levitating on the chest. "That guy over there is in the tantra
group," Leela said as she sat down. "The one I told you about
that I did that exercise with."

"You never tell me about any of the exercises you do in
group, remember?"

Kate's attention appeared to be on the dusty gray cat
making its way toward an abandoned plate of assorted *pako-
ras*. Even though there was a cigarette burning in the ashtray,

Leela watched as she lit another.

"Look," Leela said. "Don't take it personally. You know we swore not to tell anything that happens in group. Oh forget it, it's not such a big a deal anyway. We were in pairs doing this breathing exercise, standing up, one person rapidly pushing air in and out of the third chakra." She put her hand on her belly. "It's supposed to have something to do with power, your own personal power. The other person supports you while you do it. I was paired up with that guy over there, Jack." She pointed at Jack who was still detachedly checking out everyone who passed.

"Air in and out of the third chakra. Right."

Leela decided to ignore Kate's sarcasm. "That's correct. Anyway, when I was his partner he totally ignored me. I guess since I wasn't one of the young voluptuous girls, I wasn't worth paying attention to. Very businesslike and dismissive at the end."

"I'm sure that's not it," Kate said. "I'm sure he has a problem. You always take things personally."

Leela turned toward Jack, and at that moment their eyes met. In that instant, with the interlocking of their eyes, she felt a kinship as if she could see inside to who he really was. He broke their gaze and turned away, furtive and mole-like.

He's shy, Leela thought. *That's what he is. Shy. A little bit scared.* "Now I see that there's something sweet about him," Leela said turning back to Kate. "Like he's really trying to see his stuff, wants to heal whatever he has going on with women. I mean, why's he doing this intensive tantra group if he isn't trying to go deeper?"

"My god, you can be so naive sometimes," Kate said, brushing her honey hair back from her face. "Is it still a mystery to you that guys get involved with tantra so they can get laid a lot? They don't care what it's called, they just know there are lots of girls willing to put out."

"Sometimes you can be a real asshole," Leela said. She stubbed out Kate's still-burning cigarette into the ashtray. "You still buy into that old dichotomy about men are looking for sex while women look for love which is incredible Western bullshit. It dehumanizes everybody. Everyone is looking for love, ultimately everybody, men and women alike. Men just try to find it with their dicks. There's nothing wrong with that, it's just different from how we are."

"Whatever." Kate got up to go. Her nipples stood out prominently through her T-shirt. She brushed some crumbs from her skirt and picked up her bag.

"You don't have to get all offended, Kate," Leela said. "There's just stuff I'm learning in the group that makes me see everything differently. We've got it all wrong, all that crap we learned in the West. If it makes things better between men and women, heals our split, what's wrong with that?"

Kate sat back down. "Okay, okay," she said. "I just don't want to deal with it right now. What do you say, want to go to the swimming pool? It's getting hot, and there's nothing like that cold water against the skin."

As they left, Leela glanced back at Jack. He was still sitting pulled back, the observer of the scene, not involved, a dark presence in a light-filled room.

tHE BOY FROM GOA WAS DANCING BY HIM-self. *He's attractive in a kind of boy-next-door way*, she thought, *but he's much too young for me*. She crossed over to the other side of the room. A slender girl from Denmark shimmied by, smiling as she passed. Leela threw back her head and shook out her hair, rotating her hips in a figure eight. *I hope someone caught how sexy that move was*, she thought. She remembered dancing in clubs back home, and how often she had been told she was a great dancer. The music was a slinky Afro-Cuban beat, and everyone was trying hard to look their erotic best. After all, this was a tantra group.

"Stop!" Bashir called out. The music came to an abrupt halt. He gestured for them to come and gather round. "This is all fine as it is," he said, lowering his voice so they would move in closer. "You all look very hot. However, we are here to learn to go a little deeper."

Leela looked at the Rastafarian man she had been eyeing earlier. He had taken off his shirt and his shoulders shone with sweat. A pendant in the shape of Africa hung against the nappy hair on his chest. *Now there was someone who personified hot.*

"Most dance is focused on entertainment," Bashir said. "Everyone look at how beautiful I am, how sexy. It is focused outward on the other's perception." *Guilty*, Leela thought. "When you begin to dance for yourself," Bashir continued, "a whole different world can arise. If you stop dancing from the mind, you may get to a moment when it's instinctual, when it's real. I want you to stop thinking with the dancer's mind and allow the body to dance its own dance."

Leela remembered seeing Bashir that night in the meditation hall and how at home he had appeared to be in his body. He had moved gracefully, without any note of seductiveness. He had seemed entirely uninterested in who was around him, and complete in himself in his dancing.

"People in the West focus on looking attractive, not on being attractive," Bashir continued. "They treat their body as an object, an object to attract. Personally, I'm interested in who you are in your body, not in your body itself. I don't care about the dancer; I care about the person."

The music began again, a *qawwali* mix with its invitation to enter a state of trance. "Practice staying inside," Bashir called out. "Open your heart; take a risk. Find out what your body wants to dance, just for itself."

Leela closed her eyes and scanned down inside: her arms, her stomach, her thighs. She lifted herself up onto her toes, then rocked back on her heels. The *qawwali* singer began a scat improvisation, tripping all over the Arabic scale, sustaining a note here, a moaning vocal there. It helped shut off the mind not knowing the meaning of what he was singing.

When she let her body lead, Leela noticed it didn't seem to want to dance fluidly, let alone act sexy at all. The moves it was making were stilted and cloddish, and as she went deeper in, she felt it to be an elephantine plodding, a dance of heavily rooted things. Soon enough the weightiness morphed into a cobra, slithering up from its coils. She felt her sex energy rising and spreading through her pelvis.

"If you don't love your body, how can someone else love it?" Bashir intoned over the microphone.

Leela felt the snakiness calm into a slow stomp, and then she wasn't there anymore. The body was dancing on its own, and she followed its lead where it went.

Then she noticed something entirely new, as if she had taken off glasses she hadn't known she was wearing. All that she had done to her body: Staying thin, going to the gym, eating healthy diets; all this had been imposed from the outside. All were disciplines she had been doing *to* her body, enforcing from the outside whether the body wanted to or not, never asking or respecting. It all came from the mind, the mind deciding what to force upon the body. This was what the West offered, and although it was better than no body awareness, nothing had been from the inside until this moment. She saw with the greatest amusement what incredible ego she had about her body, while she actually knew nothing.

This must be what Raúl had been trying to teach her. It was necessary to get into the body, learn to love her own body. Not the way it might be someday if she continued to improve it, not compared to anyone else's, or how it used to be, but me, my body today. All the ways that Raúl had pointed to: Massage, dance, the sauna; and yes, now she could see what the group was indicating, being naked to challenge the ego's hold, and sex, wherever they would be going with that. This was it. The path that lay in front of her.

The music stopped. Leela turned to face the raised platform where Bashir was leaning back on the Persian rug.

"The answer is not the body," Bashir said, "but it has to be gone through. It's a stage on the path, a certain beginning level of awakening."

Leela looked around the room at the other physical beings taking this journey with her. Fat, tall, short, skinny: all sweaty and happy and full of endorphins. They were all much more sexually attractive than she had noticed before. Bashir's dance class ended for today, and they picked up their towels and headed for the door.

"When you leave the ashram this morning," Bashir said, "be gentle with yourselves. It's a different world out there. Here inside the ashram, people have been meditating; out there, the rickshaws, the madness. You may not be aware of the shock this is to your body, especially now that you are more open. Be gentle with yourselves as you leave this protected space, gentle like water."

EELA PASSED THE OUTSIDE CAPPUCCINO BAR on her way out of the ashram.

"Hey, I've been seeing you around a lot." Jack grabbed her and pulled her onto his lap. He smelled of coffee and fruit as she took him in. His breath was hot on her neck; his skin damp with a light film of perspiration. "I was thinking," he whispered in her ear, "that we could get together and practice tantra."

Jack was fleshy and headed toward plump, and his body felt like a soft cushion as she leaned back against his chest. What he said was confusing. The exercises they had done so far in group hadn't had anything to do with sex, directly. She had been learning a lot, and it was great and all, *but there wasn't actually anything one would get together to repeat. Was there? They had been practicing opening up, mostly with their clothes on and always safe. Did he mean continuing that? Do more chakra breathing exercises? More ecstatic dancing but in her room, or his?*

She remembered when their eyes had met, and she had seen his vulnerability and shyness. In her mind's eye, she saw their bodies close, enveloped in an embrace, holding each other's gaze with complete trust. In the present Jack shifted underneath her, settling her more squarely on his knees while he lightly wrapped his arm around her waist. Her breath quickened with the excitement of his wrist lying against the exposed flesh of her belly.

A picture appeared of them both naked, sitting face-to-face practicing what she imagined to be sacred sex exercises, breathing together so respectfully, learning and growing together. Whenever she had heard about tantra in the West, she had fantasized this: herself with a lover, sitting in *yab yum* making love ever so slowly, so intently focused on each other, breathing as one, eyes locked, deliciously attuned to every movement of the other, each masterfully controlling the degree of the other's arousal for maximum pleasure.

Leela thought Jack must know about stuff like this because he was so self-assured. She felt the warmth rising up into her body from his lap, and was aware of his mouth so close to her neck. She imagined the sacred sex with him, saw him naked with her, smelling like he did, felt his perspiration against her skin and his desire, his desire for her, Leela. How smooth his skin was, with very little hair. He would touch her so gently, so skillfully, the tantric pleasure she had only dreamed of before.

"I might be into that," she said turning to face him. She restrained herself from reaching out and taking off his glasses and running her hand over his buzz cut. "That might be cool. I'm on my way to an appointment with Dr. Tsenpo, but maybe some other time, later." She edged off his lap and stood to go. The light glinted off his glasses and she could not see his eyes.

"Just let me know when," he said.

ᴇᴇʟᴀ ᴅᴇᴄɪᴅᴇᴅ ᴛᴏ ɢɪᴠᴇ ᴛʜᴇ Mᴏᴢᴀʀᴛ ᴀ ʟᴀsᴛ whirl before heading home. The café was the usual late-night mass of bodies choking with smoke, laughter, and sexual innuendo. She passed Ethan gesturing emphatically to a table of Kenyans. Beyond him Kate was cozied up with her paramour of the evening, looking as if she didn't want to be interrupted. As Leela kept walking, she noticed Jack on her left against the wall surrounded by a hive of boisterous Israelis. He belonged with them by virtue of speaking their language, but he sat as though alone. He motioned with a nod of his head for Leela to come and sit beside him.

"You're burning the midnight oil," she said. There was so little room she scrunched right up against him, thigh to thigh.

"You're coming from a class?" he asked. There was a light sheen of sweat on his forehead. Leela suppressed the desire to run her hand over his closely cropped head. His hair was so black against his olive skin, and it looked like brushed velvet.

The dreadhead on the other side of her shifted, pushing her body even closer against Jack's.

"Yes," she nodded. "I'd never done contact improv before. Have you?" Jack shook his head no. "I've seen couples doing it out on the dance floor, of course. All that rolling up and down each other's bodies; it always looks so smooth. And fun. The class showed me you can tell a lot about a person, and about yourself, from how you contact someone else in the dance. How you resist, or how open you are, or whatever."

"Uh-huh," he said. He leaned closer and smiled. "Actually, you caught me on my way out. I was just about to leave. Would you like to come over to my place for some tea?"

"No," she said. Her previous picture of the two of them "practicing" loomed up in her mind. The present situation had none of the elements of the way she had envisioned it. "Thanks, but no, I want to get an early start tomorrow, and I was just on my way home myself."

"C'mon," he said. He reached across her and touched her arm. His voice softened. "I'm lonely and homesick, and I just want someone to talk to." His hand slid down and stroked her wrist, then clasped her hand. "I feel like I can talk to you."

Ah, he wants to get to know each other first, she thought. *This might be perfect.* Still she hesitated. "You'll bring me here after the tea?"

"Whenever you want." He raised his right hand. "Just say the word and I'll bring you back."

They walked out into the still sweltering night. There must have been fifty scooters parked up against the side of the Mozart with Jack's bike indistinguishable from the rest. Since Laxmi Road had no streetlights, Leela wondered how he found his bike so quickly. He backed it out of the pack, started it up, and motioned to Leela. She threw her leg over, wrapped herself around him, and they were off.

Vedanta House was one of the largest apartment complexes around the ashram and also one of the most expensive. The grounds were well lit and maintained, even if what could be called landscaping consisted of barren plots of earth with potted plants in the corners. Jack led the way up the stairs to the penthouse. He opened his door to a room four times the size of her flat. At the far end, arched doorways led to a balconied terrace. On the left was a seating area flanked by a shelving unit crowded with items; and on the right an alcove that held his bed and nightstand. A mirrored wardrobe demarcated one from the other. There were luxurious carpets and wall hangings of a quality she had not seen since leaving the West.

"Please have a seat," Jack said. He picked up a bottle from the shelf. "May I pour you a brandy?"

"Umm, you said we were going to have tea."

"Tea it is," he said without skipping a beat. "I'll be back in a minute."

While he was out of sight, Leela inspected the pantry-like shelf brimming with goods carrying labels in Hebrew: tins of cookies, plastic packages of halvah, jars of cashews, almonds, dried apricots, and figs. A pair of ornate liqueur glasses matching the brandy bottle sat on a mahogany tray next to a stack of ceramic plates.

Leela had just positioned herself on the couch when Jack came in carrying two cups of tea. He must have either brought all this posh interior decor or had it shipped. "It seems like you were a bit of a success back home," she said.

"I did all right." He settled back on the couch and put the cups and his feet on the coffee table.

"Yeah, okay. Doing what?"

"I was involved in the first rollout of applets for the enterprise," he said. "You see, before me, different departments were using different operating systems and different protocols, and the IT department was pulling out their hair."

"Um, you were in tech?"

"Yeah. By coming up with a cross-platform model, which was distributable and scalable, I saved the company millions of dollars and got two patents out of it. Let's just say they were nice to me, and now I can afford to have some fun."

Leela felt relief that they were moving on to a topic she understood. "So what do you do with your time?"

"Well, I'm here now for a few months. Every winter I ski in Gstaad. Maybe from here I'll go on to Thailand, one of the islands like Koh Phangan or somewhere. You don't have to be anywhere, right? Want to come with me?"

She laughed, but filed the invitation away for later. "So do you have a woman in every port, or are you married with a long-suffering wife waiting patiently at home?"

He smiled. "There was a woman I lived with for two and a half years while I was building that business. But no, I'm on my own. Available, you might say." He gave her a wink.

"Want some more tea?"

Leela looked down at her empty cup. "Sure," she said. He hadn't asked her anything about herself. Typical.

As soon as he turned the corner, she got up and slid over to the mirrored wardrobe to surreptitiously check out her appearance. Hair looking good, skin a bit pale, tiredness showing as puffiness under her eyes but overall, presentable. She turned sideways to gauge if her stomach looked flat, and as she stood inhaling and sucking in her belly, a pair of hands covered hers from behind.

"You are so hot," Jack was saying. His tongue reached out and flicked her ear. His body pressed up full length against her back, his knees bending in and keeping hers from buckling. "I really want you," he said. He thrust his hips slowly and deliberately against her bottom while he tightened his arms around her middle.

The strength of his desire made hers rise up against her will. She looked to the image mirrored back of the two of them, him encircling her. She arched her head back to meet his as he nuzzled into her neck; holding her hips, he gently pumped her from behind. His hands were hot as they brushed her belly, and he reached down and began unfastening her pants.

"No," she said. "No, stop." She wanted him to stop, but then again, she didn't.

Jack responded with another long slow thrust and by moving his hands up toward her breasts. "Ummm," he whispered. "This is gonna be so good."

With one swift movement she prevented his hands from reaching their destination and swirled around to face him. "This isn't right. This isn't what I was wanting. You said we'd just talk." She realized she sounded shrill so she softened her tone. "I mean, I do want it, you are very sexy, but it's not right. I want to go home, right now."

"Right now," Jack said. His posture straightened to a businessman's stance. "Just as I said, whenever you want."

As she was trying to fall asleep later that night, Leela had trouble forgetting the feeling of Jack's skin against hers. *It hadn't been right. But the future might be another story.*

You'RE SO EASY TO TALK TO, *bella*," STEFANO said, putting his arm around her. "I'm so happy to be in this group with you." The morning crowd had begun straggling into the Mozart, rubbing their eyes, anxious for their coffee.

"You too," Leela said. "I love how easy it is. By the way, what did you think about this 'Feet Dance' Mevlana had us do the other day?"

"Ah, so beautiful," Stefano sighed. "I learn that if you can make love with feet only, the rest of the body—well, what to say?" He brushed his hand up and down her arm. "*Bella*, are you cold? I warm you up."

"You two look cozy," a voice said. Leela looked up to see Kate standing over them, waving her cigarette. "Will you save a place for me while I go get breakfast?"

"Actually, I must leave," Stefano said. "You can have my seat." He turned to Leela. "I must to pick up notebook before group starts. See you in a bit, *ciao,*" he said kissing her cheek, and then he was gone.

Kate sat down, flagged the passing Nepalese boy, and ordered a fried egg sandwich. "Way to go," she said. "This hottie's obviously quite into you."

"I don't know," Leela said. "He keeps talking about how great it is with me, but he hasn't asked me out or anything." She picked up her coffee cup and set it back down.

"Are you kidding?" Kate said. "The chemistry coming off you guys is so hot it blisters anyone standing too close. I would've had to sit at the next table if he hadn't gotten up to leave."

"We have a good connection, that's for sure," Leela said. "We'll see what happens."

"He's so good-looking," Kate said, lighting another cigarette. "I'll bet he's good in bed."

"Because a man's good-looking it means he's good in bed? Really? I don't think so," Leela said. "I'd say it's more of a sign he's never had to make an effort. Mevlana said the other day that if we weren't so focused on looks, we'd probably all have partners by now."

"Right. Like I'm going to be with someone ugly," Kate said. "That's really going to happen."

"There are guys in the tantra group who aren't particularly handsome who are really sensual. More so than the lookers."

"Good for them. I'm not going to be with somebody like that."

Leela looked outside and saw the young guy from Goa giving money to a beggar. She watched as he entered the café and made a beeline for their table. By his side was the bleached-blonde Japanese girl. Leela quickly averted her eyes hoping he wouldn't see them, but it was too late.

"Hello there," he said, looming over them. Leela could see well-defined arms peeking out from his shirt.

"Well, hello yourself," Kate said, looking sideways at Leela. "Have we met?"

"I'm afraid we haven't yet had the pleasure," he said. "My name's Dylan, and my sidekick here is Sasha."

The bleached-blonde Japanese girl made a little curtsey.

"Your friend there and I once shared an intimate encounter," he went on, nodding at Leela, "but until now we've never been properly introduced."

"Wait a minute," Leela said. "I wouldn't exactly call dancing together at a rave 'intimate,' and for the record, we've never partnered in the tantra group."

"That can be arranged," he winked.

I'm too old for him, Leela thought. *I don't want to see him hating on me for my wrinkles. Please go away.*

"Dylan, you sound like a lot of fun to me," Kate said. "Why don't you the two of you sit down and join us?" Leela glared at her.

"What's your story?" Kate persisted. "How did life lead you here to this perfect moment, meeting us here in exotic

India at the Mozart Café?"

"Life's completely unpredictable, isn't it?" he said. "A year ago I would never have imagined it. But a girlfriend introduced me to tantra, and that was it for me. Regular sex seems so pointless now." He grinned and glanced sideways at Leela, who was suddenly finding the colon cleanse poster fascinating.

"Love that," Kate purred. "Good taste. Where are you from?"

"Austin, Texas. I'm between jobs—I got tired of being an account manager. After group's over I'm going back to get my MBA."

"In what field?"

"Electronic entertainment. You know, video games."

"Ambitious," Kate said. "I like that, Tex. If I can give you tips on business or anything else, be sure and let me know."

"Thanks. Anyway group's starting, and we don't want to be late. Just wanted to say 'hi.' The group's damn amazing, don't you think?"

Leela nodded and took a sip of her cold coffee.

"All right then, off we go." They started out the side door and Dylan called back, "See you later."

"Why aren't you friendlier to him?" Kate said. "I'd do him."

"The whole thing doesn't interest me," Leela said. "He's just some young guy who wants to get laid."

"What's wrong with that?" Kate said. "He seems nice enough. Look, if you don't want men to be age prejudiced, then you can't be either."

"Hmm . . . good point. But I'm still not interested," Leela said. "I know we're supposed to kiss a lot of frogs and everything, but he seems more like a tadpole. Hey, I gotta go, group's about to start and I need to head out."

The Nepalese boy set down Kate's breakfast, and she fished out a few rupees to pay him. "I'm going to stay here and see who else comes along. The Mozart is a whole parade of personalities, isn't it? You just sit here and the whole world comes to you."

"Yeah, it's great," Leela said, getting up. She gathered up her bag and stepped over the bench.

"You don't mind then?" Kate asked. "If I go for him? Dylan, I mean."

"What do I care? Believe me, I have less than zero interest."

Leela took a step out to Laxmi Road and reeled back as an oxcart swerved perilously close to the café. As she looked out at the street, she saw Jack riding by on his scooter going in the direction of his flat with a woman on the back. Sitting calmly, her arms were wrapped around his waist, hands resting on his stomach, her straight dark hair barely moving despite the velocity of the bike.

HEN YOU TRACE IT ALL BACK THERE ARE only two paths," Mevlana was saying, "tantra and yoga. All traditions stem from one or the other root." Leela propped herself up on her elbow as she leaned into her cushion. The morning meditation had just ended, and all had settled in comfortably around the group room.

"The paths stemming from yoga are those that teach there is something to *do* to arrive at ultimate fulfillment," Mevlana went on. She was sitting on the dais with Bashir at her side. "The seeker needs to learn to restrain the passions, discipline the body and breath, and refrain from indulging in pleasures, including sex. One must mold and sculpt oneself into something worthy of God in order to progress along the spiritual path. This mindset becomes apparent in the whole Western ethos of striving, making, doing, or trying to get somewhere, anywhere or anyone other than who or where you are.

"Tantra on the other hand," she continued, "is the path that teaches that all is divine. In yoga, some things are holy and some things are not. In tantra, everything is perfect just the way it is, including darkness, death, difficult emotions, and sensual pleasures. No matter what is happening, it is celebrated as part of precious Life. The path to ultimate realization is in the full acceptance of the perfection of the present moment. There is nowhere to go; nothing to do, no one to be; all is as it is, and realizing this, one can surrender into a deep let-go."

Leela looked around the room which was quivering with everyone's rapt attention. She located Jack lying with his pillow doubled up under his head. A woman with curly brown hair was sitting suspiciously close.

"In its central worldview that all is divine, tantra accepted our sensual nature as an essential facet of being human. *Tantrikas* would experiment with what was forbidden by other traditions such as eating meat, drinking wine, and having sex, as a way of experiencing that *all* is a manifestation of the Divine, that the distinctions taught by society are false. These activities were performed in special ceremonies as specific occult techniques, much like the homeopathic remedy of ingesting a tiny bit of the poison that caused the illness in order to cure it."

Mevlana took a drink of water from the crystal goblet on her side table and resumed. "Of course, today when all is permitted in Western society, the performance of such 'forbidden' actions carries no meaning. Eating meat, drinking alcohol, and having sex are activities that no longer teach us anything and have, in fact, become stale. Instead, many people's lives have led to a sickening over-satiation of sensual pleasure, causing obesity, degenerative disease, and rampant boredom. Engaged in the desperate pursuit of stimulation, only a very few consider living beyond the search for more and better entertainment. Modern life by definition lacks connection to anything sacred and meaningful.

"This is particularly true of sex today. Great psychologists such as Sigmund Freud and Wilhelm Reich pointed out that the majority of people are starved for sexual fulfillment, causing all kinds of ills such as child abuse, rape, frigidity, compulsive sexuality, and obsessions of all sorts. This starvation, however, is not from lack of opportunity as it was in the past. The modern world offers plenty of images of sexuality, plenty of messages that to be sexually active is to be healthy, but little information about the connection between love, spirituality, and sex. Pornography has replaced nourishing sharing. The worship of lust has overshadowed the esoteric purpose of sex, which is to heal and purify and ultimately dissolve all into love.

"Thus, in the West, tantra has lost its meaning and has come to be a marketing slogan for better sex in a technical sense, because that is something that one can *do*. Not that there's anything wrong with better technique or bigger orgasms, I quite like it myself." Mevlana smiled at Bashir who replied with an impish grin of his own. "But it's not really the point. It is easy for the West to digest because it's something else to acquire, as one procures a house, a car, a toned physique, a trophy husband or wife. One is bored with life and wishes to obtain the identity as a tantra person. It all serves the ego and the epidemic narcissism, doesn't it?

"So, on the one hand, you have the yogic paths that condemn sex, and on the other there is the tantric path which elevates it to the level of a sacrament. Both roads have their dangers. The probable pitfall of the yogic path is an enormous inflation of ego. The yogi identifies with all that has been accomplished. The tantric path was forbidden because the danger is that one will become enthralled and addicted to the sensual circus. The pitfall with tantra is the fall into dissolution from which one may never emerge.

"Many paths today attempt to be a combination of the two. You will notice some tantric schools that are billed as 'the yoga of sex.' These approaches are arduous and involve much training of the body and breath. The original meaning of 'tantra' however, and what we teach here, remains as I have taught you."

Bashir reached around and adjusted the pillows behind Mevlana's back. She cupped his cheek in her hand and they exchanged a full loving eye connection before she continued.

"When the great yogis of the past taught that *brahmacharya,* or celibacy, is required, this is in fact a fact. However, forced celibacy before one is ready creates all kinds of ills. When sex is allowed and encouraged, one will eventually come to the point where they discover that the fulfillment one is seeking from sex is not to be found in sex. The search for Union with the Beloved can only be realized through union with the universal, not with another person, and not through the body. The body and the beloved can offer glimpses, but not the ultimate. That is for what we search. Sex leads to what we are seeking only in the transcendence of it. When one is complete, sex disappears on its own."

Leela glanced back at Jack. The woman's hand now lay across his belly. Leela's breath quickened, and as she swung her head to the front of the room, she fought to turn her attention back to Mevlana's teaching.

"In tantra, we go deeply into sex in order to complete it. When there is no repression left, no desire because it has been seen through, no more interest, we see that there is nothing there. We go beyond. We become complete. Those of us on the tantric path prefer to go through sex to get there, that's all. But we can get lost, very lost, if we expect sex to give us the answer.

"In our explorations here together in the group, we hold the possibility of completing with sex. If one is sexually fulfilled, sex will go away on its own, followed by a natural celibacy, not enforced. Actually, if from the onset of puberty one developed naturally and healthfully, which is not possible in the West, one's sex is designed to go away after age forty-two. Since very few get to the point of sexual fulfillment, we see this frantic preoccupation with the delay of aging, because if one is not sexually attractive to partners, the belief is that one will never become sexually satiated. There is a certain poignancy to it, yes?

"So, the purpose of tantra is to go beyond sex, but it seems difficult to interest anyone in this aspect of it."

"I hope I don't get there in this lifetime," a man's voice called out.

"Yes," Mevlana said. "Many people would prefer not to develop to the point of transcending sex in this lifetime." She smiled fondly at Bashir. "But my teacher said that unless you have gotten to the point where you are no longer looking for love, you haven't even really begun."

Class was over and everyone began rustling around, finding their backpacks, and returning the pillows to the heap against the wall. Leela sat up and stretched and as she did, lifted her eyes to Mevlana. Around Mevlana's head there appeared to be a halo of golden light, radiating out in spokes and faintly shimmering. Leela shook her head. *I didn't really see that*, she thought. *There must be something wrong with my contacts*—she glanced back at Jack only to see him and the woman embracing—*or this place is making me weird.*

tHE ONLY SOUND WAS THE WHIRLING FANS. With a start Leela noticed a leg lying across her chest; for a moment, she couldn't figure out whose it was. The atmosphere hung suspended with an odor of pomegranate and desert air. A hairless chest appeared in her line of sight, and with the sickening thud of an elevator dropping, Leela realized that Jack had been successful at bagging his prey.

After the last few syllables of the morning discourse, she had headed down to the lotus pond for some quiet reflection. Almost immediately Jack had appeared, sat down beside her, and started in stroking her arm and massaging her neck.

"Stop it!" she had protested in a voice too loud for the meditative space. A bald man wearing a *lungi* scowled at her and put his finger to his lips. "Stop it," she repeated in a whisper. "You are incorrigible."

"I want you to come over to my house," he had said. "There's something I want to talk to you about."

And although she could hardly believe it, she had taken his bait and was now sprawled out among Jack's thrashed sheets that were of course of such high thread count he had to have brought them from Europe. Dammit.

As soon as they had walked in the door, he had been all over her: licking her neck, squeezing her breasts, sliding his palm down to the 'V' between her legs. The impact of his desire had pounded her good sense into submission as he led her to the bed. He had swiftly put on a condom, rubbed her perfunctorily before he entered her, thrust and thrust and thrust until he came and then it was over. Her body rose up to meet his with some degree of pleasure, but she had barely begun to feel aroused. It certainly hadn't anything to do with anything "tantric." Rather, what it had been was a horny guy with an insistent little button of a cock using her to score.

She looked over at the tiny bits of coarse black hair around his nipples and navel. His hands and fingers were plump and stubby like his dick, as were his toes. He hadn't even bothered to take off his glasses.

She pushed his leg away and got up to get her clothes. Crossing the room she felt ashamed of her body, ashamed to be naked. Slipping on her favorite blue *kurta* and drawing the gauze trousers up around her hips, she heard him stirring behind her. She dreaded turning around but took a deep breath, picked up her bag, and faced him.

"You don't mind if I don't go with you?" He was leaning back against the wall, his genitals exhibited prominently with the arrogance of a bullfighter.

"That's all right," she said, as she unhinged the lock. "I know how to flag down a rickshaw all by myself."

"ЯEADY TO GO STIR UP SOME TROUBLE?" LEELA asked as she scooped up the last bit of *palak paneer*. The lure of the Mozart Café and its shady inhabitants had become an addiction. She could no longer make it through the day without seeing who was there. *Maybe Stefano would appear? One of the hotties from the group? An exciting new stranger?* A mosquito landed on her arm and with a loud whack! she turned it into a trail of smeared blood. "Hah! Take that! You pesky little bugger."

"God, the mosquitoes in India are unstoppable," Kate said, laying down her fork. "As are we." She shook a Marlboro out of its pack and struck a match. "Let's linger a bit and have a coffee. The boys will have to wait." Twilight had turned to dark as they sat at Ananda's Restaurant, sharing the spinach curry, a *Kingfisher*, and as many rumors about ashram inhabitants as they could remember.

Votive candles and the lit ends of cigarettes were the only sources of light on the patio, unless you counted the faint glow of mosquito coils smoking under the tables. It was hard to tell which was worse, suffering the incessant bites or inhaling the air made poisonous by the bug-killing devices. DDT was still legal in India, and Leela wondered if that's what they were breathing from those spiraled green disks the waiters lit at dusk.

"Oh, here's something I almost forgot," Kate said, taking a long drag on her cigarette. "Did I ever tell you about the brief encounter I had with Bashir?" She drew out the exhale for impact.

"You? No, you're kidding. What's the story with that?" Leela shifted in her seat, turning full attention to Kate.

"Well, it was at a party at that guy's house, you know that guy, fortyish, says he used to be a history professor?

"That guy with the long ringlets, balding on top?"

"Yeah, him. Gross. Anyway, nice enough guy once you get over the hairdo. He was having this party at his house, small soiree-type thing, not the usual techno bash you find around here. So there I was," Kate continued, "alone in the kitchen and Bashir comes in saying 'I knew there was something good in here to eat.'"

"Bashir would actually say such a stupid line as that? And you fell for it?"

"Well," Kate said, blushing, "it was one of the dumbest things I'd heard in a long time, granted, but it came from the famous Bashir, you know? I'll admit to having had fantasies of being with him. We all know how hot he is. But it's more than that: I wanted to be with Mevlana's man. I mean, she can have anybody. I'd like to have that kind of power."

Leela felt her stomach turn over. "You'd like to have that kind of power, and you think it has something to do with sleeping with another woman's man? That's disgusting."

"Well, I wanted to taste what she has," Kate said. She lit a new cigarette and put it in the ashtray where it joined another one still burning. "You're sounding awfully self-righteous all of a sudden."

The waiter appeared bearing two cups of Nescafe, black. He took a silver-handled brush out of his pocket and cleared the crumbs off the table. "Madams," he said, clicking his heels and making a bow as he left.

"Bashir and I didn't actually complete the act anyway," Kate said. "I mean, we rolled around on the futon in the next room nearly naked for a while. He's really sexy, you know, his kisses were like . . . he tasted like apricot jam. He was wearing one of those tank tops he always wears, and I could feel his definition. He has virtually no body fat . . ." she drifted off, her pupils narrowing into pinpoints. Then she shook her head. "But when it came right down to it, it wasn't quite special enough, you know what I mean?" She smiled. "At least not yet."

"So you left?"

"Actually when I did leave, he was flirting with that Australian bitch we both hate, that one with the perfectly augmented body and collagen lips. I can't stand to be in the same room with her."

"C'mon, she is lovely; you have to admit."

They paused to peruse the other tables, all of which were full by now. Most of the diners looked vaguely familiar, ashram visitors, but the people who frequented Ananda's Restaurant were not the folks on Leela's A-list. *Maybe they're the true A-list,* Leela thought, *but they're not my chosen few.* No, Leela's type was now the folks who hung out at the infinitely sleazier Mozart Café. The thought of the possibilities in an evening at the Mozart was delightful, fraught with intrigue and naughtiness. Maybe this was the night that the Perfect Beloved would find his way from across the universe to land at the Mozart, as all third world travelers eventually did. You never knew. It was seldom dull, because if it wasn't your night for something to happen, you could observe the never-ending soap opera of it happening for someone else.

"Let's get the check. This place is so over."

"Yeah, time to up the ante."

On their way out they stopped by the table of a heavily tattooed Brit Kate was having a flirtation with. "There's a big party Friday night at the AGM Farm," he said, smiling into her eyes. "Will you be there?"

"If you'll be there, I wouldn't miss it," she replied, flipping her hair. "Starts around midnight, as usual?" He nodded. "See you there, if not before."

Entering Laxmi Road was always a shock to the senses. As Leela and Kate began walking toward the Mozart, she tried to ignore the frenetic scene whizzing past, the motorcycles, cars, rickshaws, bicycles, other pedestrians. They walked past the dogs that looked like they were dead, past beggars who looked like they would soon be dead, and past the Greek heroin addict who looked worse than an Indian beggar, all forlorn and evil.

The gossip had run out, so they must have been talking about something else. Leela wouldn't have noticed the disheveled Brown man ride by on a rickety bike if he hadn't reached out and grabbed her breast as he passed.

She stopped. All movement on the street stopped. Kate stopped beside her, with a questioning look. "Did something just happen?" There was a crack in the wall of time, then languidly, in slow motion, people and rickshaws and motorcycles began to move again.

Leela had promised herself that the next time her body was accosted, she would not freeze. In the short time she'd been here, it had happened three times by Indian men: Once a man had come up after meditation, given her a hug, and wouldn't let go, pressing his body closer and closer before she could wiggle free; another time two young men on a motorcycle had sped past her on the road behind the ashram and swatted her butt hard as they passed. Once a man had run up and started kissing her neck while she was sitting under a tree. Each time she had been stunned into paralysis, not knowing how to react or even what had happened until she had time to think about it. She had vowed that next time, she wouldn't just accept it like a victim.

I never speak up to men, Leela said to herself. *I never say anything. I don't speak my truth. I need to start now.*

"Fuck you! You asshole!" Leela yelled at the man on the bicycle. "Fuck you!" She yelled impotently, knowing he didn't speak English, but certainly he would get the gist. Feeling overcome by a confused mess of futility, shame, and the inherent femaleness of it all; at least she hadn't stood there mute.

"What? What happened?"

Before she could answer Kate, a man on a big shiny motorcycle pulled up. Leela noted that he was a well-groomed Indian man in his early fifties wearing the fleshier body that denotes affluence in India. "Madam, what is wrong?" he asked.

"That man, he touched my body as he rode by." Leela gestured to her breast to show him how it happened. "It was no accident. He meant to do it." The words shot out in short bursts. "He insulted me."

"I see," the man said, and nodded to them. Without another word, he took off on the bike, U-turning around in the direction the other man had gone.

"What was that all about?"

"Haven't a clue." They started walking toward the Mozart again. "I just had to say something. It really pisses me off, how they just get away with it." Leela said.

"I know, it's happened to all of us."

A little Indian boy ran right in front of them, his body barricading their progress. "Madams, please, they want you to come over there."

"Who, what?" Dimly, as they turned behind, they saw a crowd gathering across the road, and someone gesturing for them to come over.

"They want you to come," the boy repeated. His shiny black eyes reflected the glint from the headlights of the passing traffic. "Please, madams, please come."

As she peered at the crowd and tried to make out what was happening, Leela thought she saw a group of Indian men standing in a circle. "Oh no, now this is getting too big," she said to Kate, "I don't know that I want to get involved. I mean, all the guy did was feel me up, for chrissake. Let's get outta here. Shouldn't we just leave?"

"Look, it's happened to me; it's happened to you; it's happened to all of us. If you don't say anything, they will just keep doing this."

Leela knew Kate was right. Every Western woman she'd met had some tale of how her body had been accosted by Indian men. In some ways, it must be an affront to Indian culture the way Western women felt free to show their bodies, striding around taking their sexual pleasure in ways forbidden not only to Indian women, but to Indian men as well. There were the imported Hollywood movies promoting the idea that American women will have sex with anyone at the drop of a hat. It may have been the men's sexual starvation, it may have been their desire to grab at a freedom beyond their comprehension, but it was also a way that in all cultures men have asserted their right to power over women's bodies.

"I guess you're right. We have to say something or it will keep on happening. Will you come with me?"

When they got to the circle of what was now a dozen men, the man from the big motorcycle was standing in the center under a streetlight. Cowering beside him, bowing his head, was her aggressor. He looked small and feeble and wouldn't make eye contact with Leela or Kate.

"Tell us what happened," the motorcycle man ordered politely.

Leela looked around at the assembled group and made a decision to be bold. "He touched me here," she pointed. "He meant to. It was no accident. He grabbed my body; he insulted me."

"Okay," the man said, "you can go."

That was it? Leela looked at Kate, who looked at Leela. It was over; they were dismissed. They shrugged and started walking away, naively thinking it was all over. Then there was a loud whack! and a man's scream pierced the night air.

I have never heard a man scream before, Leela thought. *In movies I have heard the screams of many women, but never men. I have heard myself scream at the sight of innocent insects in my room; I have heard the shrieks and cries of injured children. I have heard old people wailing, yelling at things that weren't there when I visited my grandmother in the nursing home, but never in my life had I even imagined the sound of a man screaming in pain.*

Another smack and the terrible sound of the man screaming again, screaming in agony, and a slap, then a punch. The assembled men had metamorphosed into a group of vigilantes, like a posse from the Wild Wild West, only these men were small-boned and brown with the blackest of hair and eyes. An impromptu judge and jury had been set up in their midst, and they were wreaking justice upon the man who had transgressed the law.

More and more sounds of flesh bludgeoning flesh, then worst of all, the sound of a crack. *My god, was that a bone breaking?* Leela wondered. The man was howling and the men were shouting, and Leela and Kate didn't want to think what they were doing to him as he screamed again and again.

The commotion was still roaring as they scurried away. Long after they were out of range of hearing, they could still sense the din from the crowd continuing. "My god, did I do the right thing by speaking up?" Leela began to cry. "That poor guy, I never would have said anything if I knew this was going to happen."

"No," Kate said, looking pale and tired, "you did the right thing. You had to do it for you. How they handle it is their business. That's one guy who won't hassle women anymore."

As each went home to her separate flat, the Mozart and its imaged pleasures were a distant memory. *I don't know,* Leela thought. *All these terrible, painful things happen so you can grow as a person?*

EELA KNOCKED ON THE DOOR OF JACK'S PENT-
house. She could tell he was home because the padlock
had been removed. No one answered. Maybe he was taking a nap, or what if he was in there with someone? She
knocked again.

There was the sound of the deadbolt sliding and then
Jack was before her, bare-chested and scratching his stomach
which bulged softly over his white drawstring pants. The
contrast of the white fabric, his olive skin and black hair
was beautiful, Leela thought. He didn't say anything, just
stood there looking.

"I want to come in and talk," Leela said. "There are some
things I have to say to you."

Jack yawned and held out his arm to show her the way
in. "Something to drink?" he asked.

"No, thanks." She walked over and sat down on the
couch in the same spot she had inhabited before. Jack
sprawled out on the other end, cocking one leg over the

other knee. The feel of his skin so close was inviting and it occurred to her to snuggle up next to him, but she reminded herself he was not that kind of guy, even if she wanted him to be. "No time for drinks and polite talk," she said. "What I'm going to say you might not like very much. But it must be said."

She took a deep breath. "*That* didn't have anything to do with 'practicing tantra.'" She uncrossed her legs and put both feet on the floor. "That was more like what they call date rape. I told you numerous times I didn't want to. You just kept pushing on, taking advantage of my confusion." She paused to see if he was tracking.

Jack shrugged. "What can I say? You seemed like you wanted it."

"Part of me is attracted to you, that's true. But that doesn't mean I wanted to have sex with you. I went out of here feeling used and disrespected, and what you did hurt me. Let me put it more globally, because I know it's not just me. What you do hurts women."

Jack shook his head. "I don't hurt anybody. They all get what they came for. They all have orgasms." His smile was smug and self-congratulatory.

"I didn't," Leela said. The silence in the room felt loud. She let the pause take its effect before continuing. "Nobody will tell you that, will they? I faked it so you would stop. You don't know. How would you? You had no regard for my feelings. I went home hurt, humiliated. I said no, and you didn't listen. You didn't respect me or my limits." Despite the gulping of air she had done to try to hold back the tears, they began to slide down her face without permission. He sat there immovable. "You don't even mind that it upsets me so much I'm crying. How is it you can sit there and not care?"

"I don't like feelings," he said. He reached over and flicked on the music. Leonard Cohen's sonorous voice began to hold forth.

"I mean, what are you doing here at a spiritual ashram?" Leela asked. "Trying to screw as many women as you can? What's that about? What does it get you? You know, some people are here for serious reasons."

She reached over and took off his glasses. "I saw into your eyes once. I saw your true nature. Your vulnerability. I want to see that man now." His eyes were soft, blinking, as though he were seeing the sunlight after waking up from a dream. He reached to get his glasses back, brushing her thigh on the way. "No," she said, moving over and putting them on the shelf.

"I want to have a real conversation with you," she said. She leaned in closer. "Look, we're in a 'relationship' whether either one of us wants to be or not. We're connected due to the fact that we're in this group, that we live in this community together, that we are part of the *sangha*. There's a potential here for friendship, and you are willing to settle for so little."

Without his glasses his eyes were soft and fragile. Now she understood why he had to leave his glasses on during sex, at least the type of sex he was used to. He had to hide how

much was revealed behind his glasses, the tender unprotect-
ed quality of his eyes.

"You know, most women won't tell you," she continued, "and I understand it because I've been that way most
of my life. Men are always right, and our feelings are always
wrong. But I'm learning a lot here and it doesn't help me
or anybody else to keep quiet any more. It's like, I demand
that you acknowledge the relationship you have with me.
You don't get to just use me. You hurt me, and I'm going to
tell you. So hear it: it hurts to be treated like that. You can't
do it around me."

The afternoon sun pouring in the arched windows had
mellowed to a mustard hue. Jack walked over to the shelving
and retrieved his glasses. As he put them back on, his posture
straightened, and his belly seemed to retract. He stretched
his arms up to the ceiling then swung them loosely a few
times before he sat down.

"It's a funny thing," Jack said. "I'm not that good-looking, but I've never had trouble getting women. Lots and lots
of women, wherever I go. I don't know what it is."

"First of all," Leela said, "I don't believe that you don't
know what it is. I think it's calculated and studied, like other
guys I've met." He was looking straight into her eyes. There
was no smile.

"Second, it's because there's no uncertainty in your pursuit. It's the lack of ambivalence in your desire. A normal
man isn't sure, is tentative about being rejected, but with
guys like you, there's no doubt. You're not afraid of rejection.

You know what and who you want, and you are going to get it. To be the object of that much desire, well, that's what women have been fantasizing about since girlhood. You play on that to avoid any real type of relating."

"Okay, enough," he said. He turned and fiddled with the music, and Leela couldn't tell if he'd turned it up or down. "Okay. It has occurred to me more than once that I might want, might have, well, might be what some would call a sex addict." He crossed his arms across his chest. "Sometimes it's like I don't know what to do. I know if I go find somebody and make something happen, I'll feel better. The payoff is good, what can I say."

Leela felt a strange mix of revulsion and desire. "Look," she said. "You've acquired a lot of power in your life. You've got the money thing down, you've established enough career-wise to have proven yourself, and you can get laid any time you want. What good is it? What is it for? Just an endless stream of more and more women? What for? What good are you contributing, what was all that you accomplished for? Have you ever let anyone love you? Loved anyone? Been with anyone longer than a week?"

"There was that girl I lived with for two and a half years when I was working."

"That girl? Does she have a name?"

He looked away.

"When you had made your money you were done? That life was over? Thanks for helping and supporting me but now I'm moving on? Like those movie stars who ditch their wife once they're successful, not realizing she's the reason they made it?"

"I don't know what to do next," Jack said. His fingers were drumming out a beat on the arm of the couch twice as fast as the music. "I really don't know. I'm thinking maybe I'll go learn massage with these people who have a school in the Thai islands. Or maybe I'll go back and make some more money, I don't know."

"You don't need to make any more money, for god's sake. You're just going backward because you don't know what else to do. You're a powerful being and doing nothing with it, just feeding your own stupid ego.

"You need to change," Leela continued. "Be a different kind of person. You use people. You abuse your power. You're like some kind of a black magician or something. You've learned and mastered the ways of power, but then you use them for your own ego gratification rather than for good, and at the expense of other people. That's why you're burned out and don't know what to do."

She felt exhausted. Jack, on the other hand, was examining the hem of his pants with great interest. He got up and returned with a pair of scissors, sat down and cut off a loose thread. Then he leaned back and looked at Leela. She smelled the faint odor of oranges. He reached out for her hand and this time, it was devoid of manipulation.

"I don't know what it is about you," he said, running his thumb over the back of her hand. "I never asked anyone to 'practice tantra' with me like that before, and it struck me as strange when I said it. We have something to learn from each other, I guess."

They sat for a moment, holding hands, watching the shadows the setting sun was throwing against the wall. Leonard Cohen intoned his last note.

"I guess the way I look at it," Leela said, "is that this ashram experience is all one big experiment in doing things differently and taking risks. Then we go back to the West and our lives there changed by the experience. We need, that is, I need to try to say things and relate in a more real way than I've ever done before."

He didn't say anything but squeezed her hand.

"I guess you could say that we did ultimately 'practice tantra,'" she said, "if tantra is defined as sex through the heart chakra rather than through the genitals. Because now, whether you want to admit it or not, we have a heart connection."

Sheepish, he looked away. "C'mon," she said, "admit it. Give it up." He wouldn't say anything, but his smile gave all the confirmation she needed.

LEELA DECIDED TO TAKE THE BACK WAY HOME. Behind the ashram many Indians lived, first the compounds of rich families guarded by frail old Indian men sitting on folding chairs 24/7. Then came a depression of land gorged with tiny huts where the less fortunate resided.

Adjacent to the settlement, she passed an enclosed shrine to Ganesh, the elephant god who brought material wealth. The miniature tin building held a garishly painted statue behind a locked screen. Devotees had spent many a *rupee* on strings of marigolds and *burfi* sweets left as offerings on the steps.

As she neared the corner to turn to her flat, an Indian man in his mid-twenties stopped her. He wore a stiffly starched Western-style shirt, immaculately white, and black trousers. His little mustache quivered. He came up to Leela's chin.

"Please, sir," he said, addressing Leela. Leela wanted to scream at him that she was not a "sir" but she bit her tongue. *Was the only honorific in Hindi masculine?*

"My wife and I," he continued. His voice was insistent and firm, determined to get what he was after. "We are married new. Please, sir, honor us, bless our marriage."

Behind him was a shy Indian woman, dressed in *punjabi* and beaded sandals, her glossy black hair gathered into a thick braid. Her eyes were downcast and she clung to her husband's arm. Leela wanted to laugh. *Her bless a marriage? Ludicrous. What was with these people?*

Then she realized that to them she was a *sannyasin*, a person on a spiritual quest, which in India denotes a holy person. She laughed to think of herself as holy, yeah, celibate and all. *But then again*, she argued with herself, *I am dedicating my life to spiritual search.* In the West, this may have made her an uncool person, but here it was honored as a respected life path. Maybe her spirituality was not that of a celibate monk dedicated to hours of *pranayama* or late nights studying the dharma. She was equally as determined as he was to see it to the end. Maybe she ought to regard her own life choices with a little more respect.

How did one bless a marriage? "All blessings for your marriage," Leela said. "May you live long and happily together." She waved her arms around as she imagined a priest would. *Would that do?*

The man smiled at his wife who nodded. The newly married couple walked on into their life together, and Leela walked on into her life alone.

EELA RECOUNTED THE VIGILANTE STORY FOR Helmut, the big-bellied guard at the front gate who seemed in the know.

He pondered a minute. "It's a caste thing," he answered.

"What do you mean, a caste thing?" Leela remembered her assailant, how his clothes had been rumpled and dirty, and that the man on the motorcycle had worn a cleanly pressed shirt and well-cut hair.

"Well, it was an excuse for men from one caste to beat up someone from a lower one, all in the name of protecting women."

"What do you mean?" Leela asked, feeling her anger rise. "You mean to tell me that those men were not avenging the disgrace of a woman? That it wasn't a chivalrous act, to ensure that women are treated respectfully?" She thought of the great Indian goddesses, of Saraswati and Kali, of Durga riding her tiger, of Shiva and Shakti, a male/female pair, communing in divine sexual congress throughout the ages.

"I thought they worshipped women in the Hindu religion, held them in a sacred place. It seemed as if they were punishing that guy for insulting a woman's honor."

"Things in India are often not what they seem." Helmut checked a gate pass and nodded the man inside. "It was really an issue among men, one man getting out of line, and the other ones ensuring that the hierarchy of the caste system persists. You were just an excuse for them to enforce their superiority, even to the point of violence. The higher caste enforcing its power over the lower, whatever it takes. A lesson to all that the status quo will not be interrupted."

As Leela walked over to sit by a tree, images of what she hadn't seen began forcing themselves into her mind: rivulets of red running down the man's face, blue welts rising on his torso, his arms, a finger broken backward, the man being beaten into a bloody mass by the ruling caste. One after the other, the pictures came unbidden, interspersed with scenes from violent movies she had tried not to see in the West—a trailed smear of mosquito blood, a broken evil body lying by the side of Laxmi Road. She heard screams, and howls, the pain and repulsion crashing through her brain and blinding her inner sight. She felt lost in the terrible blindness of the world as it swirled around her. She struggled to tame her fear and horror of man's cruelty to other men, and the knowledge that women were immaterial in the men's game of power over each other.

I don't get what's going on here, Leela thought. *The relationships between men and women, East versus West, all that*

I've been taught that doesn't seem to work versus the tantric worldview. The stakes are getting really high when people are being beaten to death. Now it's not just my heart getting broken repeatedly, it's bones and souls getting beat down. Women's seeming powerlessness in the scheme of things juxtaposed against the sexual power of Mevlana . . . What have I gotten myself into?

tHE MUSIC HELD OUT ITS HAND IN A WEL-coming gesture. Leela peered in through the walls of the meditation hall, wondering whether or not to enter. The schedule for the day had posted a Celebration Event at seven this evening, but celebrating *what* it hadn't said. Musicians had been tuning up for twenty minutes, and a crowd of a hundred people was already swaying to the beginnings of a melody. Leela closed her eyes as the tune seemed to lift her up and carry her toward the door. She swallowed her isolation and entered the room.

The floor and the podium at the front of the meditation hall were made of ice-gray marble with black veins running throughout. The stone lent a clean cool atmosphere no matter how sweltering it was outside, or no matter how much heat was being generated from the exhilaration of dancers. The hall was big enough that one could remain anonymous, but not so big that one couldn't be located if someone was searching the crowd intent to find you. Which Leela often found herself doing when she was supposed to be meditating, scanning for men she had seen earlier that day at the Mozart or at lunch. *That's the kind of spiritual aspirant I am,* she thought, *looking for men when I'm supposed to be meditating. Well,* she rationalized; *if I can't get over my patterns I might as well go into them all the way.*

People, at least a couple hundred more, were streaming in from all four doorways to join the crowd behind the musicians. A large area of the room in front of the podium had been roped off and covered with Persian rugs. Six pillows were arranged in two rows in the center. People were leaning up against the velvet ropes as if they were waiting to view celebrities at an event they dreamed of attending, jostling and jockeying for the space with the best view.

The tantra group was on break, and Leela had been attending several active meditations a day which meant she was fully oxygenated from all that aerobic activity. She could feel her pants looser around her hips which always made her happy, but she reminded herself it wasn't really the point to focus on here in India.

The anticipation in the air was sweet and thick and sticky. Leela had no idea what people were waiting for, although she supposed it had something to do with the vacant pillows. People were now six persons thick against the ropes, then seven, then eight; then they were standing so far back that folks had given up on the idea of being able to see and were just dancing in a ring along the outside. Leela took a deep breath and with the intention of a rock concert attendee, pushed boldly through the crowd right to center front.

People were undulating and singing along with the music, dancing, and flailing their arms about hippie-style or cupping their hands around their hearts as if the music could channel right in. Palms were upright and open, signifying a readiness to receive. Everyone knew the words to the songs, and Leela was catching on. The tempo was increasing, and the group's energy rising right along with it.

All eyes turned toward the door behind the podium as Mevlana entered, hands in a *namaste* gesture to the crowd, smiling widely, followed by Emma and another of the female assistants. All three were middle-aged, large-bodied by Western media standards, and dressed in white gowns. Leela could see that they were calmly and strikingly beautiful, all three.

The crowd began cheering as the women seated themselves on the row of pillows facing the audience. Then the women closed their eyes and disappeared inside, away from the music and the general high energy surrounding them. They sat very still, having gone where the surrounding excitement did not exist.

"Why are they sitting on those pillows?" Leela whispered to the man standing beside her.

"Watch. They're going to be channeling," he replied, not taking his eyes off them. "Just feel what happens. They'll be receiving and transmitting divine energy."

The crowd was dancing now with arms extended in the air, and some of the bodies dripped with sweat. The musicians were in charge of manipulating the emotional tone of the room, and the steady percussion would not allow anyone full relief from the mounting tension.

The women at the center opened their eyes. They smiled beatifically at the crowd, turning their heads all around the inside rim of the circle, *namaste*'ing all who met their eyes. Then there was silence. Three persons, a young boy in his twenties, a slender girl not much older, and an Indian grandfather were led by three men to the cushions in front of the mediums. The three arranged themselves facing the women, while the men kneeled behind them for support.

The music picked up. The women turned their attention to the supplicants, then went inside and started swaying. One by one, they lifted their arms skyward, heads thrown back. This continued while the music regained its former rapturous quality. Then Mevlana, followed by the two flanking her, reached out her right palm and covered the young boy's forehead, tipping his head back.

He began to go into convulsions, his body jerking around like a fish out of its bowl. The man behind him ensured that he was not hurting himself. Mevlana had her eyes open now, staring intently, and she was beaming whatever it was into the boy's third eye. When he finally came to a place of no movement, she removed her hand and sat back in meditation posture on her cushion.

The girl next to him had swooned, lost consciousness, a blissful smile on her face. The grandfather sat as though paralyzed. The look on their faces after they had been zapped was so utterly relaxed and soft that Leela wondered how she could volunteer. The music soared and the crowd resumed dancing, clapping, and singing the lyrics they all seemed to know.

The men helped the three to their feet and led them out while another three were brought in, with the process repeating itself. The crowd was going wild celebrating the energy transmission, going up and down with the music, which was at times soft and mellow, at times orgiastic and tribal. *Either the women had some special powers that they were channeling to the supplicants in front of them, or hundreds of people were colluding to make it seem so,* Leela thought.

The beat once again reached critical peak, and she was dancing as crazily and euphorically as anyone else. Leela looked at Mevlana who at that moment was placing her hand on a forehead before her. As palm met flesh, Leela felt a rumbling at the base of her own spine. Her head tipped back, seemingly to clear her throat so that more air could get in, and she was aware of feeling hot and flushed. Her breathing became full and gasping. *What was going on?* She was taking in huge gulps of air, the exhales forcing themselves out, when suddenly, there was no mistaking this, her vagina started contracting in strong hard pulsations, one after the other, multiple orgasms happening right there in the crowded room. Little pleasure noises wanted to come out of her mouth, but she stifled them as the contractions continued. Her eyes teared up at the wonder of it; she felt all at the same time confused, joyful, and afraid. The energy pulsed and subsided, and she knelt down on the floor.

She reached out her arms along the marble and prostrated herself to whatever had entered her and fucked her and given her this experience. She was completely spent, limp, and her mind had short-circuited: She didn't know what to think or feel, and she didn't have anybody to tell. A cosmic orgasm, an orgasm without a man or herself giving it to her, no manipulation, no making it happen. She stayed like that on the ground, surrendered, barely noticing that the celebration had ended and feet were scurrying toward the exits.

A pair of arms slipped around her from behind. She was gently lifted up and shifted into someone's embrace, while she kept her eyes closed so as not to break the spell. Whoever it was smoothed her hair and stroked her head, held her in its arms and softly rocked her. It didn't matter who it was; Existence had sent a Perfect Beloved to her at this life-changing moment. Leela couldn't believe her good fortune, and she cried with joy.

After some time, she turned her face up to see who it was. The shock made her turn away, for it was the guy from the tantra group, Geno, the gym rat who had ignored her in the walkway. They shared a long eye gaze, then without a word, he slid softly up and away.

The revelation washed over her that orgasmic energy is independent of sex, rather, it is pulsating infinitely, always, underneath everything. *Maybe these tantra people were on the right track after all.*

Leela sat up and looked around the meditation hall. There were a few couples spread out around the room, lingering before they went out into the night. The musicians were carrying out equipment and rolling up rugs. She felt a wave of immense gratitude and at the same time, a pleasing sense of her own insignificance in the whole scheme of things. It was enough to be allowed to just be a being, not to have to be anyone special, just one little person having one little life.

tHE MUSKY SMELL OF INCENSE GREETED them as they filed into the room. Light streamed in through the tiny windows close to the ceiling, streaking the walls in shades of peach. The assistants stood in a line to welcome each participant as they entered. Leela smiled at Travis who responded with a wink.

"Today we will perform *latihan*," Mevlana said, after they had all settled. "Or rather, if we are fortunate, *latihan* will grace us with its presence. Let's see," she continued, motioning to the assistants to take their places in the corners of the room.

"Let's have the men choose partners this time."

Leela felt the momentary junior high school fear that no one would choose her. Such a relief when she felt a touch on her arm, and even more when she saw it was Stefano. "*Ciao, bella*," he whispered. She returned his smile, and then furtively looked around the room to see who had partnered with whom. Ian was still with the perfect Swede while Jack stood next to Sasha, the bleached blonde, looking straight ahead and not at her, which was, Leela thought, as much closeness as he could handle.

"*Latihan* is a word indicating the hidden power in all beings," Mevlana said. "Today we are going to observe how this power can manifest in spontaneous body movements, if, in moments of stillness, we allow for them. When one practices *latihan*, there is no plan, no direction, no force in any way. You will simply receive the pulsations from the center of your being, in whatever form they come."

Leela shifted from one foot to the other. She looked at Stefano who was watching Bashir select a tune. Bashir stood up, stretched lazily baring his sculpted torso, and exited out the side door.

Mevlana instructed one person from each couple to pick up a bedsheet from the pile lying where the musicians usually sat. "Now face your partner, and tie the ends of the sheet diagonally across your shoulders." For a few minutes all Leela could hear was the swishing of sheets, embarrassed laughter, and her own heart beating nervously.

"Standing as close as you can to each other without touching, you will allow the movements to arise from within," Mevlana said. "They will be so slow as to be imperceptible to an observer. Neither of you will guide the movements. Allow yourself to be moved instead of doing the moving. No speaking, no sounds at all. Just be with the movement coming from inside. Enjoy."

Stefano put up his right arm, and Leela matched it with her left. One of the assistants started the music which was barely music at all. Faint electronica: it was so slow it was more like silence than music. Sometimes it sounded like a guitar string plucked listlessly, sometimes like plops of water into a pond. The notes resonated throughout the room, moving out in concentric circles, echoing out from the center of Leela's being.

Were they moving? Leela breathed in the pleasure of standing so close to Stefano. All his morning hugs in the Mozart, leading up to this intimacy. Here they were, chests almost touching, breathing together, bound to each other by a sheet. She became aware that their arms had moved down nearly to their waists, but she hadn't noticed it while it was happening. *Was he leading? Was she?*

There was nothing to do, nothing to focus on, so the breath in their bellies became foremost in her awareness. She felt his inhales and exhales, when his breath stopped momentarily, or when it speeded up. It was a heady mix being so physically present with nothing to think about, nothing to do, so close to another human being. Especially one she liked as much as she did Stefano.

There was movement happening, surely. Around the room couples spiraled around each other like seashells. The movements their bodies made were barely visible, microscopic whorls. The music now poured out as infinitesimal tinkly sounds, while a wave seemed to wash the room with a faint, staticky quality. It was all an exquisite Chinese water torture.

The bodies tuned into each other and moved by themselves, from inside. Leela felt a quiet joy, waiting to see how the movements would shape Stefano's and her bodies. It was an ecstatic surrender to the place deep within that was the source of all movements.

Leela slowly turned her head to look at Stefano at the same time he turned to look at her. His eyes were a glimmering, moist soft brown, and as they met hers, they each fell down the rabbit hole of the other's eyes. Somehow it was the closest embrace even though their bodies never touched. *We are making perfect love*, Leela thought.

The music ended, and Mevlana asked the couples to close their eyes and sit together in silence. Leela's awareness was deeply rooted in her *hara*, and her breath came full and freely. She felt Stefano next to her, breathing in unison. The thought crossed her mind: *This had been better than sex.*

Many minutes had passed when Mevlana whispered, "These movements will transform you if you let them." A few more minutes passed in silence. "When you are ready, slowly get up. Go with your partner to the park and be together in nature."

Stefano tenderly removed the sheet that bound them and replaced it on the pile. He took her hand, and silently they left the room. The park had been built next door to the ashram as its gift to the community. At certain times of the day, it was closed to visitors from the outside. Stefano and Leela got permission from the guard to enter and slipped past the gate.

It was so densely forested inside that the air was darkened, in stark contrast to the blazing sun outside. A stream curled next to the pathway, and Leela and Stefano paused on the bridge. Hand in hand, they walked past a tiny statue of the Buddha in a field of moss, and past a thatch of bamboo. When they caught up with the stream again, it was edged by big black stones they sat down on.

Leela looked at Stefano. His wispy hair lifted in the light breeze. Light filtered down through the trees, illuminating their little sanctuary. A bird called out to its mate. *It is absolute perfection*, Leela thought. *Nothing else is needed.*

THE MORNING AIR WAS SO BITING THAT LEELA shivered inside her thermal anorak. The Mozart was quiet this early; the traffic hadn't started up yet. She was on her second espresso when Stefano eased onto the bench next to her.

"I couldn't sleep, *bella,*" he said.

"Neither could I. It was just so perfect, all of it." She looked shyly over at him to see if she was embarrassing herself. "I mean, it was so high, being there with you, so surrendered. It was perfect, one of the most perfect moments ever." She hesitated, and then asked, "Was it like that for you?"

"Let me get a coffee, then I will answer you." He got up, went over to the counter, then came back and sat down. They sat together in silence until the Nepalese boy brought the coffee and collected the money. Stefano took a sip, then put the cup down.

"Yes." He turned to face her. "The *latihan* was one of the highest, most total experiences of my life. Thank you for sharing it with me." He reached over and kissed her neck, then put his arm across her shoulders and pulled her closer for warmth.

Yes, Leela thought. *Yes.* The traffic was moving. It would be full daylight soon.

ait," Mevlana called out. The room was full of the exit sounds of group participants rustling through backpacks, zipping up jackets, and unscrewing water bottles to take a drink. There was instant silence as conversations were put on hold. "I have homework for you for tomorrow," she said. Class had already run over an hour, so Leela hesitated, unsure whether they were supposed to come back and sit down or not.

"You can stay where you are," Mevlana said. She looked even taller than usual as most of them were kneeling. She may have been fatigued from the long day's teaching, but her eyes were merry and bright. "When you go out into your lives in the world tonight, I want you to observe who you can have."

Leela realized she had no idea what Mevlana was talking about. She turned to Jack next to her and whispered, "What does she mean by that?" Jack didn't answer but was staring at Mevlana expectantly with a smile flirting about his lips.

"What do you mean?" Sasha's voice spoke for them all.

Mevlana smiled and paused, moving her eyes around the room to connect with each one in turn. Then she dropped the smile. "Exactly what it sounds like," she said. "Go out and observe who you can have. In precisely the way you think I mean it."

LEELA SAT HAVING BREAKFAST OUTSIDE THE meditation hall. The walkway was lined with lush green shrubbery and bamboo trees, and the people sat silently in white lawn chairs balancing trays on their laps that held oatmeal or scrambled eggs, watermelon or papaya, cups of coffee or *chai*. Some days one could catch a glimpse of the "moon dogs," as residents called the silvery mongooses with their striped feathery tails, trying to steal food from a breakfast tray. Leela loved the whole scene; it had become her favorite time of day.

Enjoying the cool air of the morning, Leela watched as Mevlana entered the walkway, breakfast tray in hand. She was alone and looking for an empty chair, smiling perfunctorily at several of her fans who wanted attention. As she passed by, Leela again noted Mevlana's lined face and scraggly hair, her dumpy body and slight stoop. She stopped in the middle of the walk. There was not a single seat left.

A man stood up and offered his chair. He had an air of executive sheen, and his formal manner was of a class rarely seen here among these laid-back spiritual seekers. His silver hair was expensively cut, and his casual clothes were pressed and immaculate even in the humidity. *He looked rich and at the height of his power*, Leela thought, and *that's a guy who can have anybody he wants*. It was not too hard to imagine that he wielded a lot of power in the West, and Leela wondered what he was doing hanging out at an ashram.

Mevlana nodded and started to walk over. The man was standing, smiling, gesturing to his chair. Then to Leela's utter amazement, as Mevlana stopped in front of him, he dropped to his knees, prostrated himself before her right there in front of everyone, and kissed her feet. He stayed there, bowing, while Mevlana reached down and softly stroked his hair. Then he got up, joined his hands together and held them up to her like a prayer, and moved over to sit on a bench by a flaming bougainvillea.

"OKAY, EVERYBODY, CLOTHES OFF."

Oh god, not again. I don't know if I can take it, Leela thought. Fear clogged her throat and made her hands cold. She looked around the room and saw everyone else beginning to comply. Mevlana was sitting in her chair on the dais, and the assistants stood at each corner, all as usual. A smooth Indian raga played in the background, its beginning slow and calming. Leela dropped her trousers to the ground and peeled off her top; then deposited them on the heap where everyone was tossing their clothes.

"Assistants, now pass out the blindfolds." When Travis handed her hers, Leela grasped his wrist and gave him a weak smile.

"Ah, don't worry," he whispered. "You'll be all right."

I'd be all right if I could spend some "quality time" alone with you, she thought, then jerked herself back to the present. *Just the way to escape whatever was coming up, creating a fantasy future somewhere else.*

"Blindfolds on? Okay, assistants move everyone to the center of the room."

A pair of hands guided her forward, and she felt a tiny breeze as bodies were moved into place next to her. She felt calm knowing that at least she was next to Sasha. They had come in together after breakfast at the Mozart, and on her other side was that safe older man, Rolf.

"Assistants, mix everyone up."

Leela was spun gently around and guided to one part of the circle, then swirled in another direction and transferred to the left. She heard others being moved around amid nervous laughter. Now no one knew who or where anyone was. The group stood in a huddle, blindfolded and confused. Leela could feel the presence of the others around her, and that someone was breathing very close. *Whose exhalation was that, and who was standing to her left? It didn't matter now; they were all going along for the ride.*

"Out in the world, we do not have permission to touch each other," Mevlana said. "Consequently, most of the West is rabidly hungry to be touched. Remember those monkeys you studied in school, the ones that died for lack of being stroked and hugged? Humans have needs just like that, and most people in the West are starving to death, starving for touch.

"Look around you in the third world. People touch each other all day long. The poor hang on the street corners, arms around their families, patting, caressing. Men walk hand in hand without worrying whether this means they are gay. Babies spend years strapped against their mother's chests, feeling their heartbeats. Here, people starve for food, but are rich and satiated with the sensual touch of other beings. You see, it is a Western phenomenon, this longing for touch, this skin hunger.

"Here today, in this room, you have permission. However you wish, touch the bodies around you. Feel them, and feel what it is like to be touched by them. Feel the different essences, the individual smells, the varying energies. These are your friends, your lovers, other beings on a journey like yours. Be with them, be how you are. Be present also to the response you receive from your touch, but be yourself, touching others. Enjoy this beautiful and rare experience."

The music swelled as Mevlana stopped talking. There was a momentary stillness, then the soft padding sound of people as they began moving around each other.

Tentatively, Leela reached out and felt a forearm. The skin had fine hair on it. *Was it a man or a woman?* Her hand slid down to the fingers, and back up to the bicep. At the same time, an elbow grazed her back. This arm she was touching seemed to be a woman's, whose? Leela reached up and stroked her face. The skin was moist and smooth, and fine-boned, and she reached up and felt hoops in her ears. Leela decided to give up the desire to figure out who it was and just feel this skin, touch a woman's face other than her own.

She turned to the elbow behind her, and ran her hand up to the shoulder. Man or woman? Taking an in-breath, she slid her hand down the front of the body and felt her breasts. They were firm, and sweet, and moved freely. It suddenly seemed strange that she had never felt any of her girlfriends' breasts before. Girlfriends so intimate, but with a closeness born of words only. She moved her hand down and felt the outline of the woman's ribs.

"Keep moving," Mevlana said. "And make sure your blindfolds are in place. No peeking! This dance is not about looking. It is about feeling, and feeling your enjoyment." The music was making itself known; the *tablas* grew gradually more pronounced.

The next body was a man, as Leela could tell from stroking the coarse hair on his chest. Probably black hair, she thought as she traced it down his belly. He was running his hands down her arms and then down to her hips. Ah, why not, she thought, I've got the chance, and she reached down and took his penis in her hand. It felt so soft, so trusting. It was new to touch a man that way, just because she could, not to lead somewhere. She cradled his balls in her palm, then let go slowly, patted his chest, and moved on.

As much skin as I want, she thought. She breathed in the smell of lemon, of yeast and sweat. Someone was caressing her ass, and she stopped to feel what it was like to not know who, just feel the pleasure. She felt how there were different levels of attraction with each being, *attraction not based on the eyes, but merely on essence, on touch: an animal sensing.*

She ran her hand up the side of another man's body. He turned toward her, their torsos so close she could feel his breath on her face. He encircled her waist with his arm, then ran his hand up her back and softly tousled her hair. She moved even closer to his chest, skimming her nipples against his. He pulled her close, moving his lips to graze her cheek, her nose, her lips. His breathing deepened, and she felt how magnetic this attraction was, far more so than the others. They were kissing, and their tongues anxiously sought each other out. They could hardly stop running their hands up and down each other's naked bodies, and Leela could feel his hardness press against her hip.

This attraction is so remarkable, so intense, Leela thought. *This one, I need to know who he is.* She reached up for his hair, trying to find a clue. His hair was wispy and fine, and to his shoulders. Only one man in the group had hair like that. *It can't be. It can't,* Leela thought. Pretending she was brushing her own hair away from her face, she moved her blindfold just enough to be able to see that it was, indeed, Stefano. Stefano, utterly surrendered to their pleasure together, his enjoyment of his physical connection to her, Leela.

"Keep moving," Mevlana said. "Don't stay too long with any one person."

AH, THERE YOU ARE *bella*. I HAVE BEEN LOOKing for you." Stefano sat down on the bench across the table from Leela. "I've been wanting to ask you a question."

It was late afternoon, and the Mozart was hopping. Every table was so full that some girls shared seats with their boyfriends. The air was thick with cigarette smoke, rickshaw exhaust, and grease from fried food. The Nepalese boy came by to pick up empty plates and cups, and Stefano ordered an espresso from him. Leela marveled at his ability to drink them at any time of day or night.

"I want to ask you something," Stefano said. "You know me pretty well by now." He looked around to make sure the other people at the table were engaged in their own conversations and not paying attention to theirs.

"What is it?" Leela questioned. "You can ask me anything."

The coffee arrived and Stefano reached into his pockets for the money. He gave the boy a tip, which Leela thought must have been generous by the smile on his face. Stefano turned to her squarely and cleared his throat. "*Bella*, why is it so hard for me to talk to women?"

Leela was confused. How many mornings had they sat here, huddled together, talking about every sort of intimate subject, talking freely about their insecurities and what they were learning in the groups, about their mistakes and halting successes. He had shared so many personal things with her, and seemingly so easily. In fact, it had seemed unusual in a man to be able to talk so freely about his emotions. Some Italian thing, she thought.

"I don't know what you're talking about. You don't seem to have any trouble at all talking to me about just about anything."

"Of course, *bella*," he said, laughing as if it were the funniest thing in the world. "It's easy with you because I'm not attracted to you. I'm talking about with women to whom I'm attracted."

My god, she realized, *he truly doesn't know to whom he is attracted.* She could still feel his urgency in the blindfold game, how when she would try to move on to switch partners, he would keep her there with him, wanting more of her mouth, her skin, and her energy. When he couldn't filter his experience through those false friends, the eyes, his body made it very clear to him what was true.

The fact that he doesn't think he is attracted to me has everything to do with him, Leela thought. *It's not a comment on my level of attractiveness or on me at all.* It was a comment on his own state of development, that he filtered his experience through his eyes, instead of trusting the truth of the energy of the moment. This whole idea that "men are more visual" only speaks to the fact that they are more out of touch with their feelings. It spoke to the brainwashing of the West that attraction is measured by the eyes, not the body's true response.

This is one of those moments when everything in your life changes, Leela realized. Mevlana had tried to teach them not to choose with their eyes, but she had scoffed it off. End up with someone "ugly?" Never. Like Kate, she had thought she would rather be alone, and so she had been.

Stefano was looking at her expectantly. "I don't know what to tell you," she said, getting up to leave. "You're going to have to figure that one out for yourself." She walked out into the sharp sunlight and took a good look around. She couldn't wait to find out what she was going to learn next.

As Leela approached the Mozart, she spied Kate and Dylan together over where the bikes were parked. Kate was speaking animatedly, and Leela watched as Dylan kept shaking his head "no" and inching backward. Kate looked like an actress playing a seduction scene, pursuing him with an enthusiasm Dylan did not match.

The way things were looking Leela didn't want to interrupt, so she sat down in the nonsmoking section even though there was no smoke. The Mozart was empty as if readying itself for the evening onslaught. Two girls poked their heads in but promptly left when they saw there was no action.

"I'm going to get laid tonight," Kate said, sitting down and blowing a long trail of smoke out the side of her mouth. "Somebody new."

"Good for you," Leela said. "Is Dylan the lucky victim?"

"Not tonight. I have a few suspects in mind. If all else fails, there's the dance in the *dojo*."

Leela looked at the stacked bracelets on Kate's wrists. Everyone here wore loads of cheap jewelry bought from the vendors outside every venue. Turquoise beads, coral shells, cowhide bands: ethnic jewelry at its finest. "There *is* a feeling in the air that something is about to happen," she agreed. "Like a premonition or something."

The air was languid and thick, with nary a breeze. Light dappled through the thatched roof of the café painting little pockets of brightness on the graffiti-scratched tables. Espresso cups were still piled up from lunch and ashtrays overflowed.

Leela sat up alert as the tall, trim, impeccably groomed man walked in the side entrance heading for the counter, following a much younger woman with magenta hair. He was dressed all in black, which no one else did here, looking Western and sleek amid the tie-dyed ex-pat gear. His silver hair was groomed in a cut that was expensive and up to date, and except for the heavy bags under his eyes, his beauty was enhanced by his age.

"That's the guy."

"What guy?" Kate picked up her glass and took a sip.

"The guy that bowed down to Mevlana. I told you, that morning in the walkway. He got down on his knees and she touched his head. It was like . . .he knows something."

"I guess he knows something. That's Andrew. You've heard of him, right?"

"He's 'the one all the girls want to be with?'"

"Yeah, that one. He and Mevlana used to be lovers. They say that's how they learned everything—together. They broke up a long time ago, but the hush-hush is that they're involved in some kind of ongoing secret work together."

"Like what?"

"Who knows? Some kind of esoteric self-realization thingamajiggy."

"Have you been with him?" Leela asked.

"No, but I've heard women are waiting in line. He's supposed to be the best."

The redhead got a coffee to go and left. Andrew placed an order, then turned and scanned for a table. Catching Leela's gaze, he nodded as he walked over to sit by the door.

"C'mon," Kate said, stubbing her cigarette out on a plate. "Let's go over to the pool—there's at least a good hour's worth of sun left. Plenty of candidates there to choose from." She picked up her purse. "If we want to meet someone, our best chance is to move on from here."

"You know I don't like that whole pool scene." Leela ran her hands up her bare arms. She watched the Nepalese boy who had begun clearing the tables. "I'm going to hang out here and have another coffee. You go on."

"You're going to miss out," Kate said, getting up. "You never know what kind of magic synchronicity could happen." Her blouse exposed her navel as she stretched, and the top of her thong underwear.

"Good luck and happy hunting. I'm sure you'll have a hot story to share tomorrow."

Leela's coffee arrived, and she scanned the café. When her eyes got to Andrew, he looked up. Leela willed herself to smile, the smile that said she was available and friendly. *The more you were interested in someone,* she thought, *the harder it was to give that smile, the one that gave the impression you were totally harmless.*

"Hey," he said softly, nodding, acknowledging her. He looked away, then back, and Leela willed herself to smile again. His eyes were the darkest brown, almost matching his shirt. He must even have his T-shirts pressed, she thought.

She struck up her courage. "You're a friend of Mevlana's, aren't you?" she called across the café.

"Yes," he said, not breaking her gaze. The Nepalese boy was setting down a plate of food and a glass of carrot juice on the table in front of him. Andrew reached into his pocket and handed the boy a few coins. "Are you enjoying your solitude, or may I join you?"

As he sat down, he brushed a few crumbs off the table in front of him. She noticed the black and silver hair on his arms, and that his watch was a Cartier. His nails were well tended, immaculate.

"How do you know Mevlana?" Leela asked.

"We're longtime friends." Apparently that was all he was going to say.

Okay, Leela thought, *that's the end of that one. What to say next?* She looked down at her bare arms and wished she had a few bracelets. "I'm in Mevlana's current group," she said. "That's why I wondered." It was always a risk telling men you studied tantra. They usually took it as a sign that you were eager to jump into bed, particularly at that moment, and of course with them.

"And how are you finding it?"

"I'm learning things I never imagined. Far more than I ever expected to know in this lifetime."

"And what were you expecting to learn in this lifetime?"

As their eyes connected, Leela suddenly felt the sensation of his body next to hers although he was sitting in the seat across from her the same as before. She shivered as she felt his skin against her torso, his chest hair tickling her breasts. She felt the sigh of his breath against her neck, and with a whoosh his energy seemed to enter her and take a look around, checking her out. It was startling and an utterly novel feeling, and although she felt naked and exposed, she welcomed it.

"Oh my," she said, catching her breath. He was sitting innocently as if nothing had happened. "I don't know what I was expecting, but this is definitely more than that."

He bit into his veggie burger and took a swig of juice, leaving orange traces on the sides of his mouth.

"How long have you been here?" she asked. "In India, at this ashram?"

"More than ten years now."

"What do you do here?"

"Mostly, hang out. Hard to imagine how it could be any better, living here in heaven. I do a little teaching now and then."

"Classes at the ashram?"

"No, informally." He reached over for the ketchup bottle. "Please, share these fries with me."

"Ah, no," Leela said. "Too fattening. Not to mention what they do to one's skin."

"Here," he said, offering a fry up to her mouth. "They make them here with the perfect degree of greasiness, don't you think?"

Perfect, she thought as she chewed.

He sat back and pushed his empty plate away. "What would be perfect now is an after-dinner cup of tea, don't you think? We could share one here, or you could come back to my flat for one. I live by the river. It would be beautiful to sit out on the balcony and watch the sunset."

Out among the field of scooters parked up against the café, Andrew maneuvered his Enfield motorcycle. They took off in the direction of the bridge, past Leela's favorite cybercafe, inside which Ian was probably leaning back in his chair and tweaking his songbook. They passed the man with the fresh fruit stand loaded with melons, papayas, guavas, and apples from a box marked Washington State, then the grimy Westerner who looked worse than the Indian beggars.

"That guy gives me the creeps," Leela said.

"Him? He got here about five years ago. He's a fixture on the scene—Greek, a heroin addict. It's sweet in a way, how his countrymen who come to the ashram take care of him, give him money and get him washed up. Part of the local color."

Andrew lived in the building all the way at the end. As she had surmised, his place was spotless, all white tile and linen. A screened-in balcony overlooked the river gleaming in the late afternoon sun. His bed was white; the curtains were white; the dresser was covered with a luxurious cloth of white brocade. A tiny teddy bear poked its head out from the couch.

"Who's this?" Leela asked, picking up the bear and holding him against her heart.

"She thought I should have it," he answered with a bemused smile, as if that were an answer. "Why don't you relax out on the balcony while I put on some water for tea. If you'll excuse me while the water is heating, I want to change my clothes. These are a bit sweaty, and I'll just be a minute."

She looked out at the river and at the black Indian cows peacefully grazing on the banks. The afternoon heat had cooled considerably, and the sun was low in the sky. The washerwomen had finished packing up for the day and could faintly be seen climbing the stairs by the bridge in their red and blue saris. Leela felt a surge of love for the beauty of India, for moments like this when the mind stopped its incessant chatter and one could surrender to an effortless joy of being.

She turned around to look for Andrew to share the moment. The room inside was dark which highlighted the bathroom where he had left the door ajar. There, because of the clear view, with the room so dark and the light of the bathroom so bright, she was surprised and delighted to see him in the midst of stripping off his clothes. He was completely unselfconscious, apparently unaware that she could see every inch of his skin.

His body was beautiful, lightly muscled, well proportioned, slim, and very male. He was the kind of man who looked better with his clothes off—his clothes, although tailored and expensive, did little for him. She saw how vulnerable his soft cock looked, hanging there waiting to be covered by the yoga pants he slipped on without any underwear. Leela sighed as he pulled a fresh T-shirt over his head. There had been no ego to it, no strutting, no look-at-my-beauty. It was all very ordinary and matter-of-fact.

She turned back and faced the river. A cowherd had appeared and was swatting the animals with a switch, prodding them to move up the banks and onto the road home. The sun was almost at the horizon, the air still and weighty. A waft of incense pricked her nostrils, and then he was there, standing beside her, setting a silver tea service on the table between her chair and the love seat.

Without speaking they watched the sun flatten down into the horizon, and the mist rise up to meet it. Andrew rose and lit some candles that cast an amber glow. *I know I look better as the light goes down,* Leela thought. The air hung with expectancy, and she became aware of their breathing. She heard the sound of a distant train, and realized she felt as intoxicated as if they had been drinking wine instead of tea.

"Do you ever hear that guy singing in the morning?" Leela blurted out. She had awakened several times recently to an eerily beautiful song cutting the smoky silence of the dawn. When she had asked others if they knew what it was, no one seemed to be up that early. "I've never heard anything of such exquisite unearthly beauty."

"He's singing *Al-Fajr*, the Muslim morning prayer," Andrew said. "It's one of the most precious things about this place."

The tea was finished and the sun had set, and there seemed nothing to do but go. "It's been wonderful," Leela said, getting up. "I've enjoyed it very much."

"It's a pleasure I'd like to continue," Andrew said. "Shall we pick up where we left off? Will you have dinner with me on Friday?"

Will I ever, Leela thought. *I can't imagine how I'm going to wait.*

tHEY KNELT IN PAIRS ON THE MATS, THE MEN behind the women as per Mevlana's instruction. Dylan had asked politely, and Leela decided not to fight it. He was in back of her now, his hands resting loosely on her hips.

"All right," Mevlana said. "Women, raise your arms and feel your longing. All the longing you have ever felt. Reach, reach for the sky."

Leela lifted her arms to the ceiling and felt the stretch along her ribcage and the sides of her breasts. Her head fell back and her left hand covered her right as her fingers strained upward. Longing. She felt her longing. So many things she had desired in her life: beautiful clothes, that pair of silk pants with the silver braid, that boy at summer camp, what was his name? Ice cream, and world peace, and for summer never to end.

"Really reach for it," Mevlana coaxed. "Long with all your might."

Leela remembered her ambition for career success and

the trappings that were supposed to come with it: a designer-decorated home, a luxury car, and tropical vacations in Fiji, or Bali, or Kuala Lumpur. She had fantasized being as rich as Oprah, and craved the opulent life that magazines extolled. Her itching for this consumerism had gradually declined as she began to realize it was all greed stoked by the marketing machine.

"Feel your longing," Mevlana repeated emphatically. "Really feel your longing."

Leela strained harder. The air in her chest pushed down against her diaphragm and her arms elongated up, further. Her fingers spread wide toward the ceiling, grasping, reaching.

So much effort and money and work spent aspiring to be beautiful, hoping to be loved and cherished by a man. Where was he? The dream of the Perfect Beloved. Desire to be united with him. The pining to be held, to be made love to. The coveting of other women's boyfriends.

"Feel all the longings of your life," Mevlana urged. "Don't hold back."

There was the yearning to stop the search and be flooded with love and finally feel satiated. Leela reached even further. To understand what was really going on. Why life had to hurt so badly. Why it never worked out the way you hoped. To know the secrets of death, and life, for that matter. A passion to get to the place they call enlightenment, and to understand what the heck it is we are all doing here. How she hungered to know the Truth.

Leela tensed, exhaling the air out from her lungs, hard.

She lengthened her arms above her head, further, farther—up as high as they would go.

There was a rustling on the dais and for the first time, Leela became aware of the soft *bhangra* Bashir had chosen as the music. Mevlana stood and called out an instruction. "This is to the men. Rise up behind your partner and let her feel your support. Unmistakably, let her know the full degree of how much you encourage her in her longing. Hold her and incite her to go even further in her pursuit so that she knows that this time, she does not endeavor alone."

Leela felt Dylan's body rise up behind her, felt his warmth against the curve of her back. His hands slid up, grasped her forearms from behind and urged them up a little further. Leela gasped. The effort was intense. *This is what it felt like for longing to be okay and not secretive and humiliating.* It had never occurred to her to ask that her appetites be supported, by girlfriends maybe, but not by men.

"Really let yourself be supported in your longing, in your passion," Mevlana said.

With Dylan holding her, Leela let herself relax and permit his solidity to carry her. To be supported like this allowed for a modicum of trust; trust that her prayers might be answered. *It is tremendously healing,* Leela realized, looking up at Mevlana with gratitude.

The yearning and stretching continued. *That's got to be enough now,* she thought. *Surely this exercise must be almost over.* But no, it was not. The effort was beginning to wear. *Dylan's got to be tired of me by now,* she thought. *He must be thinking what a dolt I am to be so full of lust. He must wish this would end, feel a hankering to move on.* She peered around. His eyes were glistening with kindness. The shock made her disappear back into her striving.

"You'll notice that longing is always attached to pain," Mevlana called out, "but what to do? That's the nature of it."

Leela suddenly realized that even if she never got what she hoped for, as she actually never had in the past, everything would still be all right. The longing itself was the point. *It really wasn't about the objects of desire. That was the error, seeing the object as the point, rather than the longing itself.*

"All right," Mevlana broke in. "Take a moment to make sure you have exhausted all longing and get ready to switch places. Men will become the long-ers and the women will be the support persons."

They switched. As Leela put her hands on Dylan's body, she smelled his scent, and admired the definition of his arms. As the exercise proceeded, she noticed how much easier it was to support a man in his striving compared with how it had been a completely unfamiliar experience to be supported by a man in hers. She felt how sexy she considered a man to be in his longing, how noble, and honorable. It was hard to feel the same way about herself. She had experienced her own longings as pathetic, but a man's as worthy of support. She felt now, and had always been, happy to be there for him, whoever he was.

As the late afternoon sun cast shadows across the group room floor, the exercise came to an end. All members of the group came to relax in a circle in front of the dais at Mevlana and Bashir's feet.

"Now you know more about longing than ninety-nine percent of the world," Mevlana said. "Use this knowing wisely. Realize that if your love has any motivation in it, it is not love. Life is fulfilled by longings, not by ambitions.

"The longing that men and women have for each other," Mevlana continued, "you have to understand its true nature. There's nothing wrong with it, but it's really longing for God, for the Ultimate. The longing has to be completely frustrated, or we wouldn't get on to what's real."

Leela looked over at Dylan and smiled. Behind him sat Ian, cuddled with a Brazilian girl, then Stefano, then Jack who sat by himself. *Completely frustrated.* She could truly say that she loved these men without any longing, although that may not always have been the case.

"A ND THAT WAS THAT," ANDREW WAS SAYING. Leela suddenly realized she had spaced out imagining his life in Switzerland. She wasn't sure what 'arbitrage' meant, but it sounded glamorous. "All it takes now is a few hours each week in the cybercafe to manage my investments," he said.

She listened to the faint sound of the river lapping at the shore below. The first quarter moon beamed overhead, and a pleasant breeze cut through the evening's humidity.

Leela shifted in her chair. Her body felt a heightened sense of aliveness here, sitting across the table from such a handsome man. She had never been attracted to anyone with silver hair before but really, wasn't it about time?

She pushed aside her plate with its remnants of *masala dosa* and took another sip of wine. "Wasn't that kind of schizophrenic," she asked, "being a spiritual person while working in that environment?"

"Indeed. I'd been leading a double life for years. At five every morning I was faithfully sitting *zazen* at the local Zen Center, then off I would go to work as this cutthroat trader seeing who I could kill." He shook his head. "It's tragic to look back and see how lost I was, trapped in the typical *Playboy* conditioning that life is all about who and what you can screw. I was your typical Western dickhead, totally awash in ego. Even the way I was using my work at the Zen Center was contributing to how special I thought I was, superior to everyone else."

He topped off Leela's glass and poured himself the last of the wine, placing the bottle upside down into what used to be ice. "I probably could have continued that way for years, immune to the toll it was taking, if Karyn hadn't come along."

"Karyn?"

"Mevlana before she was Mevlana. I was captivated by her from the first moment we met. Never before had I encountered a woman of such radiance, possessed of such a mature sexiness. The male culture doesn't teach us to see wisdom as erotic, so it hit me in spades. I found myself turned on by how much she knew, by what she had studied. I would have followed her anywhere. She took me to India and introduced me to tantra. I was a tough nut to crack, but between the two of them, Mevlana and the *dharma*, I became capable of surrender."

The waiter came up and removed their plates. As neither of them looked up, he left without asking about dessert or coffee.

"Our relationship was the catalyst for me to open my heart," Andrew continued. "Before that I was pretty much a confirmed bachelor. I experienced reverence for the first time, and I learned to sit at a woman's feet. I was rescued from a life of self-absorption, and by grace, now I can say I know who I am."

The waiter set down the check. He bowed his head and exited silently.

"In sum, you could say that the life I had been living before wasn't my own."

"Yes," Leela said. "I know what you mean. That's exactly where I've been at."

Andrew stopped. He turned his razor gaze to peer deeply into Leela's eyes, down past all the layers of resistance to where her soul lay like a wrapped-up Christmas gift waiting to be opened. This is some kind of alchemical process that's happening, Leela thought, some kind of lead into gold, a mingling of essences. She looked at the light-filled being in front of her. Leela knew that this was good; it was right.

Andrew broke the spell. "You definitely have the Thirst," he said.

Moonbeams reflected off a spoon lying to Leela's right, next to the salt shaker. "I have the what?" she asked.

"The Thirst," he said. "The thirst for the divine nectar."

Leela reached for her wine glass, and to her horror, watched it fall to the table. The wine bled out onto the previously pure white tablecloth. "Whatever," she said and shrugged. The waiter rushed over to mop it up, but the wet spot sat staring her in the face like guilt.

Had he been reading her thoughts? Did he know she had been thinking he must be the Perfect Beloved? It was as if she'd been dreaming of him of all her life, but didn't know it. Be careful, Leela thought, *your longing is running away with you*—but then she remembered Mevlana: *stop protecting yourself from love.*

Andrew took his napkin from his lap and placed it over the spill. One hand reached over and covered her hand, the other picked up the check. "Will you excuse me for a minute?" he asked, and he was gone to settle the bill.

Leela looked out at the shimmering river lit by the stars overhead. The quiet hush blanketed the noise from the market across the way. Her reverie was suddenly pierced by a dirt-stained beggar standing at the table, holding her baby to her breast.

"*Baksheesh, baksheesh,*" the woman insisted, gesturing from the baby to her mouth, "*baksheesh.*" Her hand was clenched like one of the scrawny chicken feet Leela had seen for sale at Chinese markets, motioning back and forth between her mouth and the baby. Her teeth were askew and her sari was bedraggled and stained. As their eyes met, pain stabbed into Leela's heart so strongly she couldn't breathe. "*Baksheesh*," the woman droned on, "*baksheesh.*"

Then the waiter was there, shooing her away. "*Chalo*," he ordered. "Stop bothering this lady." He made sweeping movements with his arms as he herded her out the door. "So sorry, madam, this will not happen again."

"Ready to go?" Andrew asked. Leela looked up, grabbed her purse and followed him out to where the motorcycles were parked. The beggar woman was standing there, and she reached out her chicken's foot claw to grasp Leela's wrap. The waiter ran out. "*Chalo! Chalo*! Be gone!" he ordered and the woman moved on.

Andrew angled the bike, jammed down on the kickstart, and headed them out onto Laxmi Road. Leela was confused about where they were going, so decided she would wait and find out. The first thing they passed was the turnoff to her flat. He was not dropping her off at home. The bike was heading toward the Mozart Café, were they going there? No, Andrew turned down the lane. They were going to his house. Leela wondered if she should stop him, after all, she shouldn't be going back to a man's house she'd just recently met. But there existed this cult of instant intimacy here at the tantra ashram, and anyway, it was what she wanted, so why fight it? The bike continued down the lane going where both of them knew she wanted to go.

After lighting candles here and there, and putting on light trance with the volume down low, he slid onto the couch and sat not saying a word. She had chosen a single chair to his right. Neither of them spoke as they watched the lights sparkle on the river, listening to the calls of the merchants trying to make one last sale before packing up for the night. Leela savored the dampness in the air, the heat spreading out through her body, the flow, the waves. Silence hung heavily in the air expectant, his waiting, and hers.

Finally she got up, went over to the couch and sat down between his legs, her back flush against his chest. He adjusted a bit and moved her into the concavity of his arms, enveloping her in them. As her head relaxed forward, he massaged her neck and shoulders with one hand, running his hands through her hair and scratching her scalp, the other arm still wrapped around her body. His hands made their way up to caress her face, the fingers rubbing gently while the thumbs made more emphatic statements.

"Shall we go into the other room?" he asked, scooping her up in his arms and carrying her to the bed. Kneeling above, he began undressing her, making soft sounds of pleasure as he discovered her breasts. She watched as he slid open her zipper and dropped her pants to the floor. Then he stood full height and pulled his T-shirt over his head exposing his lean torso, all the while not breaking eye contact. He untied the drawstring to his trousers and Leela was pleased to view a repeat of the private striptease she had been privy to before. This time, however, it was not solitary, but for one purpose only—that their skins could taste each other's aliveness.

Their first kiss was exactly the way she liked it: languidly slow, full deep tongues, around and around, all over the face and throat. Over and over, around and through and again and again: She was good and he was good and it was the two of them being good together. It was heady being matched with someone whose hands knew exactly where to go, someone who really inhabited his skin, his body, whose consciousness was not blocked at the neck: It was divine. He was divine. *We are divine*, thought Leela. It just went on and on.

And his tongue was going round her belly, making circling swirly kisses with the full of his mouth, orbiting a wide oval around her navel. It was anguishingly slow—he was torturing her with slowness. Every so often his chin would brush her pubic hair, and it seemed like the goldfish she had kept as a child were swimming up to her belly and brushing against it, kissing her with all the affection she had then known they had but couldn't express, kissing her with their puckered lips, sucking, she was swimming with the fish, swimming in their bowl . . . she was losing it, where was she? And then out loud, "Ahh . . . like little fishies. . " she breathed.

"Yes," he said.

She pulled on his hair; how did he still have such thick hair? Felt his slippery scales, inhaled the salty smell of the sea, flipped her tail . . . and then she was coming and coming it kept coming in crashing waves, crashing waves rippling out from her core as she released, released and surrendered, let go more and more and then the sacred *amrita* was flooding, the holy elixir of love, the sweet nectar of the goddess.

They lay there in the quiet together. She opened her eyes to his eyes inquiring into hers. Reaching over, she ran her tongue around his earlobe, rubbed her cheek against his jowl. Perfect. It was perfect being there with him—perfectly beloved in the way she had always dreamed, that she had searched for all her life.

With a jolt she realized he hadn't said anything, hadn't expressed any preference, any desire. He had been masterfully satisfying her and giving so generously, but not asserting anything for himself. How odd, how unheard of, for a man to act this way.

"Now for you," Leela said.

"Shh," he whispered. "My pleasure is your pleasure."

She reached down and began fondling his testicles, moving over to his penis. He pushed her hand gently away. "It's not like that," he said. "Not some sort of scorekeeping, or 'I've got to get mine.' When I said your pleasure is mine, that's really how it is for me." He tucked a lock of her hair behind her ear. "A woman's orgasm is so vast, so inclusive. It's everything to me."

He leaned up on his elbow. "I also don't have intercourse with women I don't know. It's much too intimate." Leela looked at how his lip glistened, at the shadow of his silver-gray stubble reflecting the light. "There's everything else; what's the hurry? We'll only be at this acute level of anticipation once, so let's enjoy it. We have plenty of time."

He was stroking the insides of her thigh as he spoke and kissing her neck. "More?" he asked, slipping his fingers inside, stroking her Sacred Spot. This time she was driven to beg, please Andrew, please, begging please let me come . . .

After she heard his faint snoring, Leela got up and dressed, yearning to sleep in her own bed. Back in the familiar room, she glanced at the clock and shook her head, surprised to see that it was half past two. What time had they had gotten to his place? It must have been what? Nine-ish? They had sat for a half an hour or so, then the walk home—it must have been four hours she and Andrew had been making love, and they had never even "had sex."

GYELTSEN WAS KNEADING HER ARM AS SHE idly gazed at the cartoon map of Tibet. "You more relax than anyone who come here," he said.

"Thanks to you," Leela answered. He moved over to her shoulder and was manipulating the muscles behind the scapula. "Gyeltsen," Leela asked, "how did you get here?"

He dug into the trapezius connecting her neck to her shoulder. "I walk."

"You walked over the Himalayas?" She winced as he dug deeper into the deltoid.

"Yes, walk."

"It's all snow and everything, right?"

"Yes. Great snowstorm. Almost die." He lifted her shoulder, then pushed it into the table, loosening all the tension out of her neck.

"I can't even imagine such conditions. What did you want so much that you would risk your life?"

"Freedom. I want to live in freedom."

Usually it was a story you read in a book, something happening in the 1800s, people risking their lives for freedom. Here was an unassuming man, a masseur catering to affluent Westerners, with such a dramatic longing to be free that he was willing to risk dying for it. The extraordinary bravery of ordinary people, Leela thought, the heroism encountered in everyday life. You would never know about it if you didn't ask.

"And your wife, Dawa, she walked too?"

"Yes. I send for her later. She walk too."

He was massaging the occipitals at the back of her neck now. "Gyeltsen, will you tell me another story of Tibet?"

"Okay. I tell you about special lama. From his powers he shrunk to size of child only. He live in Potala Palace. All small. Live in a box."

"Why would he shrink up like that? What for?"

"Very special," Gyeltsen said. "Very great power."

He said no more as he repeated the strokes on the right side of her body. Leela could hear the faint rumblings of traffic from Laxmi Road if she tried, so she decided not to. It was so delightfully warm in the room she found herself dozing off until it was over.

"Gyeltsen," she said with a start. "Could you straighten my back?"

Her spine had had a slight S-curve since childhood, which never caused her any pain, but interfered with her flexibility for yoga and dance. "Uncorrectable" she had been told, but she had always had a sneaking suspicion this was because the person pronouncing it so didn't know how.

Gyeltsen stood over her naked torso inspecting her backbone. He pressed against the vertebrae here, then there. He tapped along the coccyx, then stood back. "I push now, okay?" he asked.

He pressed forcefully against her spine from left to right. Leela exhaled deeply as he exerted more pressure. It hurt, but she could take it. "Good for today," he said. "You come every day. We see what we can do."

"I can't afford to come every day," Leela said. The truth was she could, but it would be a stretch. Still, to have her back straightened? What would that be worth?

"You come every day. Days between massage we just push, a few minute," Gyeltsen said. "No charge. We see if we make it straight."

Here I am this rich Westerner, Leela thought, and this magnanimous man who walked on foot over the Himalayas is going to treat me for free.

"Okay," she said. "We see what we can do."

THEY HAD BEEN RIDING ALONG IN THE HOT sun for what seemed like an hour or more, out in the country on his motorcycle, no other traffic, just sailing along. Green pastures, falling-down fences, signs in Hindi; the mind stops and it was exquisite in that silence. There were no thoughts, only the sound of the air as it swooshed by. Leela felt her legs wrapped around Andrew's thighs and squeezed a bit tighter; he answered back by putting his hand on her knee. She thought that maybe she would like to kiss the back of his neck but decided against it. The sun shone off his silver hair.

He had brought her to a little village, and as they slowed down on the bike to enter, a crowd of tiny girls swarmed out to meet them, saris flailing. "*Baba, baba!*" they cried, and other Hindi which Leela couldn't understand. Their mother and several other women set down their pitchers and ran out to the gathering, clasping their hands before their chests in the *namaste* gesture as if making a prayer.

Leela could tell by the reception that they didn't see too many foreigners here, and thought that this must be what it was like when rock stars arrive. For the first time she saw that even to conceive of the ease of mobility to go wherever you wanted and show up here, in this medieval village, was a luxury Westerners had no idea they had.

With the shutdown of the motorcycle the village was richly silent, so unlike the India around the ashram. Other than their arrival, there was little going on in the heat of the day, and probably not much at other times either. The little huts had dirt floors and holes in the walls instead of windows, but the space around them was swept clean. Even though everything was dirty, there was an air of the immaculate.

"*Paise, baba, paise,*" the women chanted, and Leela watched as Andrew reached into his pocket and came out with a handful of change. He smiled into the face of the prettiest one, who demurely dropped her eyes. Holding out his hand, he let them take whatever they wanted. *Look at that*, Leela thought, *he is a god wherever he goes.*

Andrew took his camera from over his shoulder, adjusted the lens, and photographed the girls. "You should get a picture of this too," he said.

"So lovely," Leela said. She took the camera out of her bag and snapped the girl with the bundle of handmade brooms over her shoulder. Then she took another of Andrew taking pictures of the girls.

He kickstarted the engine, and they waved goodbye to the little crowd. As they progressed along the path of the village, others ran out to see them: a bent-over old man, small shirtless boys covered with dust who ran after them shouting in Hindi, wanting them to stay, perhaps to dole out more coins.

They turned right onto the main road and headed back toward the ashram. Leela settled in enjoying the perfect sky with the weightless white clouds, the empty field with the lazy cows, and the total lack of air pollution. After a while Leela called out over the roar of the engine, "What was that word they kept using, *paise*?"

"That's the name of the coins I gave them," Andrew said.

"Those coins, the ones with the 'five' on them? You rarely see those around the ashram. They're a quarter of a rupee!" Leela calculated the arithmetic in her head. There were five rupees to a dollar, so a fifth of a rupee was about four cents. "Those people were begging for four cents?"

Andrew's eyes were moist as he turned back and smiled at her. Then he gunned the engine and put his full attention on the road. They still had at least an hour to go before they would be back at the ashram.

THERE WASN'T MUCH OF A CROWD IN THE walkway these days, and Leela had it almost all to herself. She sat as she had for so many mornings, balancing her breakfast tray on her lap, waiting for the recorded discourse to begin. The chill air cut through her cotton clothing so she pulled her wrap more tightly around herself. Pashmina shawls may have been a high-class and stylish luxury worn by rich fashionistas in the West, but here so close to Nepal they were cheap and plentiful.

The air was damp and the soil around the palm fronds in front of her chair was wet with dew. Leela inhaled the morning's freshness and listened intently to the silence. The only sound was a slight cough from a man sitting far down at the end of the row. One other soul was waiting for the discourse to begin, an old woman sitting behind her quite a bit to the left. It was the end of high season so most people had gone home or were packing to leave.

Suddenly the sun burst through the mist. First the heat hit the top of her head, then spread down her shoulders and arms. Leela closed her eyes and felt it warm her, remembering that by afternoon all would be sweltering. Ah, she thought, the many surprises of India. Opening her eyes, she looked down at her food. She took a sip of coffee, then decided on an egg and started to peel it.

And then it started again. The familiar pulsing began in her groin, spread out through her legs and hips, and ran up her spine. Her backbone elongated as her head fell back, arching to receive the inner explosion. Her breath exhaled forcibly as the orgasm rose up all the way from her tailbone out through the top of her head. The stillness of the morning had hardly been ruffled. She had had a full-body orgasm in public from no doing of her own, and no one had noticed. *What is happening to me?* Leela wondered. *I'm turning into someone else.*

EVLANA SAID, "FOR TONIGHT'S HOME-work you are to go on an old-fashioned date to the flamenco concert in the meditation hall. In case some of you have forgotten or never knew, this is how a date works: Gentlemen, you are to ask one of these beautiful women for a date, someone new, someone you have not done any exercises with and are not seeing on the outside. You will each go home separately to dress, then the man will pick up his date at her house and take her to dinner. After the concert, you are to go home, with nothing more than a goodnight peck on the cheek. You are to be courteous and respectful at all times. Please have a wonderful evening." She stepped off the dais and exited by the rear door.

The kindly older man from the Heart Dance tapped Leela on the arm. "Hello, my name is Rolf," he said, bending slightly at the waist. "May I have the pleasure of your company this evening?"

"I would be delighted," Leela answered, and the truth

was, she would. A date with a gentleman would be refreshing.

"I want to let you know right up front," he said, keeping a respectful distance, "that I'm here at the ashram with my partner. She has given her full agreement for me to participate in this group. If we see her at the concert tonight, I don't want you to feel awkward." It was so kind and considerate of her feelings Leela could hardly believe her ears.

He continued to prove chivalrous in his behavior. Later, when he stopped to talk with a friend on the way to the meditation hall and therefore didn't give Leela full attention, he apologized. *This is it,* Leela thought. *I'm going to raise my standards so only gentlemen are allowed from now on.* At the concert she snuggled in with him, curled up like friends.

The guitarist came out and played a passionate solo, then the box-drum player joined him. A raven-haired woman in a flaming-red dress with yards of black lace came stomping out on the stage. Everyone, artists and audience alike, found their pulses quickening, and spontaneous clapping broke out in the crowd. A darkly handsome male dancer dressed in black joined the quartet and the fever pitch rose and kept on rising.

As at all ashram concerts, there were those who could not keep from dancing themselves. A few lone souls had stood up amid those seated on the floor, grooving and swaying. People danced in the back in the empty space behind the crowd. Leela turned around to see and sure enough, dancers were swirling around the perimeter.

Closest to the stage, she caught sight of Mevlana and Bashir. Whirling in an embrace together, they were grinning widely and looking into each other's eyes, dancing what appeared to be a polka to the flamenco guitar, seemingly oblivious to the crowd as they lurched from one side to the other. *My god*, Leela thought, *they are the poster children for how to be married and totally in love. Or are they?*

t*his is almost better than sex*, LEELA THOUGHT, *this lying in bed together and talking. Almost better, but not quite.*

A candle shimmered in front of the mirror on Andrew's dresser. Glowing with the color of rose quartz, it enlightened the space around it, spread up onto the walls, turning the black night into pinkish gold. Against the mirror the light pulsated, flickering like the beat of an unseen heart.

He was wrapped around her side as she lay on her back, his arm resting softly across her belly, hand curled over her hip. A cotton sheet covered their naked bodies. She felt him breathing and silently aligned her breath with his. Inhale and exhale. A perfect meditation. In and out. Watching the other's breath for a change.

"Women need to be more aware of their responsibility to help men evolve," she heard Andrew say.

She hadn't heard him right, had she?

Andrew leaned up on his elbow. "Think about it, it's men, not women, who start wars, commit rape and most of the domestic violence. It's mainly White men who play the game of acquisition of money and power no matter who it hurts while keeping others off the playing field."

If this had been a girlfriend talking Leela would have laughed, but to hear a man say this was stunning.

"Women can hold the moral standard for men." Andrew moved his hand onto her belly. "It's our mothers who teach us manners, to behave like gentlemen, to pick up our socks, to take others' needs into consideration." His hand began tracing a long slow circle across her abdomen from hip to hip.

"When a man falls in love with a woman, he wants to become a good person for her. He puts aside his desire for selfish things and becomes a provider: of tenderness, of food and shelter for her and their children, of nurturance for their growth, of protection with his physical strength, of financial support and well-being."

Leela adjusted her head on the pillow. Maybe she wasn't really hearing this. But she must be, because Andrew went on.

"Women should hold us to this higher standard, but women today have given up this task." His hand came to rest over her navel. "Oh, it's because we beat it out of you, for sure. We men told you we didn't want your input as we continued our adolescent behaviors of Internet porn, gathering in packs to drink too much alcohol, talking too loud, cursing, carousing, and watching other men run around on fields maiming each other over a ball. We have belittled, despised, and convinced women they aren't powerful."

catherine auman

His hand slid up to her breast. Softly his fingers formed a U-shape around it, squeezing lightly. Then he moved so that that the palm covered her nipple and he squeezed again.

"I don't know," Leela said. "Men are always complaining that women are trying to change them. You learn real quick that if you want to keep a man, that's something you'd better not try to do."

"These kinds of men are childish," Andrew scoffed, his hand lying still on her ribcage. "A man who is truly a man wants to learn everything he can from a woman. Men who wish to remain teenagers will rebel against women whom they make into their mothers. A woman should run as fast as she can in the opposite direction from such a man."

"If we did that there would be no one to play with! Do you know how few men like you there are out there?"

"Then all the women can play with me," Andrew said. "That would be perfectly all right." Leela poked him in the ribs with her elbow.

"Okay," he said. "If a woman finds herself with an immature, selfish man, if you don't demand better functioning from him, he will lose respect for you." His eyes were gleaming in the soft light of the candle. "Look around, many of the women today are more evolved than the men. Women need to stand tall and demand better functioning from men, that we give up our Peter Pan ways, and that we mature into men with dignity. Demand that we honor our commitments, that we treat you well, that we share, and, that we act as if the planet doesn't belong to us alone."

"Wow," Leela said. "This is intense. How did you learn all this?"

"I wouldn't have become who I am without the mentoring of many beautiful and wise women. I've sat at the feet of more than one female master. But it was the grace of my main teacher that made me who I am. I was a hopeless case before she deigned to help such a lost soul as I was. A typical Western male who dishonored the feminine: using their bodies for my sexual addiction, sloppily swilling beer, greedy, domineering, my way or the highway. An utterly selfish lover."

"You're certainly not that now."

"It's been a long road. I was a hard case to crack. And I am grateful to every woman who cracked and splintered me until I broke."

He pushed the sheet away and looked down at Leela's body, illuminated by candlelight. "Ah, so beautiful," he said. He ran his hand down to her hip where it began, then lower down to the thigh. "I like that you are older. Young girls look like larvae, like they don't know anything at all.

"It was not until I was able to drop to my knees in front of Her, the divine She, to prostrate myself, to kiss her royal feet, to elevate her above myself. But that is not the right way to say it because I cannot 'elevate' that which is already so beyond me.

"By allowing me to worship her, by initiating me into the tantric mysteries, she transformed a boy basically illiterate in the ways of existence into a man. A man humble enough to admit what he doesn't know. Wise enough to surrender. Surrender when in the presence of something greater than himself, such as the great and mysterious *yoni*."

He turned away from her and reached behind to the bedside table. The candle was still sputtering. Leela watched as he opened a bottle of oil and lubricated the first two fingers of his right hand. With his thumb he rolled the oil around, spreading it thickly and evenly. He smiled at her, cocking his head to look more deeply into her eyes. He reached down between her legs, his fingers brushing over her pubic hair on the way to their destination. With agonizing slowness, they began a sliding stroke along the sides of her inner lips.

"The *yoni*," he whispered. "The divine gateway to the secrets of the universe."

With his tongue he parted the lips of her face, and as the pressure of his finger on the sides of her clitoris increased almost imperceptibly, Leela felt herself letting go into the engulfment of his kiss in sweet full-trust surrender.

IT WAS STRANGE TO SEE THE COFFEE BAR deserted at this time of day, except for Paloma over at a table under a tree. It appeared that she was just sitting, and when Leela approached her, smiling. Sitting and smiling.

"Can I talk to you, Paloma?" she asked. She tried to keep the anxiety out of her voice but feared she was unsuccessful.

"I need to talk to someone. May I talk with you?"

Paloma smiled wider and patted the seat next to her. Her silver hair and baggy clothes felt nurturing and safe. Paloma sat waiting, and smiling.

"I'm so afraid," Leela blurted out.

"Hmm. Afraid of what?"

"I don't know. Everything's changing so fast! It's like there's this force beyond my control that is changing me; I'm becoming someone else and there's nothing I can do to stop it. Well, I mean I guess I could stop it on one level, but on another, I can't. And I also wanted this, but the rate at which it is moving is terrifying. I need it to slow down, but I can't, or it won't . . . I don't know anymore!"

She looked at Paloma who was still smiling benignly. "And then I've met this guy," Leela continued, "who scares me, he's so powerful. I don't know whether or not I should trust him . . .? It's all so big, so scary . . ."

"Is it really fear?" Paloma asked. "Look deeper."

Leela looked inside. Yes, the fear sat there in an amorphous mass, looming black, with spidery tendrils and a stench of rotten things. Slugs and other disgusting creatures were oozing around in the primordial mud. There were gravestones, and a woman's blood running circularly down the shower drain, and all kinds of things that hid beneath the bed at night.

"Underneath that," Paloma said. "Look deeper still."

"I don't know how to do that . . . ?"

"Drop down," Paloma said. "Go deeper. Let your breath take you down, down beneath the fear."

Leela looked deeper, and a perfect Alpine lake of calmness appeared that had been waiting lifetimes for her arrival. She gasped at its pristine beauty, and as she opened her eyes, it was to Paloma sitting so close, tears streaming down her face. Leela began to cry too.

"What's this about fear?" Paloma asked softly. "There is no fear. Only this: so drunk on the divine."

With that their tears broke out in a waterfall of crying, a blissfulness of sweet breaking pain, a cracking of the shell that housed understanding. Leela collapsed into Paloma's lap, and the two women continued laughing and crying together until it was done. So drunk on the divine.

22

SHE WAS ON A HIGH ANYWAY. LEELA HAD been at Ananda's for *chili milli* and a whole *Kingfisher* for herself, sitting and recounting all the pleasures that had happened since leaving home. After paying her check, Leela walked the distance on Laxmi Road to the Mozart Café, ignoring the frenetic scene whizzing by. The foot traffic got thicker the closer she got to the Mozart. Standing out front she saw Bashir, Mevlana's husband. The blue of his eyes was piercing even in the dark. He waved and came up close.

"Leela, it's great to see you." His tank top exposed his chest and his chiseled arms. She noticed he was just the right height for hugging and not feeling overpowered.

"Hi, Bashir, great to see you," she answered, surprised that he knew her name. They stood looking at each other. No words followed, which was strangely peaceful rather than awkward. Their eyes locked.

Smiling, he finally asked, "Are you enjoying the group? You seem very juicy in there."

"I do?" *How did one respond to such a comment?* "Thank you." She noticed a fine line of perspiration on the seam of his shirt and the way his hair fell nonchalantly over his forehead. He was rather juicy himself. She smiled into his eyes, where she could see herself smiling back.

His body was inches away. Bashir reached out and took her hands. As their skins touched, an energy rose up from her heightened state to his perhaps already naturally high state, sexually alive and embodied. Warmth filled out from her center and encompassed all her nerves and muscles and bones. The heat spread out until it was encircling the two of them in a seething oval shape, all warm and fluffy like goose down. The noise from Laxmi Road retreated into the background, and although all was frantic around them, it was quiet and blissful inside the pillowy cocoon.

They stood there holding hands, gazing into each other's eyes without moving. If there weren't so many bizarre things going on at all times, they would have attracted attention, but as India is a constant flurry of inexplicable sights and sounds, no one noticed two people having a total bliss-out by the side of the road.

"Wow, if we can be blissed out like this on Laxmi Road," Bashir said, breaking the silence, "we can be blissed out anywhere." For a moment, the taboo of him being another woman's man dropped, and Leela felt a strong desire to hail a taxi to take them back to her place, to make love madly and forever. The moment passed. He belonged to Mevlana. There were enough men to go around that one didn't need to betray one's girlfriends.

She dropped his hands and the cocoon disappeared. "Well, that was quite something!" she laughed. "You never know what to expect around here." She adjusted the bag that crisscrossed her shoulder. "See you in the group tomorrow. It should be a particularly *juicy* day."

The connection had been complete in itself. I would have used to have had to turn this into something else with a future attached, Leela thought, but now it's just as it is. She turned and walked home to get a good night's sleep for tomorrow's group.

ake a break," Mevlana said. "Tomorrow we'll pick up where we left off."

Leela looked up from her partner. "I could use some water," she said. Brandon nodded and went in search of their bottles. She relaxed back on her elbows. Everyone was scurrying this way and that. The exercise of the day had been intense, and they all wanted to get outside to track down an intriguing distraction.

Over under the windows, Leela watched as Jack approached Sasha, her bleached blonde hair showing deep-black roots. Soon they both were leaning back on their elbows, smiling. Leela observed their lips move, their heads nod in agreement, then Jack sat beside Sasha on the mat. He is as smooth as an oil slick, Leela thought, and then she suddenly felt afraid for Sasha as Jack moved into a position mirroring her recline.

Brandon was handing her her water. "Are you going to the party tonight at The Farm?" he asked. "DJ Petar, the one from Belgium, is spinning." He took a drink and offered her one from his bottle. "The cops shut the last one down. Ha! Should be quite the scene. Want to go get something to eat and then head over there together?"

"Sure. Let's go."

Leela craned her neck around Brandon's legs to see Jack and Sasha sharing a laugh. Jack had told her he wanted to change, become a better person. It all looked like innocent play between them. Wasn't it?

As she and Brandon headed out for the evening, Leela glanced over to see what might be happening over underneath the windows. Jack's body was now nearly covering Sasha's, and their mouths were kissing passionately.

LEELA SAW AMONG THE DRUMMERS THE BIG Danish guy who had arrived at the ashram a few weeks before. It had been hard to miss his arrival with his leonine head of dreadlocks, his friendly gap-tooth smile that strangely added to his handsomeness instead of bestowing the hillbilly look it would have on someone else, and his perfectly proportioned body despite how long-limbed he was. He had completely shaved his head after he'd been there about a week, a decision due either to the extreme heat or to his desire for a completely new persona.

She interlocked her fingers and stretched her arms behind her back. The morning dance class was just beginning, and everyone seemed stiff and not-yet-caffeinated. Bending over her left knee, she noticed Sasha sacked out on the pillows, and that Bashir had not yet entered the room. Sasha was obviously trying to draw no attention to herself as she snuck a few more seconds of sleep, but the bright sapphire blue of her blouse defeated her purpose.

Leela's ears guided her back to the Dane. His playing was smooth and rhythmical, completely in tune with the other musicians, laying a beat that was starting to get them going. As she watched him throughout the class, she noticed that he turned out not to have the big ego she had expected from his larger-than-life presentation; rather, he stayed in the background taking direction from the leader the entire time.

SASHA WAS CRYING. HER SKIN IS SO BEAUTI-ful, Leela thought. It was that Asian-porcelain-doll thing, for sure. But it was also that thing you don't know when you're young and so down on yourself for your looks— that your skin is exquisite. Each single cell plumped, pulsing with blood and collagen. So good-looking, you have no idea.

Mevlana's homework had been to go on a date with a member of one's own sex. Get dressed for them, go to dinner, talk about the familiar, and feel the relaxation of being among your own gender. After undergoing so much intensity with the opposite, such an assignment felt to Leela like a relief, a place of refuge.

She had showered, dressed carefully, put on eyeliner and lipstick. When they met for dinner at Ananda's, it was obvious Sasha had done the same. Now all that carefully applied mascara was running down her face.

The stars overhead were winking, as were the votive candles on the tables. A few other couples were out having a romantic evening, but Leela and Sasha were the only two girls on a date.

It was quiet off Laxmi Road by the river. Leela could hear the water lapping in the spaces between Sasha's low-pitched sobs. "Does this have anything to do with the fact that I saw you huddling up with Jack the other day?" she asked.

Sasha looked away sharply. Her back straightened and she shook out her hair. Reaching down to her purse, she took out her compact and began wiping away the black from underneath her eyes. "I love this *baigan bharta,*" she said. "It's my favorite dish."

"What happened?" Leela asked, not letting her change the subject. "Did you guys hook up?"

Sasha's tears began washing down her face again. "You promise not to tell anyone?" she asked. Leela noted that Sasha was wrapping her napkin round and round her hand.

"I promise."

"It's all my fault," Sasha said. "Really. It was me. I should have said no, that's all. I mean, I did say no. But I should have . . ."

Leela felt her anger rising. It was as if Sasha was her younger sister who needed protection. "I'll tell you how it was with me," Leela said, "and then you'll have another perspective. Jack is very smooth. One day I found myself over at his house having sex with him when I never intended to. Is that anything like what happened to you?"

Sasha's twisted napkin lay like a cruller beside her plate. "I didn't want to, but he didn't pay any attention." Her words flooded out like a monsoon shower. "I mean, I like him, but I didn't . . . I mean, it was my fault; I shouldn't have gone over to his house. But then again, I thought it would be okay, because he said he wanted to talk. But—it was my fault for not pushing him away. I mean, I did push him away, but at some point, it was just easier to go through with it." She picked up her napkin and put it back on her lap. "It's all so confusing."

Leela remembered Jack's strange seductiveness, the way he appeared vulnerable and trustworthy at the same time he was using you for his own agenda. The way he seemed like someone to sit and cuddle with, even though he was a person who hadn't demonstrated a single sensitivity to anyone else's wants or needs. How he was so into sex but didn't know anything about how to please. His soft unguarded eyes that said, "I don't want to hurt anybody."

"In no way was it your fault," Leela said. "It was exactly the same for me, and he's done it to countless women. After I got clear on what happened, I knew I had to say something. I had to say it for me, but also for him. These men here are our brothers. We all have a spiritual connection just by virtue of being together in the same space and time. Trying to find answers, all of us together. I had to do it for me, for him, and for all the other women who haven't been able to say anything.

"You have to tell him, tell him he hurt you." Leela saw the light of the candle flame reflected in the table knife by her plate. "I know this now; it's the only thing that will make it right for you. It made the biggest shift for me. Tell him what he did to you is not okay, or he will go on hurting other women the way he hurt you, and hurt me."

"No," Sasha said, "it's not that big a deal."

"It *is* a big deal," Leela said. "He needs to know and be held responsible. You have to let him know, or he will go on hurting women. We women have to stand up and tell him that the way he is is not right. You have to do it for yourself, and you have to prevent him from continuing to harm people. Really, tell him."

"No." Sasha was a long way from crying now. The mascara down her cheeks had dried, looking very Goth. "Just forget it. It happened, and now it's over."

"Then I'm going to talk to him."

"No."

"Jack and I have gotten to be friends through all this, and I know he doesn't want to hurt anyone. He's trying to change, and he asked me to let him know if he's out of line.

Let me go with you to talk with him, or if you won't, at least let me talk to him about this by myself."

"No! You promised this was in confidence. You promised you wouldn't say anything."

"Please," Leela said. "This is really important."

Sasha was staring at her. Her intent was clear. There was nothing Leela could do because she had promised. She picked up her spoon and started in on her sweet carrot *kheer*.

THAT NIGHT, AFTER HER DINNER WITH SASHA was through, Leela took a rickshaw over to Andrew's flat. When he opened the door, it was obvious he was delighted to see her. He invited her in, into the warmth within.

And that night, he slipped it in, the divine entering. She gasped at the fullness of it, every time a surprise at the feeling of being full, complete, of not remembering since the last time that to walk around in the world is to be incomplete, that with this returning of the cock to its sanctuary they were both on their way home. That it didn't matter how many times it had happened before, that the act of entering and being entered is always a celebration of homecoming.

23

EELA SURVEYED THE ROOM. GROUP HADN'T started yet, and she felt the quiet charge of expectancy in the air. Over by the wall, Mevlana and Bashir were deciding on today's music. Travis was draped behind Emma, rubbing her shoulders. Jack stood talking conspiratorially with Nicole, his body closer than necessary. Their heads were inclined downward and toward each other. *Indeed*, Leela thought, *she's one he hasn't had yet.*

Over in the corner of the room, Leela saw that Sasha was also watching Jack with Nicole. She lay alone on a towering pile of pillows, curled in upon herself in a fetal position. Her face was ashen, and shadows made her jaw appear heavy and dark. Leela waved to her. Sasha's return gesture was a flag at half-mast.

Leela looked from Sasha to Jack and back again, just in time to see Sasha roll over and bury her head under a pillow.

I promised not to say anything, Leela reminded herself. *I gave Sasha my word.* She heard Nicole's laughter and looked over as Jack reached up and stroked her hair. Nicole tipped her chin up and angled her eyes. *That damn Jack*, Leela thought. *This can't go on.*

"Excuse me," she said, breaking into the little *tête-à-tête*. "I need to talk with you, Jack."

"Sure, Leela," Jack said. He was sporting a new tuft of hair under his lower lip. "Can't it wait?"

Leela's eyes held steady. "Nicole, you don't mind, I'm sure." She glared at the younger woman, commanding her out of the space.

"No, I don't mind at all." Nicole turned and touched Jack's hand. "Maybe later we can pair up for an exercise?" She widened her lips in an imitation smile at Leela as she left.

"What's up, Leela?" Jack's voice became gentle and concerned. He turned his full attention on her, and it was as if he had wrapped a shawl around the two of them.

Leela took a deep inhale. "Jack, you're at it again, buddy. You hurt that girl, Sasha." This was not what she was supposed to be doing, breaking confidence, but she plowed on anyway. "She was trying to say 'no' to you, just like how it was with me. And you pushed your way through, literally. She didn't want to, Jack." He had turned his head so that his ear was almost at her mouth. "She was really upset when she told me. Now she's all confused because she didn't want to, and here you are, this nice spiritual guy."

"Damn," he said. "She seemed like she wanted it."

Leela shook her head an emphatic "no."

"All right," Jack said, turning to scan the room. "I'm going to talk to her."

"No, wait, you can't." Leela panicked. "I promised her I wouldn't say anything to you." *Oh god, what have I done? The last thing I would ever do would be to betray a girlfriend's trust in me.*

Jack reached out and took her arm. "I'm going to talk to her," he said firmly.

"No, you can't. I can't let you." She put her hand over where Jack was holding her. "I wasn't supposed to say anything. You just have to change, be different."

"Look," he said. His voice was calm. "I'm trying to be different. It may not seem like it, but I am. I need to make this right. I'm going to go talk to her." He lightly removed her hand where it covered his arm, then strode over to the pillow heap. He lay down about a foot away from Sasha, uncovered her head and ruffled her hair, then began whispering to her. Leela watched as Sasha attended to Jack, then peered over at her, Leela.

Nausea rose up in waves. There was nowhere to hide. *Should she have told Jack?*

"Time to start," Mevlana called out. "Everyone choose a partner you haven't worked with before."

Leela moved through the motions of the group vacantly. She counted the minutes until she could go home, somewhere that Sasha couldn't see her. At long last the exercise ended, and she picked up her things and started the slow walk along the lane toward her flat.

"Leela." She stopped and turned. It was Jack. "Sit with me a minute. I want to tell you what happened." They sat together on the low stone wall that lined the lane.

"I talked with her," he said. "Everything's all right. We came to an understanding." He reached out and took Leela's hand, running his fingers over her wrist. "Thank you for saying something. I'm sure that wasn't easy for you."

"Oh man, I can't believe I did that," Leela said. "I said I wouldn't tell."

"You did the right thing, Leela," Jack said. "Things had to be set straight."

"I don't—"

"It was the right thing," he repeated. "The right thing to do."

IKE A HOMING PIGEON, LEELA HEADED straight for his table although she had no conscious idea of where he sat. She found him talking to a woman she would have in other circumstances been jealous of, a Latina goddess sporting a magnificent *décolletage*. The chatter in the Mozart was muffled in a pleasant hum, as Leela stood in front of them, silent, waiting for his attention to shift.

Sofia Vergara threw her head back and laughed so hard her breasts rippled above her tube top. Andrew looked up and when he recognized Leela, instantly diverted his focus. "Leela, what is it?" he asked.

Leela stood full, the energy overflowing. "Take me out of here," she said.

There was boundless happiness for no reason at all, but how could one say that? How to communicate this need to burst open, to expand beyond one's skin? To leave this consensual reality in the dust, to travel to some place that didn't exist?

Andrew turned back to Sofia who was not laughing now. *"Ciao,"* he said, kissing her on the cheek as he stood up, taking Leela by the hand. He led her out through the cacophonous conversations, out through the café cloud of cigarette smoke into the street cloud of traffic exhaust.

They stood in front of the thirty or more motorcycles parked against the café. "What is it?" he asked, squeezing her hands. "Tell me what it is."

"Let's get out of here, and go get lost in the city," she said. "I want to get lost."

He smiled and dropped her hands. He backed his motorcycle out of the bunch, and revved it up. Leela threw her leg over the back and positioned herself around him. They cruised slowly to the end of the lane where he turned left into the lunatic flow of traffic.

The rickshaws were so close one could easily reach out and touch the passengers inside. Andrew darted the bike in and out in a delicate ballet, swerving between cars, buses, turquoise carrier trucks sporting *malas,* cows, carts, and a wedding horse. Blaring horns sounded their warnings constantly: Leela remembered them described as "the official language of India." There was the sound of the rushing wind by her ears, and the intoxicating adrenaline rush of speed.

The night was black, lit only by taillights and garish neon signs in Hindi. Andrew steered the bike past every bit of the outskirts Leela had seen before into the unknown depths of the city. He seemed to know where he was going, down cobbled streets with tiny shops, Internet cafés, banks, and street vendors selling cashews and grapes. The blur of lights became so loud, Leela felt sufficiently lost. She had never been in these parts of the city before, and certainly not at night.

They drove for nearly an hour, or was it more? In and around the Indian city in which the ashram was only a small island. Leela saw more people strolling at night than one could ever count, nearly all men. She estimated there was one woman to every hundred men, and then only out at night if she were arm in arm with her husband.

They whipped around a corner and a most magical street spread out before them, a matrix of tiny white lights crisscrossed on wires over the whole breadth and width of it. Andrew slowed the bike and they floated along block after block, as the lights kept going on, strung out on the horizontal grid hanging over their heads, sweeter than Christmas.

"Thank you for bringing me here," Leela gasped with the wonder of a six-year-old. They left the fairyland and picked up speed. She went flat up against his back and close to his ear. "C'mon," Leela shouted above the roar. "You still know where we are. Let's go someplace that you don't know either." They were passing a temple with *sadhus* walking down the steps. "I want us to get lost together."

She craned around to see the side of his face. He was smiling a warm grin she could see even from behind. She had never quite seen him share such a look of delight before.

"You," he shouted back, over the traffic and rushing wind. "I'm lost in you."

The night blurred and she disappeared into it. She no longer knew or cared where they were, or whether or not he had experienced this before. She drank in the narcotic of his body between her legs, resting her head against his back as she held on tight and gave up all to his lead, lost in him.

tHE DISTANT TRAIN WHISTLE CUT THROUGH the smoky air. Leela couldn't remember hearing a more erotic sound. Muted light filtered in through the holes in the curtains, casting shadows of illumination in her tiny flat, barely big enough to hold a single bed and dresser.

The whistle blew again and Leela let out a low moan. She lay paralyzed on her back on the bed: The bliss energy had her completely in its velvet grip. Large gulps of breath came pouring in and out, each one more euphoric than the last. They rolled lengthwise through her body: rushing down her spine to her toes, reversing to billow up and spill out her mouth and nostrils like molten lava. Around and around it coiled—time had stopped, or had it? There was no other time than now.

How could anything ever have been other than this— this awareness of the omnipresent ecstasy, this bliss residing, usually hiding in the body? It made itself unmistakably known as it circled in its loop, entering and exiting. Her neck arched back as if she were having an orgasm when the next big inhale took her. Leela felt herself to be just one thing and one thing only, a blissbody ecstatically alive in the dark Indian night.

24

"**t**HIS ASHRAM WAS BUILT ON THE SITE OF AN ancient tantric community," Mevlana said. She clapped her hands. "All right, everybody wake up. I know it's getting close to lunchtime and your blood sugars are low, but I want you to get how serious this all is." Leela snapped to. "The *tantrikas* who lived in these parts were actually burned alive for their beliefs and practices. This is a profound esoteric legacy we honor today."

Mevlana brandished an elegantly manicured hand down the front of her tunic. "One of the practices of the region was that the tantric couple would live their lives together in one garment. Yes, their bodies together, inside one robe, for the lifetime." A wave of curious murmuring coursed through the room.

"Sharing their lives that way, together in one dress, performing all the daily activities: patting out *chapattis* or throwing a pot, hoeing weeds or singing prayers to God, without time off for oneself. Week after week, year after year, togetherness; working inch by inch for the taste of ultimate intimacy.

"Think of it—modern couples can't even stand to be in the same room together for long. We start fighting during a meal. The other's otherness begins to jar, to appear wrong to our eyes. Too much time together breeds irritation, the need to get away and be on one's own.

"Of course, you'll say, we are a different kind of people today. But are we? What if instead of seeing the other as always 'in my way', we saw this as an opportunity to become aware of how much we make the other's way of being wrong? To see that it is all projection? What would it be like for the ego to bump up against itself every moment of the day? Uncomfortable yes, but a path of purification by fire, a *tapasya*. A rapid route for those willing to burn themselves out on the fast track."

Leela tried to imagine someone, a lover, invading her space all day and all night. *I need so much time alone!* she thought. *To do my own thing, and find out who I am.* She felt an urgent desire to leave the room, take a break. She remembered a therapist who had once told her that whenever she got this urge to run, to sit with a blanket over her head and breathe.

Mevlana laughed. "Breathe, everyone. No need to panic. You aren't going to have to live this way! Today we give you an opportunity to taste this discipline of intimacy. After that, you may return safely to your separate ways. You will spend the afternoon with a partner, not in one dress, but as one unit. You will not let go of hands during lunch and for the duration of the afternoon. For this brief moment in time, you will experience what it is like to share togetherness in everything."

Mevlana motioned to Bashir to start the music. "Now stand up, and pick your partners."

Leela looked vaguely to the behind and to the left and was surprised to see Dylan. *Had he been sitting there all this time?* She didn't remember him being there before. He raised his eyebrows, smiled, and held out his hand. She smiled back and took it, pleased by how strong its grasp was. These two hands would not break contact for the rest of the day. Leela found herself suddenly shy, unable to meet his eyes, so instead she focused on watching Brandon and Sasha choose each other.

"All right," Mevlana said, quieting the din of the room. "This will be a great opportunity to watch what comes up for you. Observe the ego trying to assert its importance, convince you that your way of being is the right way. Contemplate on what your ego constructs as a barrier to truly being in the present moment with the Beloved.

"Any last questions before we begin?"

"Just to clarify," came a voice from the back, "we don't let go of hands until we come back for this evening's session?"

"Right."

"What about when we have to use the bathroom?" somebody yelled out. Nervous laughter coursed through the room.

"I expect you to honor the essence of the activity," Mevlana said, "which is to experience togetherness in all things, *especially* when it is uncomfortable for you." She exchanged a glance with Bashir, then addressed the room. "You will accompany each other to the bathroom, but you may have your privacy if you wish."

Leela felt the collective sigh of relief meet her own. She looked at Dylan who squeezed her hand.

"One more thing," Mevlana said. "You are to conduct this exercise in silence. Everything is to be communicated by touch and gesture only, not by talking. This will add awareness to your experience."

Bashir turned up the volume, and the soft jazz drowned out the rustling noises as the couples left the room and headed out for lunch.

Leela followed Dylan to the ashram's main dining area. The path was strewn with leaves and she delighted in the sound as they scrunched under her feet. When they arrived at the line leading up to the cafeteria, people who weren't in the group were talking and giggling, and it seemed that she and Dylan were alone together within a bubble of silence.

Gleaming steam trays offered up the entrees. Dylan pointed to the eggplant parmesan with his free hand; Leela declined. He took a large portion for himself, then indicated the curried spinach, did she want some of that? Leela nodded yes, and he placed a serving on her plate. *As typical with men,* Leela thought, *they choose the really dense food, while girl food consists of salad and veggies.* Dylan picked up a baguette, Leela a cucumber. Slowly, together, they proceeded to the counters with the side dishes, condiments, fruits, and breads, where he gently offered and scooped up food for her.

It all grooved along in slow motion. Each action took so much longer, twice as long; it was definitely not an efficient use of time. Everyone else suddenly seemed to Leela to be rushing insanely, to be ridiculously in a hurry, even though they moved at a tenth of the pace of the West. As she and Dylan walked through the cafeteria, not separated from the Beloved, making time above all else to be together, the individual people appeared to her to be isolated and alone.

Perhaps this is one reason it's hard to find a partner in the West, Leela thought, *and that relationships didn't work there. Everyone focused on productivity and making the most of their time; everyone was built for speed, wanting to get things done fast and expeditiously.* Leela noticed that although it took much longer to decide if you took someone else's preferences into consideration, it made the space for an exquisite tenderness. *Tenderness takes a lot longer than efficiency.*

"You've found a perfect one there," the voice behind her said. Leela turned to see Andrew elegantly leaning against the salad bar. He pointed to Dylan. "That one's a keeper."

Leela looked at Dylan, who was trying to decide between *tiramisu* and chocolate cake. He didn't appear to have heard. "What do you mean, a keeper?" she whispered at Andrew. She wasn't supposed to be talking and she didn't want Dylan to hear. "You mean a keeper for now, or for the long run?"

"For forever, that one," Andrew said. "If that's what you're looking for."

This one? Leela blinked her eyes and shook her head. Dylan tugged on her hand lightly, and she turned her attention to him. He was pointing to the dessert counter, and she shook her head no. As they headed to the cashier, Leela looked back at Andrew to see him ladling *dahl* into a cup. She wasn't sure what he meant, but she felt a ground swell of peace ripple through her, just seeing him.

They joined Sasha and Brandon and another couple at a table under a big blue umbrella. Wide smiles were exchanged all round as Leela and Dylan took the empty chairs. The couples had already begun feeding one another, keeping their married hands locked in embrace. Dylan picked up a portion of the curry, wiped the spoon on the edge of the bowl, and slipped it into Leela's mouth. She savored the coriander and cumin, the cinnamon and garlic. He smiled and wiped the corner of her mouth, then slowly licked the end of his thumb. Leela gave him a mouthful of the eggplant, then picked up the baguette. How to tear off a piece, let alone butter it for him? Dylan grabbed the other end and tore, picked up the knife and buttered while she held the bread. Leela nearly laughed out loud at the awkwardness but managed to maintain silence.

The people sitting at the tables around them seemed to fade; their attention was only on each other. The silent bubble now seemed to be a shelter of safety. Leela and Dylan and the couples in the group were the only tribe, the only ones who could understand this shared reality. Leela felt a new relaxation hanging out together as one entity. It was not the usual franticness of being among single people, all unfinished and looking for their other half, living the life of independence and toughness, rather than spending it learning what now seemed of utmost importance: how to live in tenderness with the Other.

They communicated through their eyes since speaking was not allowed. Dylan put a forkful of cake up to Leela's mouth. She automatically shook her head no. When he persisted, she succumbed and the chocolate exploded in her mouth, reaching out and massaging all her synapses. She closed her eyes to savor, and when she opened them, it was to Dylan taking care of her, affectionately, protectively. It had taken them a long time to finish their lunch.

Leela found herself enjoying the relaxation of letting Dylan lead. She shut off her mind and surrendered control. *Surrender*—a concept belittled in the West, but a cornerstone of spiritual teaching. If one couldn't surrender to the Beloved, how could one ever surrender to existence?

Dylan led the way to the back of the ashram where there was a meditation garden overlooking a pond with lotus pads. They sat together on an iron bench, watching a swan gliding by on the water with apparent effortlessness, leaving a wake behind. Its eyes were ringed in black, its bill a bright orange. Another stood on the bank preening, scratching under its ruffled wing, arching its neck and shaking its head.

Leela had heard that swans were rumored to have knowledge of the Supreme Being Brahman. They were beloveds of the goddess Saraswati and were said to dine on pearls. Their name in Sanskrit was *hansa*. Swans mated for life.

How sweet this tenderness is, Leela thought. *Tenderness. Tenderness is what has been missing. Taking the time for the*

Beloved. Making the time above all else, over all the things we think we have to do and get done. Precious time to discover the other's preferences, how to delight, how to support; making this knowledge one's own.

Reluctantly, it was time, and she followed Dylan back to begin the evening group. As they neared the entrance, he stopped and faced her. Their eyes met and they exchanged a deep full-bodied smile. Leela looked closely at his dark hair, and the way his beard was showing its afternoon shadow. He squeezed her hand, then divided them into two, bringing her palm up to his lips and kissing it. He took her in his arms, and as he held her close, she felt his body against hers for the first time. For a moment they breathed together, his arms around her; then Dylan broke apart, turned, and walked through the waiting door. Leela paused for a moment recalling the familiarity of separateness, then walked alone into the tantric temple.

25

EELA SAT PEOPLE-WATCHING AT THE COFFEE bar at the ashram. She had long ago lost interest in her book and didn't have a single thing left on her to-do list. *In fact*, she thought, *I haven't had a to-do list since I left the West.* She assessed the man who had made her cappuccino and talked her into adding a heart-shaped cookie. She had seen him that day whirling in the meditation hall and wondered if that vortex of energy translated to his sex life, since he didn't seem much interested in hers.

A butterfly landed on the corner of her cup, tasted the sugar on the rim, and fluttered away. It was so nice to have a moment to enjoy by oneself.

"We've been looking for you." Leela looked up to see Kate accompanied by Nicole.

"Okay if we join you?" Kate asked, sitting down before Leela could answer. "Nicole asked to meet with you when I told her your report of what's been happening."

The blood drained from Leela's face. That conversation

with Kate had been strictly confidential. She looked from one woman's face to the other.

"We were chatting after painting class this morning," Kate continued, "and I told her how you're having orgasms without sex." Kate gave one of her devilish sideways grins and cocked her head to the left. "Nicole said, 'I want some of that.'"

Leela couldn't be sure that Kate wasn't mocking her, although that didn't make sense. What was up with Nicole was never clear. Her poker face belied nothing, whether she was really into learning anything, or whether this was just another way to prove her superiority.

"How do you do it?" Nicole asked. The women looked at her expectantly. "I've heard such a thing was possible, but I've never met anyone who could do that."

Leela considered. *Would they understand? Would they have the patience to let themselves unfold?*

She decided to go for it. "First of all," she said, "it's not something you do. It's something you prepare for and then allow to happen." She pondered for a few seconds. "You can get primed by doing Kundalini Meditation every day. You know, the one with the shaking of the pelvis? Mevlana says that if you have any trouble with your libido that will really wake you up."

She pursed her lips and paused again. "Then I guess it has something to do with how we live around here, the daily practicing of ecstasy. You could call it 'the disciplines of pleasure'—bodily delights and sensuous treats. All these enjoyments we have to choose from: hot, sweet-smelling soaks in the tubs, alone or with friends, receiving a massage, sweating in a sauna or steam room, stretching like a cat, dancing with wild abandon. Anything that increases the oxygen in the body increases pleasure.

"Practically a prerequisite is keeping your body oiled and running like a smooth machine with various dietary and exercise disciplines. In the West, I had done all these things, but I had done them *to* the body. I didn't know until I was here at the ashram that it has to do with experiencing them *in* the body."

Leela felt a sense of caution, and she looked at both their faces to figure out how to continue. All she knew was to jump right in. "Everybody knows all these activities help make you healthier, but they don't of themselves make the orgasms possible. For that, it doesn't have anything to do with sex or the body but with opening to Existence." Leela looked to the sky, scanning for words. "It's like I got blessed with an awareness of the inner orgasmic space that is always there underneath. Or like, it's about opening to the Great Orgasm that is always happening. The orgasm inside that is always going on *all the time.*"

The women were staring at her. Kate looked in her purse for her lighter and lit a cigarette. Leela felt that somehow she had blundered, but she stumbled on. "It's about surrender. When I got here I had this experience where I totally let myself relax into whatever was happening, and I've mostly been able to stay in that space. Orgasm is really just a big letting go, isn't it?"

Neither Kate nor Nicole was looking at her any more. They wanted some kind of magic pill, but there wasn't one. It was available for them, but they weren't willing or able to open that way.

"I told you it was quite a story," Kate said to Nicole.

"How lovely this has happened for you," Nicole sneered. "Thanks so much for your time."

Kate exhaled and stubbed out her cigarette. "We were on our way over to the Mozart when we saw you. Want to come with us? We're on a mission to meet a man who knows a thing or two about orgasms."

"You two go on," Leela said. She had a date with the orgasm master himself tonight. There was nothing she could do if people didn't want to hear.

YOU'RE NOT REALLY ON A SPIRITUAL PATH," Andrew said. He looked straight into her eyes until she had to force herself to look away.

"What in the *hell* are you talking about?" Anger ascended up her spine. "Not on a spiritual path! That's the *only* thing my life has been about." She glared at him. *How could he know so little about her after all this time?* "Ever since I can remember, I was trying to figure out what all this shit is about." She gestured from one side of the Mozart to the other. "When I was six years old, for god's sake, I used to lie in bed imagining infinity and feeling like my head would explode. All through adolescence I was this weird bookish kid, reading philosophy and debating with the youth minister about how evil could exist. That, of course, and studying the sex manuals under my parents' bed."

Andrew kept looking at her, not moving a muscle.

"As soon as I got to college, it was Transcendental Meditation and the Maharishi, group therapy and Esalen, reading all kinds of books about Eastern religion. Becoming a vegetarian, going on these extended fasts that were supposed to purify you—they only made me weak. Visiting Ram Das, and Hari Das, and Swami this and Swami that. Dabbling in black magick, Aleister Crowley, tarot, astrology. All the time trying out everything, committing to nothing because my identity was being a Seeker, a seeker *on the path*, mind you. Always looking at my stuff, trying to improve, to increase my conscious contact with god. My *whole life* has been about being on a spiritual path." It was as if he had never known her. It made her feel hopeless and worn out.

"All of this is as it is," Andrew said. "But you are not really on a spiritual path. You think you are, but you are not."

Maybe this misunderstanding is due to our different culture and languages, Leela thought. "Spiritual path," she reiterated. "That's what I'm about. I thought you knew that. If you don't know that, you don't know me, and that makes me really sad."

"Look," he said, measuring his words." I know this hurts you, but you are not really on any path at all. Look at how you are: Anything can knock you off balance. Even this discussion throws you, makes you doubt who you are. You have ideas about your identity, but you don't really know, do you? You go chasing after this thing, that. You have no center. You're just reactive to whatever comes along."

Leela took a long in-breath, then exhaled slowly and audibly.

"Some guy beckons," he continued, "you go. Another offers you a big drama, you succumb. You hear about a new form of meditation, and you have to taste. You become angry when a beggar is particularly aggressive, then sad because it makes you think of all the suffering in the world. All day long, you are swept about by your emotions, your thoughts, first this, then that. There is no central person having these experiences."

Leela raised her head and looked into his eyes. They were opaque and crinkled around the edges. She loved the way the deep lines fanned out toward his temples.

"This is why the first step is 'yoga'," he said. "Not the way you think about yoga. Oh, I know, in America now it's about having a beautiful body and pretending to be spiritual, and a whole new way to look for sex partners. But what yoga is really about is the creation of a *seat,* a place from which to view the world that is unflappable, from which one may observe the outer and inner worlds. They have it all wrong, as usual. You don't have to assume any pretzel poses or do any twisting exercises. The stillness is the point; the still point is the only point. Only from there may one know anything."

A rickshaw pulled right up next to their table, glee-fully sharing its exhaust. Then the two boys selling drums approached, banging and yelling, "*Baba*, buy drums! Drums, *baba*, drums!"

"Not these guys again; I can't stand it!" Leela groaned. The drum sellers showed up everywhere Westerners congre-gated. "Can't we get out of here? Before we get stuck buying drums neither of us wants?"

"Sure," Andrew said, with a bemused smile. "We don't have to talk any more."

Without Leela really noticing, they headed toward the *ghats,* and beyond that toward Andrew's building. Soon they were climbing the cool dark stairway to his flat, and opening his door. Leela headed straight for the balcony and stood looking down at the washerwomen by the river below. She heard the sounds of Andrew making tea in the kitchen, and it soothed her, made her feel she belonged.

Leela walked into the bedroom and lay down on the pure white coverlet. She leaned on the pillows propped against the wall, and looked into the mirror that reflected her and any other activity that might happen on the bed. *How do I look?* she wondered. *I look good, being with him makes me look good, and I look like I really belong here.* It felt like home, her home, although it was not.

Andrew walked in with the tea service and lay down beside her, pouring them both a cup.

"You don't look down on me?" Leela blurted out. "That I am so scattered and so lost?" She felt the impulse to run, even though she felt safer than she had ever felt before with a man.

"Oh, no." He laughed, adding some sugar to his tea. "You're from the West, that's all, as we all were when we came here. Gradually we learn that the things worth knowing can only come from a place of deep relaxation." He offered her a teaspoon of sugar, which she accepted. "The West is totally against this relaxation, in fact, the West is about creating agitation. That's why they are all so aggressive and adrift. Here, there is nothing to do but relax. Like you and me here now. Let's drink our tea, and do nothing together." He settled back against the pillow next to her and placed his hand lightly on her thigh.

It got so still that Leela could hear a cow down at the river give a low moan, then the switch of the cowherd on its back. She scrunched further into the pillows holding the teacup against her chest. Its warmth on her heart let her relax into a very soft place.

"Do you think I will ever get it?" she asked, embarrassed by her plaintive tone.

Andrew smiled. "They say it's available to anyone." He took a sip of his tea, which was cold by now. "Who knows if they themself will wake up? I guess it depends on how much you want it." He stared out into the room, off somewhere in his thoughts or memories.

Leela put her cup down on the tray. She stole Andrew's cup out of his hand and placed it next to hers, then pushed the whole thing to the bottom of the bed. "How much do

I want it?" she asked. Smiling, she sat up astride him, her legs on either side of his. "How much do I want it?" she asked, keeping eye contact, watching his lips curl into a smile. "How much do I want it?" this time, as if she was asking herself. She reached down and placed her hand firmly over his groin, pressing her hand in hard, moving slowly up and down over the fabric of his jeans.

He reached up and unbuttoned her blouse, cupping her breasts in his hands. "Yes," he said. "I hear you have to really want it." He ran his hands down her sides and pulled her down so that her lips nuzzled against his cheek. Leela took a deep inhale of his smell. He moved his hands inward along her thighs, stroking in light feathery movements, working his way up to her center. When he got there, he traced a light circle round and round. Leela sat up and took off her blouse, then reached down and unzipped his pants. "What was that you were saying—that everything is learned through relaxation?" Things weren't so relaxed any more. In fact, as he picked her up by her hips and lowered her onto his mouth, then moved her onto his lap and entered her, it was quite the opposite.

Afterward they lay cuddled like spoons until he broke the silence. "Do you want to go to the swimming pool?"

The moment was over. "Nah," she said. "I have to go pick up my laundry and do errands." They got up and dressed.

"Okay," he said at the door as she left. "Catch up with you later."

Later, Leela thought. *Whatever that meant.*

LEELA SCANNED EVERYONE ENTERING THE HALL for the evening meditation. The figures silently took their places in the ghostly light, laying down mats to protect from the chill of the marble floor. They wrapped shawls and jackets tightly around themselves before settling in for the duration.

The hall held about four hundred in all, and she couldn't recognize everyone. So many newcomers every day. There was the woman from the clothing boutique, and the man who had served *aloo gobi* at lunch. There was the Sufi dancer, and that just-arrived girl with the thick curly mane and long legs that all the men were noticing. Leela kept searching, sure she would find him.

At almost the last minute, he came in, alone. The slight stoop to his back gave him away, as well as his almost invisible ordinariness. He walked to the opposite corner from where Leela sat and laid out his mat like everyone else. When he sat, she lost sight of him, but that was only with her physical eyes.

All through the meditation she tried to concentrate on spiritual subjects, but going home with Andrew was foremost in her mind. On her left two lovers, ignoring the meditation, lay entwined and murmuring softly to each other between kisses. They caressed and were gentle and obviously in love. She looked and saw their wedding bands. The meditation seemed like it would never end.

When the gong finally sounded, she sat up alert to see which exit he would take. The one he came in, of course.

She ran out the back door where she had entered and made her way through the crowd picking away at the shoe pile. She found hers lying in the flowerbed next to where she had left them.

The pathway around the meditation hall was lit with lampposts every several feet. Without them, the air would have been pitch-black. Leela ran through the damp night toward where she had seen him moving, alone, surely to retrieve his shoes before returning home. She panicked that she would not find him, but there he was, standing tall and looking so wise right in front of her. Sweat seeped through her dress as her desire pulsed in her breasts.

She stopped in front of him. He was leaning against the lamppost strapping on his sandal.

"Ah, it's you," he said. Nothing else.

"Yes," she said. "I saw you inside, and I wanted to catch up with you." She paused, breathless. "I want to be together with you again. Tonight."

He looked down and began strapping on the other sandal. He finished and stood at his full height next to her. She looked up.

"I'm with someone else tonight," he said gently.

The shock rocked her, but she remembered to be cool, cool here at the tantra ashram. "So?" she said. "Wouldn't you rather be with me? All that we had today? You and me? I want to be with you."

His silver hair shone under the glow of the light overhead. "I'm sorry," he said. "She's waiting; I have to go."

"Wouldn't you rather be with me?"

He touched her shoulder, then ran his finger down her cheek. "I can't keep her waiting any longer." He kissed her on the top of her head, and then he was gone. She watched all the way until he turned left out the gate. She thought idly about running after him, but stayed put where she was. It was a while that Leela stood under the lamppost, watching the thousand mosquitoes suicide into the gleaming light.

HEY THERE, WHAT'S WRONG?"

Leela looked up to see Dylan's dark head outlined against the leafy trees overhead. He was much taller than she remembered, or at least he looked so, standing over her like that. She wasn't sure she wanted company. "I'm okay," she said, wiping the moisture away from her face. "Really."

"No, not really," Dylan said. He walked around and sat in the chair beside her, his blue eyes meeting hers. "If you don't want to talk about it, that's all right. I'll just sit here and be with you."

Leela was taken by another burst of weeping. She felt embarrassed for Dylan to see her like this but she couldn't stop. How could she tell anyone about stretching so far she might snap? About how much her heart was being shattered? About Andrew, and what it all meant.

"I just can't take it anymore," she cried. "This place is too intense. Too much growth all the time. It never stops." The pressure in her chest felt like her body wasn't big enough to contain it. Gradually the round of tears tapered off and ceased. She sat up, dried her eyes, and began again.

"And then today. When I was down on Gandhi Road. It . . . it was just the last straw."

"The straw that broke the *wallah*'s back," Dylan said. "Tell me. Tell me the piece that tipped it over the edge."

"This guy . . . this guy I saw today, he was lying in a puddle—there are just so many people," Leela tried to explain. "So many people." The sheer number of human beings on the streets in India was hard enough for a Western mind to comprehend, but that wasn't what was so disturbing.

"It's like, every day, day after day, we're confronted with all these beggars, right? It's ghastly how their bodies are all distorted, like open sores with flies on them, and legs stuck on backward with the feet upside down: The level of misery is just overwhelming. You know, we all went through this when we first got here, right?"

The light shone on Dylan's face so that it looked to be made of ivory. He nodded.

"You find out real quick." Leela continued, "that you can't give them money, because if you do, you get targeted as an easy mark. Then wherever you go, a horde of beggars will follow you, yelling at you to give more. *'Baksheesh, baba, baksheesh!'* You see that the money you give does nothing to alleviate suffering whatsoever, because there's such a bottomless pit of need.

"Then you try the second tactic, which is to pretend not to see, to ignore. This works better in that you aren't mobbed or followed any more, but inside it feels like dying. You know what I mean, right? The underlying anxiety is always there, burrowing its way beneath the surface. Hey, do you have a Kleenex?"

Dylan reached into his pocket and handed her one.

She dabbed her eyes and went on. "What happened today was, I was in this taxi on my way to see a new Ayurvedic doctor in town somewhere. The driver went through this area where the people were living in these tiny hovels you could see right into: They were as small as closets with whole families living in there. They sat on their haunches, huddling on the dirt floors, and the filth! They were making these little pots of food or just sitting there.

"There was this zoo-like quality to it: like this rich, ugly American looking into their animal-level lives for her entertainment—it made me sick to be me in that moment." Leela glanced to see if Dylan was repulsed, but he hadn't flinched. "I don't mean to say that that's what I think about them, but the inherent arrogance of it all. I felt horrible, like I was this above-it-all rich person. Not by any means rich in my own country, but unfathomably rich in what I take for granted every day."

Dylan reached out and put his hand on her forearm. She shifted in her seat, waited a moment, and took a deep breath to make sure no more tears were starting.

"So then, you know how today was really muggy, and the sky was all gray and dark? There was a sudden downpour just before noon, one of those really heavy rains that lasts an instant but makes such a big mess; did it happen here too?

Everyone, merchants, women in saris, and beggars alike, were all running around getting totally soaked because there was no time to get prepared. I was watching it all from the safety of the taxi and marveling at how much water could come down in such a short time, but then what I saw broke the dam of my heart.

"This guy was lying in the middle of a huge puddle that had formed, and he was trying to shield himself from the rain by pulling this blanket over his head, but the blanket was totally soaked. I mean, he was totally drenched and trying to protect himself with this waterlogged blanket while lying in this puddle, and the utter futility of it all . . .and that that was the best he had available to him—I don't know," Leela started to cry again. "Why is it like this? What are we doing coming here? All I could do was hate myself and everything I have."

Dylan had seemed impervious, but now he spoke. "It breaks the heart," he said. He leaned in and his eyes were focused on her intently. "It breaks the heart, and the breaking of the heart opens us up to compassion." He took back his hand from her arm. "And that's a good thing, yes?"

Leela looked up at him, wondering.

"It all adds to the total level of Compassion in the world," Dylan continued. "As our hearts open and break, and we allow it to change us, we find a new capacity to practice compassion on a moment-to-moment basis. Then what happens is, as exponentially more people open their hearts, the Heart of the Planet itself opens up."

It was true, Leela thought, *that the Western mind can't comprehend the level of suffering in the world, so as the mind got short-circuited, the awareness went straight to the heart.* Leela understood now that the pressure in her chest had been her heart pushing out against its boundaries to expand beyond its present size. Her heart had been too small to contain this knowing.

"Yes," Leela said. "Yes." She looked at the man in front of her anew, her eyes cleansed by grief. This boy she had thought was merely a party animal, a spiritual tourist, a Goa raver; this boy was an old soul.

Jesus," Kate said. "I'm dying." She reached down for her water bottle and took a drink. "But everyone knows you lose at least two to three pounds in the sauna, and god knows I could use it."

Leela rolled her eyes over Kate's concave stomach, speckled with dew-like drops. She couldn't see a single place that could stand losing even a quarter of an inch. "Yeah, but as soon as you drank that water," she said, "you gained it all back."

The air above the stove was shimmering with heat. Leela blew a long breath out her mouth intending to cool herself which had the opposite effect. The walls emitted a faint odor of cedar.

Kate pointed to the *Vogue* she was reading, its pages ruffled from the humidity. "These two-thousand-dollar slacks are a dead ringer for what I bought at Izizi Boutique yesterday for twenty-five *rupees*."

"Great," Leela said, closing her eyes. "Where'd you get the magazine, anyway?"

"There's a bookstore downtown where I get my fix: *Vanity Fair, Bazaar, The New Yorker*. They're a month late and cost a fortune, but I need to stay current."

Leela willed her back to relax where it met the wooden slats. Her spine had felt like a steel bar ever since the moonlight encounter with Andrew. Gyeltsen was going to be disappointed with her lack of progress.

"You should read this article about hormones." Leela wished Kate would stop chattering so she could concentrate on de-stressing. "Do you think you'll take them later on? After the dreaded men-o-pause?"

"I *really* don't want to think about it." Leela shuddered, and her eyes popped open. "This girlfriend of a friend of mine said that after The Change she had no desire at all. None whatsoever. Can you imagine?"

"All I can say is we'd better have our fill now. The horror of what's coming: the crepey necks and all. Liver spots and sagging flesh. I don't think I can bear it."

"You'll always look great, no matter what."

"Thanks. You know me—hungover with very little sleep—that's my beauty secret." Kate rifled a few more pages.

"By the way," Leela said. "I received an email from my ex-boyfriend, Richard. He's getting married. It felt really weird. I mean, I don't want him anymore, but I also don't want him to be happy with someone else. And it rubs it in that I don't have anybody. That's not very big of me, is it?"

"Very normal. Endings are hard. Fuck him. Back to the present: What's the latest with you and Andrew?"

Leela shut her eyes again. "I don't want to talk about it." She suddenly felt shy and protective, as you do when something's really important.

"Oh, come on. Really. Give it up."

Leela leaned up on her elbows and faced Kate. "It's just that I feel incredibly stupid—even though I heard that everybody's been with him . . . it seemed like it was special." A bead of sweat rolled down her nose and plopped onto her thigh. "I came here because I thought I was going to learn what I needed for the Perfect Beloved to show up, but it seems like I keep getting my hopes up just to have them dashed. In the West, I always tried to protect myself from heartbreak—here that seems to be part of the program. The thing with Andrew is toast. Over. The end."

"I don't know about that," Kate said, taking another drink of water. "Nothing's over till it's over. And especially here at the ashram, you'll be seeing him again and again, so who can say?"

"I don't know. It hurts pretty bad."

Kate returned to her magazine. "This is who you should be with," she said pointing to a shirtless Indian hunk. "Rescue me, baby! Take me away from all this."

"Yeah, those Bollywood guys are pretty hot. At least until they start singing."

"Why can't I meet a guy like this? Talk about your Perfect Beloved!"

Way too hot in here, Leela thought. "You've missed the whole idea of the Perfect Beloved. It's not that he looks like a guy in a magazine. You're still buying into that Western rubbish that there's someone out there who'll meet your ego's criteria. That criteria was dictated by the media in the first place! That idiocy that you can put in your order and he'll appear just as you specified. The truth is, no matter how cute that Bollywood guy is, you wouldn't have anything in common with him."

"Oh, lighten up! I can daydream, can't I? Let me have my fantasy."

"I think it's really destructive."

"Whatever," Kate said. "By the way, I'm getting out of here."

Leela brushed her hand down her right shin, like a squeegee on a shower wall. "It *is* pretty unbearable."

"No, I don't mean the sauna. I mean leaving. The ashram. India."

"Wha—?"

"I can't take the bullshit any more. The poverty, the pollution, the dirt, the filth."

"You're just going through that predictable thing of every few weeks—that 'I can't stand it one more minute'— let's head on over for a little respite at the Holiday Inn."

"Now you're talking. But what I'm really referring to is the low quality of men."

Leela's mouth popped wide open. "You're joking?" she said, aghast. "I've never seen such highly developed men, anywhere I've ever been, anywhere I've ever imagined."

"They're all a little too much in touch with their feminine side, if you ask me. There aren't enough men here with money. I'm tired of paying my own way."

"They have enough to travel internationally. And it's not like you have any money issues yourself."

"Oh, I don't know," Kate said. "Who knows? I'm probably just in a mood."

"Stay here," Leela said. "You're my best friend. Who will I run everything by?"

"Whatever," Kate said. "Let's go get a drink. Or two. Or three."

IT WAS ANDREW'S VOICE—UNMISTAKABLE. LEEla twisted her head around, and yes, it was him, walking behind her talking with another man. He acknowledged her, but didn't miss a beat in his conversation. She felt her stomach lurch, but kept her feet moving on the path, turning back to resume her conversation with Kate.

"And then I told him to go screw himself," Kate was saying. It seemed that she hadn't stopped talking since they left the sauna or the Holiday Inn.

"Who are you talking about again?"

The sky was darkening and it smelled like rain. Perhaps

this was a prelude to one of those torrents that came out of nowhere. Leela pulled her shawl tighter around her body. Kate went on yammering with her gossip, and Leela tried to care.

As they passed a fork in the path, she glanced surreptitiously back to see that Andrew and his companion had walked off in the other direction.

"That was so weird," Leela said. "He didn't even want to talk with me." The sound of her feet against the pavement seemed loud.

"I don't think that was particularly weird," Kate said. "He was involved in talking with that guy, and they were on their way somewhere. Nothing strange about it at all."

"It felt bad," Leela said. *One foot after the other. Just keep putting one foot after the other.* "Here you can never tell if something's over. It's not like in the West, because you still see the person all the time."

"You're being ultra-sensitive. It didn't mean anything."

They passed the shoulder-high Buddha standing in the dense shrubbery. Since they had never determined a destination for their walk, they had ended up at the swimming pool.

"Is he really as good as everyone says?" Kate asked.

"He's the best," Leela said, looking straight ahead. "You should fuck him."

They walked a few more steps until Kate stopped, reached into her bag and pulled out her cigarettes. She shook one out and tapped the filter against her wrist. "I thought you have feelings for him," she said.

"I'm finished with that. It's over."

She felt Kate scrutinizing her face. "Come on, walk over to the smoking zone with me," Kate said. "I could use a cig."

They sat down in two wire chairs next to ashtrays overflowing with butts. Leela looked up at the sky. She didn't know how to tell if the rain would start or not. Kate fiddled with her matches, then lit the first cigarette. "Tell me what makes him so special in bed."

"He bases how he makes love with you on exactly what you like. It's uncanny how he can tell precisely what you are wanting, as if he was reading your mind every step of the way. I guess he's reading your body, right?"

"Ummm. Sounds delicious."

"You should try him out, really, just to see for yourself. He's amazing. Everyone here has been with him, and actually I'm surprised you haven't."

Kate took a tissue from her purse. "Are you aware your lip is bleeding? You must have bitten it."

Leela touched her mouth and felt the wetness there. Her fingertip was covered with watercolor red, and her lip stung as she put the tissue to it.

Kate exhaled a long steady stream of smoke. "Maybe I will check him out. You sure you wouldn't mind?"

"Me? Why would I mind? It's not like he belongs to me or anything. Have yourself some fun."

"You're sure about this? You know, guys who are that good in bed are that way for a reason, and it is rarely because they are monogamous."

"What's it to me?"

"All right then. Cool. I'll let you know how it goes." Kate stood up. "I'm going to get going. It seems like it's planning to rain, and I want to get safely inside before it does. Catch you later."

Leela watched her walk away. Just as she turned the corner, a picture of Kate naked with Andrew assaulted her consciousness with a crowbar, and she nearly doubled over from the pain. She jumped up in a panic, wringing her hands and bringing them to her face. "No, wait!" she called out. "Wait! I don't want you to." She ran after Kate, catching up with her at the Buddha head. "Wait, I don't want you to be with him. I can't stand the thought of it."

Kate stood appraising her. Leela flipped over into her mind and thought about how she valued nonattachment. "Well, I mean, really, what difference would it make? We're not together," she said. Then her heart thought of his sweet caresses on any other woman than her—it ran through her body like a machete. "On the other hand, please don't. I don't want you to." Then her mind thought about how she agreed that everyone should be free to do their own thing. "Oh, if you do, just don't let me know, okay?"

Kate still stood there, saying nothing while Leela cruised all over the map. The bushes rattled, and Leela looked down to see a mongoose snaking by. Only this morning she had seen one ferociously attack someone's breakfast tray to steal an egg. Mongooses might look pretty, but they were mean.

Kate took a cigarette out of the pack and lit it, even though the smoking zone was back around the corner. She took a long drag and exhaled out the side of her mouth. "Well, if you're not with him, it's not really your business who he's with, is it?" she said. She hadn't altered her steely gaze at Leela one whit. "I don't care anyway. I've got bigger fish to fry. Look, I've got to go if I want to stay dry. If you're smart, you'll get out of here too." She turned on her heel and marched away.

No, Leela thought, as she balled up the tissue and daubed at her lip. *It's not my business any more.* There was a crack of thunder, and the first drop of rain splashed on the crown of her head.

27

"STOP!" LEELA YELLED TO THE RICKSHAW driver. He careened past an elderly woman struggling with a load of washing on her shoulder, and pulled to the side of the road just beyond the Mozart. The traffic was heavy at this time of the evening, and the exhaust so black and thick that many passengers held scarves over their faces to try to filter the air.

Leela looked back at a sight she could not believe she was witnessing. There next to the Mozart, in the same spot where she had stood with him in the amorphous cocoon, stood Bashir and Kate, holding hands, gazing into each other's eyes without moving. If there hadn't been so much going on around them they would have attracted attention, but no one but Leela noticed two people having a total bliss-out by the side of the road.

Leela remembered how after the spell had broken, she had had the strong desire to hail a taxi to take them back to her place, to make love with Bashir madly and forever.

The moment had passed, however, when she remembered he belonged to Mevlana. There were enough men that one didn't need to betray her girlfriends.

Leela turned around and told the driver to continue on. That rumble in her stomach must mean she was hungry. It was dinnertime, after all, and she hadn't had lunch.

NDREW PULLED UP BESIDE HER AS SHE walked down the scrabbled path. The engine reduced to a low hum as he put his feet down and matched the bike to her pace. "There you are," he said. "Are you on your way back to your flat?"

"Yes," Leela said. "It's the afternoon break from group and I thought I might catch a little nap."

"Are you up for company?"

Leela turned her head to face him. He was wearing a shirt she had never seen before, brown like his eyes. A tuft of hair was sticking up in the back, not his usual perfect coiffure. "Is something up?" she asked.

"No, no," he said. But he didn't meet her eye.

Her flat was cool and dark as they entered. She left the light off so as not to disturb its fresh airiness. A light breeze blew in from the window, ruffling the curtains and the washing she had hung out to dry that morning. She gathered the clothes in her arms and moved them to the rack, joining her collection of T-shirts and gauze Indian wear.

He was already sitting on the bed and unbuttoning his shirt. He looked up into her eyes, reached out and took her hand, and pulled her down beside him. Kissing her neck and gently pushing her back, he worked her over just the way she liked until she came, then entered her and finished off. *The first time we've had ordinary sex*, Leela thought, *better than average surely, but run-of-the-mill just the same. There had to be a first time for everything.*

She listened to the stillness, their breathing quiet now, the curtains flapping in the wind. Every time didn't have to be special. Nothing was up. He just wanted to see her, that was all.

"My special girlfriend arrives from Germany in three weeks."

A crow cawed outside the window. "Your what?"

"My special girlfriend. From Germany."

Leela examined the crack in the ceiling that ran from the window to the light bulb. "Your special girlfriend. Arriving from Germany. If she's your special girlfriend, who am I?"

"Leela." His voice was tender as he stroked her arm. "I wanted to come over and tell you myself. You are special to me too. You and I, we are going to be together for a long time. Nothing has to change between us when she gets here."

The crack must have always been there, but Leela hadn't noticed how deeply it ran until now. "Excuse me?" she said. "Where exactly is this person going to be staying?"

"She'll be staying with me until she gets her own place." Andrew leaned up on his elbow and placed his hand gently on her belly. "She was living with me last summer but had to go back to Germany for the winter for work. Now she's back for an indefinite stay." He rubbed his hand in a circular movement round Leela's stomach. "I told her about you, and she's fine with it. We have an agreement." His hand cupped over her navel and rested there. "I don't want this to affect us; we can continue just as we are. You and I might even teach together. This is another opportunity to learn to be open to whatever happens, to flow with whatever existence brings."

Leela traced the crack one more time with her eye. She watched the curtain blowing out from the window. Then she removed Andrew's hand from her body as she stood up, slipping into her sundress and moving to the rattan chair across from the bed.

"No," she said. "No. Things do not continue as they are. Look, I understand you're not monogamous, that's just the way it is. But you said what we have is special. Now you say she's the special one. You don't get to have both. You have to choose."

"It is not up to me to choose," he said. "Existence happens and I flow with it, with whatever is the truth in the situation."

"If you think I am going to put up with this, then you have chosen," she said. "Get out. Get out now."

She watched as he buttoned up the unfamiliar shirt, and smoothed down the errant hair in her mirror. "This is not what I want," he said.

"Then tell her to stay somewhere else. Tell her that things have changed."

"I can't do that. And I don't want us to stop what's between us."

"You fool. Did you really imagine this would be okay with me? I want you to leave, now."

The door closed behind him. *This "flow with existence" thing is metaphysical bullshit,* Leela thought, as she lay back on her pillow in stunned silence.

I *must talk with Kate—I need her support,* Leela thought as she hailed a ride over to her flat. She can help me interpret all this. The entire bumpy ride there she breathed heavily and slowly so she wouldn't cry but was only successful part of the time.

Kate opened the door an inch, shielding the entrance with her body. Her hair was a rat's nest and her eyebrows were penciled even darker than usual.

"May I come in?" Leela felt dizzy from confusion and the rickshaw ride and wanted to sit down.

"No. This isn't a good time. The place is really a mess and I don't want you to see it."

"What?" Leela shook her head. Something was up. This had to be the lamest excuse ever. She craned her neck over Kate's shoulder to see that the usually meticulous room appeared as if an intruder had ransacked the place. Clothes were strewn about everywhere. Two open suitcases were situated in the middle of the floor.

"Are you going somewhere?" Leela asked. "Why haven't you told me?"

Kate tried to close the door another quarter of an inch. "Look," she said, glaring. "It's all over for me here and I need to get out. Dead, dead. Boring. I need to leave here, and that's what I'm doing."

Leela remembered the conversation in the sauna, but it had seemed like idle talk.

"Kate, why don't you open the door, and we'll talk about whatever is bothering you."

Kate frowned as she pressed herself more firmly into the doorjamb. "All right," she said. "I'll tell you what's going on. You want to know so badly, here it is. That rumor, the one about Bashir leaving Mevlana and running off to Australia with another woman? Well, that woman is me. I'm the one going with him. We're going together."

"You're running off with another woman's husband? What's wrong with you?" Leela flashed back to meeting Kate in the nail salon, rolling with laughter at the Holiday Inn, sharing confidences about men and growing older. Was this the same person she had grown to trust?

"I'm sorry to cut this short," Kate said. Her tone was ice-cold now. "I have to finish packing and be out of here by four today. So I'm going to have to say *adieu* now. *Ciao*, baby. *Hasta la vista*. Been swell. Wishing you the best."

Leela could have sworn she heard the hissing of a mongoose. "All your stupid talk about power and wanting to sleep with Bashir to get it? I thought that was all a joke.

Not that you would ever really do it. You must be out of your mind."

"I don't care. It's my life and I'll do as I wish. I will have who I wish. Mevlana can go fuck herself, or any one of her many minions. I don't care. Neither does anyone else."

"I care," Leela said. "I do completely. Mevlana is a person like anyone else, who bleeds and has feelings and her own vulnerabilities.

"You, on the other hand, are not a good person. You are hiding at this tantra ashram because you think you have license here to do anything you want, which I guess you do. But you and Jack and people of your ilk think that means using anyone to your advantage. You make me sick, the whole lot of you. Hiding your sociopathy behind spirituality, it's the oldest con game in the world. You're all just a bunch of sex addicts."

"Whatever. You can go fuck yourself." The door slammed in her face.

WHEN LEELA GOT TO THE GATE OF THE ashram there was a sign posted on an easel inside the door: *Death Celebration, 4:00 p.m.* Underneath was a high school photograph of a slight Indian man, his shiny black hair and eyes like those of any number of other young Indians his age, and a little about his life:

> *Prem Wadud, age 23, was killed on his motor-cycle on the Main Road on Thursday. He was a student at Deccan College and lived at the ashram for close to five years. Come help us celebrate his life and death.*

Leela had never noticed him around, but seeing as how Indians were second-class citizens at the ashram, they were often invisible to Westerners. It was sobering all morning thinking of him dying too early from what everyone encountered every single day—the insane chaos of Indian traffic. Learning to let go and trust—meditation may have been a good teacher for that, but Leela realized that Indian traffic had taught her more. Once in it, there was absolutely nothing one could do but surrender. It was better if you closed your eyes and didn't look, knowing that whatever was going to happen would be the only thing that could.

Leela arrived at the gate at four o'clock where about a hundred people had already gathered. Everyone was milling about looking for friends or for who else might be there, trying to position themselves next to someone attractive, or jockeying for a place next to the musicians. That's where the juice was, up close to the musicians with their mastery of building and sustaining excitement. The band today consisted of two guitar players and an internationally mixed group of drummers: White guys with African gourds, Indians with *tablas*, Brazilians holding exotic percussion instruments, and a Black man with a drum from a school marching band hanging around his neck.

Leela saw among the drummers the big Danish guy who had played for their morning dance class. She missed his previous leonine head of dreadlocks, but saw that he was starting to grow them back. All over his head were little nubs of twisted hair secured by rubber bands. Leela felt a twinge of excitement that with him included in today's drum ensemble, the music might light a special distinctive spark.

The drum corps gathered behind the corpse which was laid out on a wooden plank. The body had been adorned with strings of flowers called *malas*, and his hair was oiled and neatly combed. He had not been waxed or plucked or made-up the way he would have been in the West. Because the climate is so hot, Indians burn their dead very soon after death and do not embalm or preserve or refrigerate them. Leela remembered that when her mother had died unexpectedly years before, she'd gone to the viewing and when she touched her; the body was ice-cold from being kept in the funeral home refrigeration unit. No such luxury in hot and humid India.

The group was going to travel as a procession from the ashram gate to the burning *ghats,* about a half a mile away by the side of the river. Leela had gone back several times to the *ghats* and loved sitting there when nothing was happening. It was so peaceful, and the feeling of being alive was a little crisper around death when death was not happening at that moment. Each time she visited, the mangy dogs were still there, scratching without relief. The everydayness of life lay juxtaposed against death: the women washing clothes, the hordes of mosquitoes, the graffiti on the walls.

Six Indian men from the ashram hoisted the planked body onto their shoulders, and the music began, softly at first. There were now about two hundred people, which would double in size as they made their way to the *ghats.* The crowd started singing songs that everyone knew, well-loved songs, part of what made them a *sangha,* a community of spiritual seekers.

A groove was rising as they sang along and started dancing. The beat was building, its rising intensity barely perceptible to the mind. But Leela's body could feel it in its tissue and bone, and it was impossible for the hips not to sway, the feet not to syncopate a little step. Men and women dancing together, people dancing alone, moving down the road in the direction of the river. The music really started to jam, and slight glistenings of sweat appeared on upper lips, in half-moons under the arms, and in a single trail down a blind girl's neck. Looks of pleasure appeared on faces, looks of a blissed-out trance, a rare happiness. The dancing was getting wilder now, more primitive, less thought out and calculated to please. A little more tribal, for that's what it was, a tribe gathered to bury one of its own dead. A jungle pulse, a tantric tango, a dance of the flesh, a dance of being alive, today.

"Stop!" One of the drummers yelled out the command, and everything came to complete silence. Everyone turned inside, their attention no longer focused on the world, the *maya* that surrounded them. Leela found the silence inside blissful, as full and rich as the music had been a moment before. Then came a massive heartbeat from the school marching drum, and the music began building again. Building, building, until everyone was dancing and singing wildly with even more frenzy than before.

The procession moved on, stopping periodically to dance and celebrate, or to celebrate by stopping in silence. In the crowd Leela spied the lovers she'd had, and men she desired to be her lovers, and girls she knew, and girls she was jealous of. It felt as if all of today's dramas should have paled in comparison with the reality of death staring them in the face, but the fact is they didn't. *The ego's attachments are utterly unbreakable until they break,* she thought, *but then again, these attachments are part of what makes us human.* The dancing went on increasing in intensity, and the joy of being alive was spilling out and over onto everything it touched.

Indian merchants along the way stood outside their shops, and Leela saw Gyeltsen come out with Dawa and their infant son. They came to watch the ashram participants celebrate the wildness of life and death and the total inability to control either. *Dancing, we are dancing next to the body of the dead man,* Leela thought. *He is dead, and we are alive, and it is a blessing for death to appear in our midst to remind us of this.* Music and dance and the glorious movements of the body were what distinguished them from being dead. Bodies drenched in sweat, pulsating flesh, arms and legs, the drumbeats so hard and so happily inducing a trance of madness, death, and sexuality. The interface of sex and death, *petit mort,* the little death of orgasm, the unfathomable mystery of women and men. Leela had heard that the moment of death can be the greatest orgasm imaginable if one can only remain conscious and not succumb to fear while going through it.

There in the center of the gyrating bodies was the big Danish drummer, ecstatic, his eyes ablaze, his skin as wet as if someone had thrown a bucket of water to quench a fire. He was lost in the primal beat he was making, hitting that drum as though it would echo throughout time immortal.

There seemed to be a halo of energy radiating out from his skin, and he laughed out loud with pleasure. The music reached another crescendo and burst like a firecracker. All stopped, then silence.

They had reached the *ghats*. One of the six little pits had been filled and piled five feet high with disks of dried cow dung and fallen tree branches that had been gathered from around the village. The men carrying the body laid it on top of the pile and moved away into the crowd. People bunched up thick on the sides of the *ghats* or out of the sun under the overhang. Some people stood under the trees, and some chose to lay on the grass further up the hill, those to whom it was perhaps more of an entertainment than a holy encounter with the other side. Leela angled for a position right next to the body though she had to be a bit aggressive to get it. She wanted to be right there as close to death as possible, to learn anything she could that would help her lose her fear of the great secret.

Men came and smeared wax onto the dead man's mouth and eyes, and with that, the mood changed completely. Leela felt a sickening sense of the reality of the other part of death, the rot, the stench, the decay and the worms, the flesh falling off the bones while the hair and fingernails keep growing. The wax was thick and pasty, and Prem Wadud no longer looked like a young boy asleep in the middle of a party, but a corpse that was about to be burned.

One of the Indian men who had carried the body stood before the crowd with a flaming torch. Leela had never seen an Indian man of such dignity before, king-like, authoritative, commanding complete respect and obeisance. Indians might have been regarded as lower caste in the ashram, but apparently in the dirty work of setting a body on fire, this man was elevated as king. She felt honored to be in his presence, imagining that he possessed mastery over the fear of death. He lit the torch and walked around the body, lighting it in several places, and the dead man began to burn.

The music began again, but what had been a celebration of the physical joy of being alive was replaced by awe at the enigma of death. The song was subdued now, carrying an insistent backbeat. The fire crackled and snapped as it hit pockets of pitch in the wood, as it burned the clothes off the body, as the wax began to stream down the sides of the pyre like melting ice cream. It was a horrible sight yet utterly fascinating. The fire was licking and burning; it was orange and magenta and yellow. Standing as close as she was, Leela felt it singe the skin, burn off eyelashes and wisps of hair. *The smoke, what did they always say? That smoke follows beauty, but wait, that was in Girl Scouts roasting marshmallows over the campfire, and now she was grown up and in India and this guy had died, and there was his body in flames and the wax running down and the people singing, and it was all burning up. Like they burned Joan of Arc, only she was alive, like they burned alive millions of women in the Middle Ages just for continuing to worship in the old ways that were different from the men's.*

As the man who had once been alive burned, Leela's reverie turned to contemplation of the spiritual path's demand to be burned alive, to be crisped and die to one's previous life. They had all traveled here to this ashram to participate in the death of their egos; they had come here to learn to die. *We are all here experiencing daily little deaths, our trials by fire,* Leela thought, meditating on the big death waiting at the end, and for herself, remembering the little deaths she'd gone through back home. They were standing at the veil between this world and the other, and some of them were nearly stepping over the line.

A tortured cry broke into her thoughts, and for the first time Leela noticed the dead boy's family. The girlfriend of the boy was overcome with grief, and she had lost all sense of appropriate behavior or decorum. She looked as if she was trying to tear herself away from the man who was restraining her and throw herself onto the funeral pyre. Maybe she was responding to the ancient Indian custom of *suttee*, in which widows were forced to "voluntarily" throw themselves into the funeral pyres of their husbands. If the woman's "courage" failed, the men would pin her down in the fire with long poles so she could not escape. *Suttee* was outlawed by the British in the last century but continued unchecked in outlying areas; only recently Leela had read a newspaper account of a present-day occurrence. Women were still being burned alive today because they had no purpose without their husbands.

This time, today, the adult male was holding the woman back, and her wailing was louder than the sound of all the people singing. Among the family present were the parents, grandparents, assorted children, uncles and aunts, and a brother who was doing his best to retain his composure.

Their grief was palpable, and Leela remembered her own family's four- dimensional grief. Grief from unexpected death is so all-encompassing it can never be communicated to those who have not experienced it. One can never paint how psychedelic the grief is, how the floor no longer seems solid, how time distorts into a wave, how you see that physics tells the truth when it says that nothing is solid and everything is moving because that is how it looks to you now. The web becomes visible, the invisible web that holds it all together, the web she saw when her mother died in the water and the girl was there again crying and the web connected it all. You think you cannot possibly make it through this minute, or the next, but you do. You think that the grief will never end, but it does, much much later than you imagined. How grief can totally devastate a life and no one talks about it as if that's not a good enough reason for a whole life to go to hell. Leela had once seen an entire family fall to pieces over the death of their son, and now this Indian family was disintegrating before her eyes.

The wind whipped the smoke around in a mad swirling dust devil. The flames were billowing, swallowing up the wood, the dried dung, the body. The blaze continued unabated, but for Leela, at the sight of the family, something broke. It was no longer some ecstatic celebration party. This family had real grief, and they the Westerners had none. It was a blessing to be able to stand in the presence of death, but except for a few personal deliberations on death that day, they would all go back to their dramas, love affairs, dance classes, and meditations. This family would be carrying the grief of a too-early death for the rest of their lives. Leela had read that psychologists have concluded that the death of a child is the hardest thing for a human being to bear, and this boy had been struck down at the age of twenty-three. As ecstatic as the earlier celebration had seemed at the time, it now appeared deceptively attractive and one-sided. Certainly a better way to celebrate death than the way it was done back home, but in a way it was just another chance for people who have everything and too much to party.

The small print on the sign on the easel had said to wash your hair and clothes thoroughly after the celebration to remove the toxic ashes and the energy of death from the body. Leela went home and showered for a long time, then fell asleep until late the next morning.

About a week after the death celebration, the big Danish guy came with the musicians to play for the dance class again. The drumming and the dancing quickly got wild, really hot, and one woman began belly dancing in front of the men, turning them on. One by one, she did a dance with each of them, and when each man was chosen, he showed her what he could do with that drum. When she came to the big guy, it was like sex, the two of them communing while his drum beats responded to her dancing, and her dancing answered his beat. He never lost eye contact with her, and they stayed united until the end. It was life, a spontaneous celebration of their radiance and vitality. He was a high soul for someone so young, really embodied, really present to the precious present moment. He was emphatically alive, that guy.

A few days later Leela was privileged to witness a death ceremony in the local Indian community. It was a toned-down version of the ashram's own raucous affair. The women in their colorful saris, the men in their monotonous off-white, children, dogs, a tribe gathered to bury one of its own dead. The procession of about forty people moved down the road in the direction of the river toward the burning *ghats* just as they had. There was something so right about how the villagers were going there together, for no one had to die alone and no one's death went unnoticed. There was no shame, no sense of failure, no morbidity; death was just a normal everyday part of being alive.

29

THE NEWS OF KATE AND BASHIR RUNNING off together was irresistible, and the ashram café was abuzz. There hadn't been such delectable gossip in a long, long while.

"Such a pity," someone sitting behind Leela sniffed. "Poor Mevlana—dumped!" Her voice dripped with self-satisfied superiority.

"Well," said her companion, "it's been hard to miss that behind her back he's been coming on to scores of women. Quite indiscriminately too, I must say. Embarrassing for her, I'm sure."

Whoosh. I'm one of those women, Leela thought sheepishly. She turned a tad to hear more clearly.

"Well, what did she expect? He's the hottest man on the planet. She's too old to keep a man like that."

"Really? You think he's the hottest? I'd take Raúl over Bashir any day."

"Raúl? Whatever. It's a toss-up in terms of sex appeal.

I wouldn't kick either of them out. Seems to me Bashir has always acted like a little boy, flirting with anyone who'd give the slightest response. Pretty, but he has no character. Raúl, on the other hand, is up to something besides seduction. He has his own career helping people."

"I really feel sorry for her," the other voice continued. "Can't keep her man. It'll be hard to find someone new at her age."

Yes, Leela wondered, *what does this mean about her power? Are all her teachings in question now?*

"And that Kate! So conniving," the voice continued "What was she doing here at an ashram anyway? I was always suspicious of her motives."

"Never liked her. Always on the make. Not someone you could trust."

People haven't liked Kate? Leela felt embarrassed as she looked back on their friendship. The shock of events demanded that she view it with different eyes.

"She thinks she's so hot because she stole Mevlana's man, but the truth is, we only feel revulsion for her."

Yes, Leela thought, *I've been looking at the wrong things when I evaluate people. Maybe it's true that as women age it's inevitable we lose our power. More importantly, what does this say about tantra?*

tHE BUZZ AND GOSSIP CONTINUED AS THE crowd waited in line to enter the morning group. Would Mevlana's grief be exposed for all to see, or would she hide it, pretending not to care? Would her heartbreak lay waste to her credibility and power? Travis and Emma shushed them to keep it down. Some were expecting to see Mevlana weak, rejected, her tail between her legs. What would her teaching be like now that she was so diminished? Leela noted a few group members gloating, especially certain women, competitive, jealous and envious as they had always been, wishing to witness the downfall of a powerful woman. In the conventional world it had been bred into them to hate each other, to be ruthless to other women, especially older women, keeping each other down. All this brainwashing accomplished was to make them dread and disempower their own futures.

The line began to move. One by one they entered, and as they did, those not yet inside could hear gasps of astonishment.

When it was her turn, Leela entered and peered up at the dais. There, larger than life, sat Mevlana, resplendent, in all her queenly glory. Not an iota of self-pity, pain, or victim consciousness could be detected. Sitting next to her was Raúl, king of the gypsies, tantrika, his universal allure, radiant health and well-being emanating throughout the room. Mevlana, it seemed, had not missed a beat.

When all were settled in, in their collective state of shock, Mevlana addressed the group. "Raúl returned to the ashram several months ago as we were preparing for a change of personnel. I'm sure you will find this new energy heightened and refreshing. Ral has been my lover and an ally of this work much longer and more consistently than Bashir.

"We have been aware of Bashir's unhappiness for some time, and now with our help, he has moved on. When he was informed we needed a change, Raúl was instantly ready to take his rightful place."

She had known; she had been preparing. It hadn't taken her by surprise. She's not too old to get and keep the hottest guy, in fact, she dispatched the one who seemed like the prize but wasn't, and now here she is with the indisputable king of the hotties.

"We don't want to speak poorly about any of our friends, but we must point out that some of his activities around the ashram have been counter to our work and teaching. You may be aware of some of the ways he conducted himself.

"It is especially important in tantra where we are teaching about sex, love and intimacy, that the teachers be of high integrity, that they keep their commitments and hold firm boundaries against inappropriate involvement with students. In the West, tantra teachings have been tarnished by this acting out of those in charge, and it will not be tolerated here.

"Plans were being made to coincide with when Raúl would be able to finish up his responsibilities in Argentina and return here to pick up his duties. And his pleasure."

Raúl picked up her hand and kissed her palm. "You can be sure I am committed to Mevlana and this work of assisting you to higher consciousness," he said, addressing the group. "I will be firmly upholding safe boundaries and a loving space. I see one of the responsibilities of my job as being a role model of a healthy tantric man, free of egoic showing off or acting as though it is a component of tantra to be a sexual predator.

"Things will be right now," he promised. "The highest responsibility of a *daka* is his integrity. The previous personnel did not live up to his duty."

Together they scanned the room. Raúl stroked Mevlana's hand. "Any questions?"

The room barely breathed in its silence. Mevlana's triumph was complete, and one by one each group member internally saluted her mastery.

LEELA AND JACK SAT HOLDING HANDS, FACING each other. Their shared eye gaze had lasted for twenty minutes or longer. All the participants of the group were seated on cushions in a long line, men on one side, women facing.

"All right," Mevlana said. "Time to separate from this beloved, and share with them in words how your experience of being together has been."

Leela looked away. Her throat closed up tight and tears pressed against her lids. Everything was so confusing. But, she admonished herself; one must keep up a good front. "That was cool," she said, smiling at Jack. "Glad to be partners with you." She hoped he would accept such an offering, weak though it was.

Jack was searching her face. "Tell me what's going on," he said softly. "It's been pretty obvious during this whole practice that you're upset about something."

Leela calculated whether if she counted to one hundred she would forget about everything collapsing. Or if Mevlana would only announce the break for dinner now, she could get out of this conversation. "Ah, no, it's nothing," she said. "Everything is fine."

"Fine," Jack said. "That's a bullshit word if I ever heard one. C'mon, I'm trying to be here for you." Leela looked at him dully. He wouldn't understand. No one would. She'd deal with it on her own.

"Look," Jack continued. He moved in closer and put his arm loosely around her shoulder. "We're your friends here, and you won't let anybody help you. You help other people, but you try to handle everything you're going through on your own. I mean, I'm your friend. You're not giving me a chance to help you like you helped me. Let me return the favor. Let me in, Leela. Let me in in a real way."

She looked up at his face. His eyes were trustworthy at last. She fell into his arms as her tears rushed out from behind the barricade that had guarded them. He wrapped one arm protectively around her while smoothing her hair with the other. Jack held Leela while she cried, held her long after everyone else had filed out of the room, long after Travis had turned out the lights.

LEELA SNAPPED TO AWARENESS. THE SUN WAS pouring in the windows in the group room, and she must have fallen into a dreamy afternoon stupor. "Love is never not there," Mevlana was saying. "If you are alone and lonely, it is only because there are too many conditions on your love."

*t**hat Danish drummer,* LEELA THOUGHT, *he's always here when the music is particularly hot.* They had been dancing for ten minutes now, the appetizer for whatever the afternoon's activity was to be. The suspense in the room was charged and magnetic, pulling her first to bump with one sweaty group member, then to grind with another.

"Love is wild," Mevlana was saying on the microphone over the drumbeats. "To truly love, you must be a wild man, or a wild woman, following the dictates of the moon and the longings of your heart." She waved her hand and the rhythm picked up slightly. "Follow your yearnings; stop living in your minds." She motioned to the assistants, who began separating the men into a circle on one side of the room, with the women far away on the other. The drummers standing in the middle created a visual and a physical barrier between them. One of the assistants dimmed the lights.

"Take off your clothes, " Mevlana said, again. Leela felt the familiar fear, but it was now becoming matter-of-fact.

As they stripped and walked over to put their clothes on the pile, Mevlana continued. "Now you'll be with your own tribe, the tribe of your own sex. You are untamed women and men with full invitation to let loose your uncontrolled natures. Dance as your ancestors did around the campfires, become crazed and free within your own tribe. Let it out! Find out who you really are underneath all your social conditioning."

Leela shyly looked at each woman as they entered the circle, avoiding each other's eyes. All had different-sized breasts, bellies, butts, and hips. Long hair, short; some were old, some young, but they all had one thing in common: all were beautiful, and not a one knew it. Except maybe the perfect Swede, whose body looked the most like those in a men's magazine—the way they were all aware they were supposed to look. The women stood awkwardly, facing each other in the circle, not knowing what was coming next.

"Start by bending your knees, and allowing your body to shake as it will," Mevlana said. The women began moving tentatively. "Let the music carry you," Mevlana continued. The drummers kept the beat steady. "If you feel moved to do so, let out a grunt, or a yell. See what happens when you abandon yourself to your primitive being."

Leela looked around as women began swinging their arms, throwing their heads back, shimmying up and down. Some let out little sounds, experimental at first. One woman danced a squat little African dance, arms akimbo, ass thrust high in the air. Another was stomping so assertively

Leela imagined her wearing war paint. Sasha and Nicole were smiling and flirting, dancing for each other. As a group, they were gaining in confidence, yelling out growls and cries as the beat grew more savage.

Group energy was building. Leela suddenly felt her nakedness as liberating, especially since there were no men around to judge. The drumbeats continued to escalate, becoming noisy and fierce. Certainly the women judged each other, but it was with male appraisals in mind.

Leela could hear the men's bass voices from the other side of the room. She looked over and tried to catch a glimpse. "Keep your full attention on your own circle," Mevlana admonished. "There is more than enough for you there." The men sounded as scary and as primitive as the women were becoming.

The fervor kept increasing. Women were leaping and whirling around the circle. Some were muttering, and Leela heard the sound of apes. A woman was rolling on the ground in apparent agony. The beat picked up at Mevlana's command.

Leela's self-consciousness was giving way to the group frenzy. She turned to the woman next to her—what was her name, Anne?—who seemed to be having trouble getting into the scene. The skin of Anne's body was wrinkled and dull, and her breasts drooped listlessly. She swayed her body from side to side, but the movements seemed awkward and forced. She felt Leela observing her and looked up into her eyes, looking for approval, or support. Leela suddenly felt contempt for her, and reached over and slapped her on the ass. *Ha ha*, Leela thought as she saw the shock on Anne's face, *that will get you going.*

Leela surveyed the tribe of aboriginal women, naked and aroused. Who was next? She saw another woman she determined was not getting loose enough, and went over and slapped her hard on her butt. The woman looked at her in total amazement and shock. "Spank, spank," Leela yelled. *Fuck her. What is she here for if she won't let go?*

The drums were crazy, getting more uncivilized by the minute. Mevlana was egging them on over the microphone, hypnotically chanting, "Wilder, wilder, go for it. This is all there is. Go for it." Leela looked around the circle at the gyrating women. There was madness in the air, an archaic primal process. Some women still held back frightened, while others were going for it full tilt.

Leela suddenly noticed that Meghan had stepped into the center of the circle, Meghan who thought she was Queen Shit, with her teeny breasts but proud posture, and that the perfect Swede, she with the enviable body, had joined her. They had designated themselves the alpha females, with an unspoken decree that all the other women would dance in the circle around them, paying homage to their inherent superiority.

Wait a minute, Leela considered. *Those bitches just demanded the alpha space for themselves, claimed it, and took it. I've never seen this so clearly before.* All the years of not being the alpha female flashed before her eyes: of being compared as less than to cheerleaders, fashion models, girls with giant breasts, Playboy bunnies, porn stars, elegant society women, rich bitches on yachts, beautiful women who made it through life only because of their looks. Rock star girl-friends, groupies, movie stars, gold diggers who knew how to marry men for money. The way that people judged the beautiful as more desirable in everything, not just looks, but personality and success quotient too. *I've never been alpha before in my life,* Leela calculated, *and it's about time. I'm going to take my rightful place in the world.*

She stepped into the inner circle boldly, acknowledging her two alpha sisters.

To her surprise, they did not shun her, but welcomed her as one of them. *What if it had always been this easy? What if I could have been here all along if I would have only claimed my space?* She and Meghan and the perfect Swede danced as a trio, as the Three Fates, the Three Graces, like the dancers on the Tarot's Three of Cups. They danced as the three most desirable women in the circle, in the ashram, and in the whole world as it existed in that moment while the other women acknowledged and danced around them.

Wildly making up for lost time, Leela exalted, *I am alpha, the alpha female and everyone else will accept it or else. In my own life story I am the center, therefore the alpha of my own drama. I reign alpha Queen in my own world, in this world, and in any world I choose to enter. Everyone else can just get fucked.*

The drummers were sweating; everybody was sweating. The big Danish guy flashed his toothy grin, and Leela wondered why she had never gotten his name. He is so alive; maybe he had a lot to teach. *I should have fucked him*, she thought, *fucked him long ago when I first saw who he was. Pounced, threw him against the wall and had my way.*

Nicole appeared in her line of vision, dancing alone along the perimeter of the ring. She was a vision with her milky skin, her soft tummy, her hair curling expertly against her shoulders. *I hate women like you*, Leela screamed inside herself; *I despise your very nature. Fucked-up females who play innocent to lure men like sirens.* Leela was pacing and wringing her hands. *You stupid cunt,* Leela thought. *I . . .*

She lunged madly at Nicole and threw her to the ground. Down they fell, Leela landing on top of Nicole, squashing their breasts and stomachs. The skin on Leela's knee broke as it hit the ground, spilling blood on the carpet. They wrestled on the floor trying to pin each other, grabbing at each other's hair. Their bodies locked together, and they rolled into the corner like a worm crawling sideways. Leela had assumed Nicole would be dumbstruck and weak, but no, she fought back with force.

"*You stupid cunt,*" Leela growled like a mantra. "*You stupid cunt who plays innocent*" She grabbed Nicole's arm and tried to push it to the ground. "It's a lure; you fucking use it as bait. You don't risk; you're a fucking phony. Your whole little innocent game; I despise you."

Nicole yelled back, "Who do you think you are to tell me who I am?" Nicole had now almost succeeded in pinning Leela to the ground. With a burst of effort, Leela flipped her over onto her back. Mevlana was taunting over the loud-speaker, "Go for it. Go for it. If you can't be orgasmic in anger, you can't be orgasmic in love." Leela sat tall over her prey in victory.

No one seemed to be paying any attention. Leela got up and released Nicole without a look back. The drumming was crazy, out of control. She glanced over at the Danish drummer, and for the first time, their eyes met. He was grinning his wide toothy grin, and Leela was enchanted by his eyes, and the strange appearance of nobody doing the drumming. The drumming was happening by itself, channeling through this huge vibrating aliveness of a man.

She walked up to one of the columns holding up the ceiling and stood before it. It was a gigantic pole, and her only experience of it before today was of trying to avoid it when she was dancing. The drums were insistent, and she looked around at the drummer. The beam coming out of his eyes reached across the room and touched her. Leela put her left arm around the pole, and wrapped her legs around it. She began sliding slowly up and down, pressing her hips up against its hardness. Up and down she slid, up and down the pole. "Fuck you," she yelled. *What if somebody sees me?* "Fuck you!"

Then she slammed her hips and began fucking the pole, thrusting hard, harder, like a man who doesn't care about his partner, harder, hardest. Up and down. Harder, harder, like a man, like an animal, howling. *What if my father sees?* "Fuck you!" *What if the men in the group see? "Fuck you!"* Up and down on the pole, she fucked it with such intensity it could have brought the house down. It was wild, and she was totally gone and ecstatic and somewhere she had never been before, gone, gone, gone the beyond, in a totally different direction, equidistant from the center.

A tiny voice from her mind came hinting *my god, you're fucking a pole* but she shouted at it "Shut the fuck up' and kept thrusting. The voice got louder and louder until under its weight she collapsed to the ground spent, exhausted. It had been a total immersion, so wild and barbaric she hardly knew who she was any more.

Leela sat up, sweating, as if she was surveying the scene of a bombsite. *Who had she been? Oh my god,* she thought, as if she was suddenly waking up. *Not only did I slap Anne and that other woman on the ass, I physically attacked Nicole who has actually done nothing except make me feel competitive. I proclaimed myself the alpha female and made everyone acknowledge me whether they wanted to or not. I ran around naked making animal noises, and I've been standing here fucking a pole in front of god and everyone.* She lay there contemplating the terribleness of all this for a minute and a half. Then a wide toothy grin crossed her face. It had been fucked up, surely, and she was as proud of herself as she could be.

30

EELA SIGHED. ANOTHER PERFECT MOMENT IN paradise. The sun blazed behind the big blue umbrella as she lunched on a pasta dense with garlic, sautéed zucchini, and garbanzo beans. Geno's tray, on the other hand, was piled high with naked raw food: at least six tomatoes, two whole cucumbers, sliced; slender stalks of celery, a mixed green salad with sprouts and jicama, pineapple chunks, and a quarter of a watermelon. Dessert, she guessed.

He looked up to see her examining his food. "Got to keep my strength up," he said, squeezing a lime over the cukes.

Geno was one of the most handsome men she had ever laid eyes on, even here at the ashram, where she was becoming rather immune to the whole issue. He stood at well over six feet with a body that spoke of years in the gym, and his hazel eyes and tanned skin glowed with vitality and health. When he hadn't spoken to her in her first days at the ashram, she had taken it as a message about her attractiveness or lack of. Now she knew differently. He was just spaced out.

Early in the group, he had informed everyone that he had a partner back in Italy and was therefore off limits, although he was available to do exercises with. Many women had shared a ping of disappointment. This morning, Leela and Geno had chosen to do the sensual massage assignment together. When it was her turn to be the giver, she had watched in amazement as he didn't even flinch when she neared the vicinity where most men would take notice. His touch on her was rough and insensitive, not at all in tune with her response or lack of it, sleepy and unaware. He got somewhat excused for this by his otherworldly good looks, but not completely.

She hadn't told him how unsatisfying it had been. In true good girl fashion she had told him it had been "nice." Someone taught her once that "nice" stands for "Nothing In me Cares Enough about you (to tell you the truth)," and she supposed that was true. It was not an unpleasant diversion, however, to sit at his table and gaze at that face. And that body.

"What's your girlfriend in Italy like?" she asked.

"She is a great and famous teacher of tantra," he said. "Right now she is giving a seminar in Tuscany."

"Oh," she said, thinking back to his touch devoid of sensuality. "You must be learning a lot about tantra from her?"

"Oh yes," he said. "She's an amazing woman."

"Then why are you here, studying tantra several thousand miles away from her?"

"She says I need to learn more about being on my own, and she is right. I want to lose my tendency of codependency."

That psychobabble, I hate it, Leela thought. "What exactly does that mean anyway? It seems to me it's a way to put down people who value being in a relationship over being alone."

"Here, I hope to deepen my aloneness," he said, "and then take it back to be with her. In a more authentic way." He moved the tray with its mound of peelings and rinds to the other side of the table, and poised his spoon over the melon.

"A relationship is like climbing a great mountain," he continued. "It is a journey that is difficult and long and takes much preparation, much training. It is the only thing in life that is of value." He dipped his spoon into the watery red fruit and took a bite. "I don't understand these men who come here just to sleep with many women. It shocks me; I don't understand it. It has no ..." He scratched his head. "Ah, my English is so bad. What is the word?" His eyes turned up into the back of his skull, searching his memory banks for an *Italiano-Inglese* dictionary.

"*Rispettare . . . no? . . . No!*" Leela shook her head. She certainly had no idea.

"*Decoro . . . stima . . . .* Ah, ah, I must know." He was frantically looking around the crowded lunch area, for what she couldn't fathom. "Ah!" and he sped off over in the direction of the fountain.

Suddenly Leela found herself sitting alone, not really understanding what had happened. She shrugged it off to just another strange ashram occurrence. First she was having lunch with a gorgeous Italian raw foodist, and abruptly she wasn't. She reached over and took a dripping bite of his watermelon, then replaced the spoon.

Geno finally reappeared holding a tattered book in his left hand. He leafed through the pages, shaking his head and muttering.

"Ah hah!" he trumpeted. "Nobility! That's the word. Nobility. It has no nobility. That's it. To sleep with so many women has no nobility." He got up and left the table to return the book.

Eeeyiii, he's exerting much more pressure than usual, Leela thought. Her back was sore all the time now, but Gyeltsen assured her they were making progress. He eased up on the thoracic vertebrae and made a last effort on the lower lumbar.

She stood up from the table and reached into her bag. "Here's the book we were talking about. I bought it for you as a present." Mevlana's face smiled out from the cover. "You said you'd been wanting to read this, right? Ever since Tibet?"

Gyeltsen handled the book, turning it over in his hands. His black eyes lit up with appreciation. "Ah, I like to go to ashram," he sighed. "Very beautiful there."

"Yes, why don't you come? Like this afternoon? I have some time; I'll show you around."

"Not possible," he said. His posture was in perfect

alignment which made him seem taller than her, which he wasn't. "Can't come every day."

"You don't have to come every day. Just come once and check it out."

"Not possible. To enter must come everyday to do meditation."

"That's not required," Leela said, leaning back against the table. "All you have to do is pay the fee, get the AIDS test, wait for the results, and then you get in."

"No," Gyeltsen said. "Different rule for us. We not from West. Must come every day one month, do meditation, have interview. Maybe then 'no' after all."

There must be some misunderstanding. He must have it wrong. There wouldn't be different rules for different kinds of people.

"Don't worry," Leela said. "We'll get you in."

ᏚHE REMEMBERED THOSE KIND BLUE EYES from the Heart Dance. Rolf was asking to be her partner for the next exercise, and she felt as safe with the fatherly man as she had before. They lay down facing each other on the mat and waited for Mevlana's further instruction.

"Begin to stroke this partner," Mevlana said, "as lovingly as you can express. Caress, be tender, and build trust for the opposite sex with the other person. See how you are with this partner, in this moment, full of gentleness."

Leela began stroking his arm. Her eyes ran along his pure white beard. It was so neatly trimmed she wanted to touch it, and she stroked his jaw, feeling his whiskers brush her palms. His neck had a light covering of sweat as her hands traveled down toward his chest, which she massaged in circular movements. Rolf had stopped caressing her and was purely receiving, hungry for touch, looking for her to take the lead.

She reached out and touched his thigh. His eyes were locked with hers, and she could see far within, far beyond language. He seemed so fragile and alone, even though he said he was with someone. She could feel his eagerness, and that he wanted more. She moved her hand further up along his thigh, brushed alongside his penis without touching it. She saw it move against his jeans. Still looking into his eyes, she smiled. He was her lover in this moment. *You are my love, right now*, she said with her eyes, *only you right now*. Yet she was relieved when Mevlana rang the bell, and the exercise was over.

WHERE COULD I FIND EMMA OR TRAVIS— you know, Mevlana's assistants?" Leela asked Helmut, the man at the front gate.

Eyes wrinkling, he looked her up and down. "Zo, do you now agree that all roads in the universe lead to the Mozart Café?" he asked. His English was impeccable with a heavy German accent.

Leela laughed, remembering the early days when she hadn't known how to connect with anybody. "Everything seemed like an obstacle when I first got here! It's all so easy now."

"Yes, people have a difficult time because the energy is so intense." He ran his hand through his beard, threaded with silver. His Buddha belly was so big the dashiki he was wearing strained to cover it. "Have you ever noticed that many of the buildings at the ashram are made of marble?" Leela nodded. "That's because marble holds and contains energy. It acts as a conductor, deepening the spiritual capacity of the people around it."

"Really?"

"Whenever people have gathered and done a lot of meditation, an energy vortex is created. And people have been coming here adding to it for a long time." He leaned down and put his elbows on the desk in front of him. "Marble holds the radiance of an enlightened person for two thousand years. It's still holding ancient energy, which is why Mevlana is here. Of course, her energy adds to it."

"Wow, that's fascinating," Leela said. "No wonder things get so confusing."

"Confusion is a very high state," Helmut said. He checked a woman's gate pass and nodded her in. "You were looking for the assistants. You know that pyramid building by the duck pond where the musicians hang out? There's a bulletin board in the back that posts people's whereabouts. That's where you'll find what you need."

An Indian man flashed his gate pass for entry. Helmut

shook his head no and stood up. "Sorry, I have some business to attend to," he said to Leela. "Best be on your way."

Leela slipped her shoes off outside the door and entered the pyramid. The air conditioning had made the marble floors icy feel beneath her feet. She entered a long corridor faced with one after another closed doors. What was going on in all those rooms? She turned a corner, and then another, all the hallways and doors looking the same. *How do I get out?* Leela started to panic. *It's a virtual labyrinth in here. Have I already been down this row? Or this one? Where's this board he's talking about?* She angled into one more passageway and came smack upon a tall lone figure with blue-black hair.

"Oh," Leela said. "I came to find one of your people, but here you are."

Mevlana looked down from her regal six feet. "I've been waiting for you," she said. Leela felt Mevlana's eyes scan her, first her body, her dress, then deep inside. "Let's walk out to the pond. It'll be just the quiet we need."

The tiny lake was ringed with flowering oleanders. The weeping willow brushed the surface of the water on the right bank, and rushes poked out their brown stalks. Mallards were idly paddling, and Leela could hear the calls of parrots and of water trickling through a tiny spout. The women sat together on a wooden bench. Mevlana was silent, waiting, her hands folded limply in her lap.

"What I want to know is . . . it seems like what I'm getting . . . " Leela said, "is that I'm supposed to learn to break my own heart so that no one else can ever do it again."

Mevlana smiled. "I've never heard it put that way, but I guess you could say there's an element of truth in it." She smoothed down a fold in her skirt, its mauve color picking up the violet of her eyes. "Your heart will never stop breaking with the pain of being human, of being witness to human suffering. That pain may even increase as you progress along the spiritual path."

"I've been experiencing that."

"Yes. It's more that you stop taking it personally. It has nothing to do with you. You come to understand that all these broken hearts are initiations, openings into a capacity for greater love. You stop being at the mercy of someone who might break your heart, or walking around tensed up against it."

Leela looked at the older woman. "It seems impossibly hard sometimes. Was it difficult? Did you have to learn painful things, to get where you are?"

A memory of Bashir flashed into Leela's mind, of how he had attempted to publicly humiliate Mevlana by his abandonment. She had been outwardly triumphant, but her private response could not be known. To Leela it seemed that the lines around Mevlana's eyes were etched more deeply, but there was no hint now nor had there been of any of the nightmare she might have been living.

Mevlana laughed out loud. "Difficult? You have no idea. But then, none of it seems hard now. It has all been a play, a *leela*, the dance of life. Just a few momentary steps in time." She turned slightly.

"The way you're trying too hard to find love, Leela, shows that you believe it's difficult to acquire. It's not; it's the easiest thing in the world. You're not really open to it. You hope you are, but the act of searching is diametrically opposed to finding. Stop rejecting love."

"But some of these men here," Leela blurted out, "are sex addicts! They're just in it for themselves. This one guy –"

Mevlana stopped her. "What difference does it make what they do?"

"What?"

"What The Beloved does or doesn't do makes no difference. What matters is the day-to-day practicing of love. Our task remains the same: opening ever deeper, surrendering to love. Not to another person, mind you, but deeper surrender to the One Love."

Mevlana looked at her watch, thick with rhinestones. "I need to be going," she said. "Group is starting in an hour and I have to prepare myself." She stood up, and the women embraced. "You are doing well," she said to Leela. "I am very pleased with your progress."

L EELA SPREAD HER ARMS BACK AS FAR AS THEY would go, let her head fall back, and surrendered herself to the utter complete-bliss perfection of the present moment. As the music swelled in the meditation hall, as the other dancers swirled past, as the tears streamed down her face, she was overcome with the realization that all the sufferings of her life had been worth it for this one, precious, extraordinarily ordinary moment.

SHE COULDN'T KEEP IT TO HERSELF ANY MORE so she decided to tell Ethan. After cruising the folks at the ashram coffee bar, the bookstore, and any leftover lunch stragglers at the café, she found him lying beside the pool in a circle of shade from a leafy bamboo.

"Hey." He lowered his sunglasses in welcome. The whites of his eyes were so bright they belied the fact that he drank as much as he did. As did his flat belly. Maybe all that glycerin they added to Indian beer acted as a solvent on fat. It had to have some good purpose, Leela thought, other than poisoning imbibers. One could count on Ethan to be spending his afternoons burnishing a hangover.

"Hey, yourself," she said, settling into the recliner next to his. The moist odor of freshly turned earth from under the tree mixed with the cheap perfume of Ethan's suntan oil. He had perfectly positioned his chair to survey the thirty to forty people lazing around the giant kidney-shaped pool, landscaped to look like the tropical paradise it was.

The trees muffled any outside noise there might have been, and although a few people were swimming, one could hear no splashing nor the raucous shouts expected at a Western swimming pool.

"You finished that tantra group yet?' Ethan always looked like he was holding a cocktail glass, ready for the canapé tray to appear. The black shorts he wore were functional and modest, unlike the bikinis on most of the men. "Maybe I'll go back and try tantra again one of these days. You guys seem to be getting a lot from it. When my Ayurvedic massage training is over next month, maybe I will."

Sure, she thought, you'll be ready after everyone else has gone home. Ethan enjoyed hanging out with her, but didn't equate that to attraction. Another ashram-ite who dated around a bit (when he got lucky), lusted after beautiful girls he couldn't have, and hadn't a clue about how the game really worked. Still a victim of his eyes.

"We have one more 'ten-day' to complete. Till then we're taking a couple-week break, which god knows I can use. A person can only take so much intensity." She heard someone's nails clicking on the arm of the chair, looked down, and saw they were hers. Normally she wouldn't share something so intimate with Ethan, but with Kate gone, Leela had to tell someone.

"You know, a lot of amazing stuff has happened to me since I've been here." The words spat out in little jerks.

Ethan looked at her over his glasses. "Yeah, that's why we're here. Nobody in the West would ever imagine the amazing things we take for granted every day." He took a drink and surveyed the nearly naked bodies tanning themselves. The ice tinkled in his glass like a highball. "Sometimes I just laugh, you know, that 'if they could see me now' kind of thing—"

"No," Leela broke in. "It's something else. Something has happened. The thing is, now I can have anybody I want."

She watched him look away, embarrassed for her. She knew he thought she was okay, just not that great. Even though when she'd been over to his house he'd invited her to lie on his bed and talk, he still imagined whatever it is men tell themselves, that she was too old, too fat, too flat, too much like his mother, or not enough like her. Not enough like a centerfold, certainly. Therefore, it couldn't be true that she could have anyone she wanted because she couldn't have him. Or so he thought.

"It's true, I can now have anyone I want. I thought that was something that only happened to models or rock stars or something, but then it happened to me. I guess it's everything I've been through here, all this tantra and all. It's like some kind of new developmental stage or something."

Ethan squirmed in his chair, looked out at the pool show, took a drink. His disbelief was palpable, thick and inert. *He actually feels sorry for me that I'm so deluded,* Leela thought with a silent laugh.

"Oh yeah, sure," he said. He rattled his glass idly, then rubbed the back of his hand across his face. "Must be great."

"You don't believe me," Leela said, this time laughing out loud. "Pick someone, and I'll show you. Ah, go on, you'll see."

Ethan's eyebrows became visible above his glasses, and he returned to scanning the scene at the pool. The afternoon had become exhaustingly hot, and Leela leaned back in her chair. She surveyed the bathers as well, realizing that she recognized probably a third of them. There were always new people traveling through, thinking they were going to stay for three days, still there three months later. She noticed that Ethan had stopped moving and looked over to see what was up.

His eyes were fixated on a blond mer-man emerging out of the pool, moving toward them. The creature's chest was perfectly shaped, his skin a golden tan, his trunks brief but not too revealing, clingy but not tight. With a casual flip of his head, he shook the water from his shoulder-length hair. He was a prototypical Southern California surfer, a bronze god, the White Boy at his finest. This is not real, Leela thought, this a Calvin Klein ad. He was so beautiful he didn't even look like he was the same species as the rest of them.

"Him." Ethan said. "Go on. Him. Show us what you can do."

"Not him." Leela suddenly panicked. "C'mon, be real. Anyone but him. He's too hard. Pick someone easier."

Too late. Ethan had gestured the surfer over to their little salon.

"Hey, man, what's up?" Ethan greeted the Perfect White Boy. "Are you still practicing any of that *chi gung* we learned?'

They shook hands and White Boy sat down on the end of Ethan's recliner. "Nah, the last time I practiced was when the group ended."

Ethan introduced them, "This is my friend, Leela, who's been telling me a story about how much she's learned here. Leela, meet Sean."

Leela smiled as their eyes met. All she did, which really wasn't doing anything, was let her eyes open so that he could see inside her. As much as he wanted to see, while smiling. That was all.

The two men reminisced about their martial arts group. Leela had given up. He was too beautiful, too elite, out of her league. If Ethan thought she had been wrong, it didn't matter. It was still true. It was all about trust anyway. She felt the warmth of the sun on her skin, and how good it felt. She felt how juicy it all was, just to be in a body, her body. She rolled with her breath, felt it rock and caress her. Looking over at the two men, Leela delighted in how beautiful Sean was, and Ethan too, at how beautiful and poignant the moment. Since there was nothing to do, she let go and enjoyed the very energy of being alive.

Sean was getting up to leave. "Getting too hot out here for me. I want to get back to my flat where it's cool and I have a nice bottle of wine chilling in the fridge." He pulled himself up tall, his body within inches of Leela's. "Lay around on a nice lazy afternoon with nothing to do." He embraced Ethan. "See ya, man, always good to see you." Then he turned to Leela.

"Would you like to come with me, over to my place, hang out for a while?"

Ethan's mouth was gaping as wide as a hungry carp. Even she hadn't known it was this easy now. She looked at

Ethan and smiled. Things would never be the same between them, and that was perfectly all right.

"You have great taste," she said to Sean. "Perhaps another time." Leela picked up her things and left. *Just because you have a power, doesn't mean you have to use it.*

LEELA PEELED BACK THE POMEGRANATE AND popped three of the blood-red seeds into her mouth. She was above ground and she liked it. The three hot men sitting with her at the ashram café were jockeying for her attention, and the talk was spicy with flirtation and innuendo. Never in the West had she held her own like this. It was intoxicating.

The lunch crowd was dispersing rapidly. Through a vacant swath of tables where there had recently sat many chattering friends, she looked over and saw Mevlana and Andrew sitting alone together at the outer rim. Mevlana was pointing directly at her. Leela shook her head to clear it and looked back. It was unmistakable, wasn't it? They were huddled together talking about her.

It stabbed her in the heart to see his beloved face. It was not the face of the Perfect Beloved—she knew that now. But that silver hair and those brown eyes, his body and all that he knew—if only it had been him.

"Leela, hello, earth to Leela," Brandon was saying. "You coming with us?"

"Uh . . . where—?"

"Ha," Geno laughed. "She was on space planet."

"We're thinking about playing tennis and we need a fourth. Or, you could come over to my place and practice massage if you like." The twin with the earring was speaking. Leela had never gotten his name.

"No, you guys go on ahead. I'll see you in group later. Got some things to take care of first."

When Andrew made his way over they were nearly the only ones left at the café. "You are glowing," he said. "I saw you holding court with those three men. Things are going well."

"Yes," Leela said. She reached out her hand and brushed his arm. "If only I'd known a long time ago that friendliness is the key to getting along with men! My girlfriends and I always thought it's about some kind of strategy, but it's not."

"You're coming out of scarcity."

"Yes, like I don't need it any more. Like I can trust that the ever-abundant stream will keep flowing. This is it."

"I'm so happy to hear it," Andrew said. He sat down and put his arm around her. She felt his warmth and breathed in his faint scent of cologne. "Unfortunately, I can't stay," he said, nuzzling her neck. "I just stopped by to offer you my congratulations."

"Congratulations for what?"

"You've reached a new level," he said. "Everything will be different now."

"What are you talking about?"

He didn't answer but stood up. "Everything will be different," he repeated. "Your hard work is beginning to pay off." He kissed the tips of his fingers and held them against her cheek. Then he was gone.

He is my lover, my brother, my mentor, my teacher, Leela thought. She lazed back in her chair and raised her eyes to the sun. *The way these people are is right. The monogamy thing is so limited. The search for the Perfect Beloved: so out of date, so last century. I'm not going anywhere,* Leela thought. *There are so many lovers here. I'm never going back.*

y god, SHE THOUGHT, *can't people see what is happening to me? Can't they see that my energy is molten, there's no mass, no bones; that it's a flowing thing, like lava without propulsion, without destruction, just flow; can't anyone see that something is happening?*

Leela looked around the Mozart. It was still early before most people were up, cold still, before it burned off. Outside, members of the lowest caste would be stooping to sweep the sides of the road with skimpy handwoven brooms. The air would blacken with acrid smoke from the roadside fires they made, tiny blazes of last night's trash including plastic bottles. Inside the Mozart was dark, the light barely reaching her table from the counter inside. She sat over her coffee as she had for countless mornings, although now on this day after the group, she felt awash in the pulsation of her own energy. Not her own energy, surely, it was the lack of boundary between herself and the quivering flow of boundlessness that was everywhere. It rolled in ecstatic waves that seemed to vibrate out from her in concentric circles.

Can't anyone see? The morning bus from Mumbai had let off the usual number of new arrivals who had scattered around the room with their coffees. At the end of the row a couple sat engaged in each other, oblivious to anyone else. A very young girl with a crew cut sat blowing smoke rings while she fiddled with her backpack. Two tables to her left sat a well-built man in his early forties who looked as if he had taken a wrong turn on his way home from the office and been magically transported here to India without any will of his own. *But then again,* Leela thought, *maybe that's how we all get here, even though we think it's volitional.*

The waterfall of energy poured over her head, spilled onto her torso, ran off her fingers and toes. It showered in waves, making her breathing slow and deepen, her mouth open to let that much volume of air pass through her. In the midst of this torrent, she noticed that the man at the next table was trying to get her attention. She turned to face him, wondering, *will he see?*

"So what do people do around here?" He looked quickly down at his cup, then back up to face her. "I mean, I heard about this place back home in Canada, eh?"

"What do you mean, what do people do?"

"Well, you know, I've heard it's pretty wild here and all. I thought I'd stop for a few hours—I'm on my way to Gurudev's down in Karnataka. I'm going there to do a month-long Vipassana retreat."

The kind where there are rules for enlightenment, Leela thought. *Rules against sex. Celibacy as a requirement for spiritual growth. You are not going to learn what you need by going there, that's for sure.*

He was gorgeous. She hadn't noticed how good-looking he was at first, but then when only the best-looking people on the planet seemed to be allowed to come to the ashram, things just took on a different perspective. *He's someone I would used to have thought I couldn't have*, she thought. None of that mattered now. None of that mattered in this gigantic wave she was riding, or that she was being ridden by. Either way, it was the same thing.

"How did you get into spirituality, and happen to come to India?" she asked.

"Well, I watched this video of Deepak Chopra. He's cool! Then I took a yoga class after work and really got into it. The teacher talked about meditating in India and said if we ever got the chance, we should go. I figured this was a good time while I have a vacation break."

A baby, she thought, *how beautiful we all are when we are just beginning.* The awareness of her breathing was so intense. Breath kept happening, coming as full as it did, wrapping around and swirling and thickening the air. She smiled at him. He must just be chalking all this up to the general weirdness of India, and particularly his expectations of this ashram here.

"Stay here," she said. "Lots of people come planning to spend a day or two and you still see them here months later. It happened to me. I only planned to come for a week and here I am—almost a year." His head was cocked toward her as he stirred his cup. "You'll find what you're looking for here."

It didn't matter if he stayed or if he left, what of it? He would go his way and not find what he was looking for, or find it later, or find something else; it didn't matter in the slightest. He would go or he would stay.

They were breathing together, couldn't he feel it? The moment stretched and expanded, became fuzzy and thick, became an accordion sound, a light show. They sat breathing, and smiling, and Leela let out a gigantic sigh.

"Want to take a walk with me?" he asked. And why wouldn't she? There was nothing else at that moment to do but take a walk with him. *Why would you ever go against the way it is?* Leela laughed that she had ever thought any differently. It seemed the most ludicrous thing she had ever imagined.

They walked out into the first light of the new morning to a house that visitors often stayed at. The smoky air singed their nostrils, and a rickshaw swerved barely missing them.

"Will you come up?" he asked.

"Yes."

They climbed the cool dark stairway, with its peeling tiles and unpainted cement surfaces. There were no light bulbs, only the gray morning light showing through on the landings. He opened the door to his flat. It was the same as all the others, except that he hadn't been there long enough to decorate it with the Hindu tie-dyed wall hangings, the shelves of spiritual books, and the rack of gauze Indian clothes. There were the ubiquitous bamboo mats and one dusty houseplant in a clay pot in the corner. The single bed stood out prominently. He pointed to it. "Please, have a seat."

She sat. He came over and sat beside her, taking her in his arms and fervently kissing her neck, her face. He slipped her whisper of a cotton shirt over her head, and lowered his lips to her nipples. Around and around his tongue went, rather artfully she thought dispassionately, as her breath pulled up into her throat, letting out a little gasp of pleasure in its escape. *I'm glad he knows what he's doing*, she thought, *although it would be perfectly all right if he didn't*.

He got up and took off his shirt, exposing a lean chest covered in silver and black hair. The hair streamed up from his navel like a fountain, curly and soft. He slipped off his Levi's, exposing his cock three-quarters erect. *That's for me*, she thought, *all for me*.

He came over to the bed and gently forced her back. She had never been so desireless, yet the desire came on its own from her body, not from her mind or her wanting, not from romantic expectations or pictures or the likeness to a movie, just simple surrendered man and woman. There was no future, no past, no longing, none of the ravenous hoping for love.

Afterward, she walked home alone. The air was still cool, smoky. The insanity that was the traffic could be seen in its infancy, a few motorcycles lurching madly, avoiding rickshaws and bikes. If this had been an earlier time in her life, or if this had occurred in the West, she would have felt used, been surprised at her own behavior, been consumed with feelings of guilt, would have had to have been drunk. Instead, what it was, was that things had come full circle since Ian. She had been used, but used by existence to change the course of things. She had shown a brother the way, welcomed him to a new world, a way of being. The initiated had served as the initiation into the secret circular world of Tantra.

ELMUT'S BUDDHA BELLY WAS HIDDEN BY the guard desk he sat behind. As she strolled up to the front gate, Leela remembered their pleasant conversation about the marble.

"Maybe today I'll go check out the Mozart Café," she said, smiling.

"Aha, there you are," he said. "Did you find someone to assist you?" His beard was fastidiously trimmed in a way she didn't recall.

"That and more. Thanks so much for your help." Leela put one hand on the edge of the guard desk. "There's one more thing you could help me with." She paused while a tall Cossack-looking man flashed his pass at Helmut and entered the compound. "I have this wonderful friend I want to bring for a tour of the ashram. He's from Tibet. Gives a great massage."

Helmut nodded two women through the gate. "He is welcome to go through the process for the locals," he said.

"Perhaps you know what this is, and that is why you are here. After he completes the required morning meditation for thirty days, he will be interviewed about his motive for wanting to come here. If this goes well, he will be allowed to enter on a conditional pass for the next ninety days."

"That's not fair," Leela said. "All Westerners have to do is show up, pay the fee, and pass the AIDS test."

"If he wants to enter, that's the way it is."

"That's not right," she said. "Why is it different? I can vouch for his character. He's a really good person, and he loves Mevlana."

"That's the way it is."

"What is this?" Her voice was becoming strident but she didn't care. "Some kind of racist thing? White people can get in effortlessly and Brown people can't?"

"Be careful," Helmut said. His brow furrowed as his steel-gray eyes pierced into her skin. "You don't know what you're talking about. You come here as a tourist with all these pretty ideals, but you don't know what these people are like. You don't live here. I've been here twelve years, and I know what's best. You have to trust us."

"This is crap," Leela said. She had heard the same racist argument when she had visited Atlanta, Georgia: *You don't know how it is here. It's different. You come here from somewhere else and don't understand.*

Helmut stood up, adjusted his jeans, and sat back down. "You don't know, do you, that nearly every day we have to take away the gate pass of an Indian for harassing a woman?

Do you want that happening to you? Or would you rather feel free to walk around the ashram and not worry about such a thing?"

"Gyeltsen's not like that," Leela said. "He's an awesome human being."

"Who wants to come here and steal business from the ashram. These people aren't interested in spiritual growth. They come here to steal money from us." He suddenly reminded Leela of a state trooper. "And what about you, why aren't you getting your massages from the ashram therapists? Keeping your money inside the ashram? Maybe we'll have to review your gate pass."

Leela cringed. *Would they really take away her ability to come to the ashram? Maybe she should shut up.* "You don't know—"

"No. *You* don't. This is the end of this discussion. The answer is 'no'. I'd be careful if I were you."

He's right about one thing, Leela thought as she walked away. *I truly don't understand.*

Y OU'LL BE STAYING OVERNIGHT IN THE GROUP room this evening," Mevlana said. "Come back freshly showered and renewed for the evening. Bring with you only your pillow and a blanket; we will provide the sheets and the mattresses." She turned to face the assistants and began rising from her brocaded seat.

"Will we need our notebooks?" came a voice from the back of the room.

"Nothing else will be needed," Mevlana said, turning back around. Leela tried to read her face for a clue of what they might expect, but there was none to be had. Mevlana joined the two assistants and they left through the back door.

"What do you think is on the agenda for tonight?" Sasha asked, coming up beside her as they filed out.

"No idea," Leela said. Their pace was slow with all the participants crowding the narrow hallway. "But seeing as how yesterday was so intense, I'm sure they're not going to go over gradient tonight." *They won't, will they?* she wondered. She looked at Sasha and exchanged a nod. "I'm sure they'll make it something easy and not too challenging."

Leela stopped in for a quick *thali* at Govinda's before heading home. With the hot water from the shower pouring down her back, she looked down as she passed the the bar of soap over her stomach, her genitals, her thighs and knees. *Our flesh is so vulnerable,* she thought. Turning around, she felt the slivers of water attack her face, fill her ears, slide down between her breasts. She dried herself and opened the bottle of perfume, then remembered that no fragrances were allowed in the group room. The smell of clean skin and breath would have to do it. She combed her wet hair in the mirror and saw how much longer it was getting. Picking up her bedding, she headed out into the night.

Back at the group room, Mevlana was nowhere to be found. The assistants, Travis and Emma, were sitting on the floor of the dais, wrapped in an embrace, obviously very into each other. They barely paid attention as people filed in, pausing once in a while to nod and greet. *Ummm, I wish that was me in his arms*, Leela thought.

As most participants were now in the room and the rustling had died down, Travis uncoiled himself from Emma. "Everyone take a mattress," he said, "and arrange your bedding where you might want to sleep. Along the wall is probably best. Don't worry, you'll be able to move it later if you change your mind." There was a bit of a commotion as all fifty arranged mattresses, sheets and pillows; no one spoke. When finished, they sat on their beds awaiting further instruction until everyone was done.

"Now take off your clothes and put them over by the statue." Out of the corner of her eye, Leela saw Sasha next to her visibly wince, her shoulders slumped, and her feet turned in, pigeon-like. Leela slipped her trousers down to her ankles, and turned to see that Sasha's face was the color of chalk. Her usually lovely hair lay spread across her shoulders like gossamer.

Next to her was Anne, whose breasts drooped almost to her waist, standing with her arms across her chest. Her stomach folded at her midsection, and large dimples of cellulite dotted her bottom. She too had peeled off her clothes cautiously. No one was meeting anyone else's eyes as they stood there naked, surrendered to what was to come. *How easily breakable we all are*, Leela thought, *and how habitual it would be to discount this bravery.*

"Have a great evening," Travis said. He and Emma started heading for the door. "See you in the morning."

"Wait, what are we supposed to do?" Fifty expectant faces awaited further direction.

"There are no instructions for tonight's exercise."

Jack came into Leela's vision. He was far across the room, yet even from this distance she could feel how smooth his skin was. His chest was raised, and he appeared a little plumper each time she saw him.

Voices came from all corners of the room. "What would be considered off limits?"

"Are there any boundaries we need to respect?"

"What would not be considered okay?"

Emma had already gone out the door and Travis was about to exit. He turned and stopped back inside. He scanned the room.

"There are no boundaries," Travis said. "Nothing is off limits." The door closed behind him.

LEELA DELICATELY ROTATED UNTIL THEIR BODies were front to front, then placed her hand over Dylan's heart. She felt the wiriness of his chest hair, the faint yet adamant beating under her palm. That his face was so unlined looked strange, like an unformed larvae, lacking the knowledge of all the pain that is to come. As she stirred, he reached over, parted his lips and kissed her without opening his eyes. *Certainly morning breath is as holy as anything else,* Leela thought as she kissed him back. After all, the ancient tantrikas had made love in the graveyards surrounded by rotting corpses, inuring themselves to the stench of death, tasking themselves to master the reality that all was divine. That their bodies were decaying was only a reminder that we are all on an inevitable journey toward the end, with the exquisite understanding that none of this, despite cultural messages to the contrary, is wrong.

She looked around the room. All was quiet. Mattresses were strewn about, no longer orderly along the walls, covered by mounds of various sizes. Some lumps were of one person, some two, some held other combinations, yet there was an innocent quality, like after a slumber party where they had stayed up all night talking about boys and playing truth or dare. Only this time, truth or dare had been for real.

Last night flashed in her mind: Anne and Jack and Nicole, rubbing, kissing. Brandon and the perfect Swede joining a cluster that included Ian and Rolf and Sasha. Breasts and butts and chests and pricks, mouths, tongues, and hips moving up and down in all directions. Coos of pleasure, screams of release. Individuals migrating from one group to another in search of more.

Leela had stood stiffly surveying the scene, wanting to grab a blanket to hide her nakedness, or to go and feign sleep on one of the mattresses. She had entered the fray and tentatively stroked Nicole's arm, feeling a captive of the situation. Then suddenly, out of the blue, she had told herself the truth.

I never wanted any of this. It's all gone too far. All of this is an accident, this hedonism, this mayhem, this baptism by fire, this breaking of taboos, maybe even this whole tantra thing. That I'll have to figure out later, but there's one thing I know for absolute certain—I never, ever, never wanted to be in an orgy in all my life.

She had crawled over to Dylan to escape. He had seemed harmless, all alone under his blanket on his mattress, far away from the main goings-on.

"Knock, knock, may I come in?" she had asked. "It seems safe over here."

"Safe?" Dylan smiled, holding up the blanket and pulling her back up against his chest. "Don't get me wrong, I want you as much as the next guy." He wrapped his arm around her waist. "But I'm not into it unless you're a hundred percent 'yes'." She felt his cock hard against the back of her thigh, but he wasn't making a move.

"This is nice," Leela sighed. "Just about perfect, I'd say."

"Yes," he said. "I've finally got you where I want you."

The mad marathon had swirled on without them. Well after midnight, to Leela's relief, all had settled down into the sweet sleeping piles of her lovers and friends, beloveds all.

Now as she returned his kiss, the terrible tension of the evening melted away. *This is what I've always wanted,* Leela thought, *to be lying snug in the arms of a man I can trust. Maybe it's not all about the Perfect Beloved, either, maybe it's about the relief of friendship, this safety, this feeling of being at home in the lotus paradise.*

"COME BACK, LEELA," MEVLANA WAS CALLING softly. "Follow my voice for the way back."

Leela came to with a jolt. *Where was she? What had they been doing?* She remembered breathing, and lying on her back . . . the group had been doing a partner exercise . . . Dylan had been looking into her eyes. Leela knew that for sure because he had been her anchor, holding the thread as she went down, down . . . *maybe something was being birthed by the way her legs were moving?* The breath had been so voluminous, so overpowering, Leela went somewhere . . . where? Down a long tunnel into another reality of which she had no memory.

As her eyes opened, she was looking into Dylan's face. *The Truth was utterly unmistakable.* "You? The Perfect Beloved?" she gasped in wonder. "You're finally here!" Her body was streaming with the energy of wherever she had been and with what had been revealed. She looked into his eyes and saw only love and awe. "We have been together before, and here you are now." She began to weep with the sheer joy of it. All the longing had meant something after all. "My Perfect Beloved," she said, reaching out to hold on to his arm.

Dylan shifted on his knees beside her and took her hand. "Yes, my love, I've been waiting for this moment."

"The Perfect Beloved only exists in the ecstatic present moment, Leela," Mevlana said. "You are the only one who can deny love. This moment is complete; this is all there is. Perfect love is always present. The bliss is always there, bubbling away underneath. The ecstatic moment is always there if you know how to open to it." She turned and moved on to the next dyad.

Leela lay in euphoric shock in Dylan's arms. He was stroking her hair, just the way she liked it. She peered up to see what he looked like, because she had only known him before the recognition. His dark hair, his strong arms; he was beautiful beyond words. All had been answered; all had been revealed. He was here with her at last, breathing in unison. Here in the arms of the Perfect Beloved, in the calm bittersweetness of the afternoon, she felt her long arduous search had finally ended.

33

LEELA PERFORMED A SLINKY CAT STRETCH IN Dylan's sheets. They were definitely not of a high-thread count, in fact, they were the same ordinary ones that everyone bought at the local shops when they arrived at the ashram, along with their mosquito spray and door locks. She rolled over and splayed out, each arm and leg pointing to a corner of the bed.

Taking a good look around, she decided Dylan's was a real guy's flat: mattress on the floor, a pile of shoes in the corner, a T-shirt lying where it was dropped. Across from the bed was a cloth banner of the type she'd seen in Goa, the blue Krishna playing his flute while embracing Radha, lovers for all eternity.

Dylan returned from brushing his teeth and plopped down beside her. He took her nipple in his mouth, slowly swirled his tongue, all the while caressing her other breast with his fingers. His cuticles were raggedy and needed a trim, and Leela didn't care one bit.

"We should get up," she said. "It's past noon already."

"Do I look like a man who wants to get up?" His left hand was making its way toward her belly.

Leela snatched his hand and brought it to her lips. "Ummm," she said, "you tempt me. Actually, please, I'm a little sore and really can't go again."

"Whatever you want." He reached up and stroked her hair, making her start to purr. "It's not just about the sex for me," he said, "although I must say that last night was cosmic. I guess it's because we'd been doing foreplay for nine months. Well, at least I have. You haven't been aware of it, maybe."

"Nine months? That's since we met."

"I've had you on my radar this whole time, didn't you know? Walking a tightrope between desire and going slowly enough to win you over. That's what I want—to win your heart."

Leela rolled over onto her stomach and lifted herself on her elbows. "You're doing a good job," she said. "You just might be earning it. Now, let's get up and get the day started."

The shower was more colorful than expected. "Yikes!" she yelled. "Green stuff is coming out of the showerhead!"

"That happens when they cut the grass next door. The clippings get caught in the tank."

"I wish I'd known before I soaped my hair."

"That's India for you."

He stood waiting with a towel. After carefully drying her off, he picked through her hair for flecks of leaf. "Cute, green dandruff," he said.

They went out and started dressing. Leela put on her halter dress from last night and Dylan picked up the dropped T-shirt and put it on.

"A lot of people now are into 'polyamory,'" he said. "That's the new catchphrase."

"What's it mean?"

"Having more than one lover at a time on purpose, kind of like free love but the people into it are trying to be conscious and have relationships instead of just sex. That seems like what a lot of people here are going for."

"Except the sex addicts."

"Yeah, except for the people out for more belt notches. Myself, I've never been into being a playboy. Always been monogamous. Serially, maybe, but not by choice. I've always been looking for the one that will last." He pulled up his pants and tied the drawstring. "My parents have been married for thirty-five years and counting. Seems pretty good to me. I've always thought that when anybody says they're into multiple partners, they just haven't found the right person yet."

"And you think the right person might be me?"

"I've been infatuated with you since first sight. But it moved beyond that as I watched you grow in group, as we shared exercises together. I had to work on my jealousy seeing you with other men. Tantra can be a cruel teacher that way."

"Tell me about it," Leela said. She picked up her bag and headed for the door. "Sorry, I've got to go."

"A few people are coming over tonight to play music. Will you come? Nothing fancy. Very low-key."

"I can't." Leela shook her head. "I have my dance class tonight. Plus I think I'm going to be pretty tired after being up as late as we were."

"Okay, baby. I'll miss you. See you tomorrow."

They kissed, a long lingering lipmeld. Leela opened the door.

"Look, Leela," Dylan said. "I want us to be together. Just tell me how you like it. I may not be perfect, but I can be your Perfect Beloved."

UTTERLY AWESOME," JACK WAS SAYING. "What a discovery to be in a group of four lovers at one time. I'd say two are essential, and the third is the sauce."

Leela rolled her eyes. This group debriefing of the orgy was not to her liking at all. She glanced over and saw Sasha crying, and Ian snuggling with his new prize. Some things never changed. Same as it ever was.

Where was Dylan? Why wasn't he in group this morning? Something must be wrong.

DYLAN WAS SITTING ALONE. THE MOZART seemed uncharacteristically vacant for a late afternoon, and come to think of it, unusually tidy. There were no plates of half-eaten food on the tables or overflowing ashtrays, and the Nepalese boys were nowhere in sight.

"Where were you this morning?" Leela sat down on the stool across from Dylan. "You look all 'serious business'."

"I guess it's pretty major," Dylan said. He looked up at her for a moment and then resumed staring at the table. "Can you believe it? They took away my gate pass. I can't get into the ashram anymore."

"What!? Tell me you're kidding."

"I wish I was," Dylan said. He glanced around the deserted café and lowered his voice. "This morning I walked up to the gate, all innocent and everything, ready to start my day. That guy Helmut was lying in wait for me, you know who he is, right? That big-bellied Nazi who's always at the front entrance? 'They want to see you in admin,' he says. Of course, I have no idea why. 'What's this about?' I asked. 'Are you sure you've got the right person?' Helmut gets someone else to watch the gate and gives me this personal escort there. Dude said nothing the whole walk over."

Dylan took a deep draught of his drink, running the back of his wrist over his mouth to catch any stray drops.

"I was having that little gathering at my house last night, right? You had your dance class so you passed." Dylan continued. "Believe me, it was nothing. Paul was playing the didgeridoo, that Norwegian guy was on the flute, Nicole was there; we weren't even smoking *bhang* or anything. Well, maybe some people were, but it was so chill it wasn't even an issue. No more than six of us there at one time, just hanging out."

Dylan drained his glass and cleared his throat. "So when Helmut takes me to the admin building, I'm ushered into this meeting with all the head honchos. It's like the Inquisition, definitely no humor allowed. The tall skinny one tells me they've received a report that I hosted a 'black magic voodoo party' the other night. I kid you not, that's what he said. 'A black magic voodoo party'."

"No way," Leela said. "Nobody would actually say that." She looked at Dylan. He wasn't joking.

"They asked me if it was true, so of course I didn't lie: I said that I'd had a little party, but that it had been low-key. They weren't having any of it. They told me this was unacceptable behavior to be going on around the ashram, and that they were taking away my gate pass. That I wasn't welcome to come here anymore."

"But people have parties all the time!" Leela protested. "All those raves with hundreds of people. What about that?"

"They have plans to shut those down. The Indian police have been hassling to get them stopped. But that has nothing to do with what was going on in my flat that night, not in any way. Now I can't go to the ashram any more. Just like that."

Leela felt like she had been run over by a rickshaw. "You have to fight it," she said. "Tell them there was nothing 'voodoo' about it."

"I did," Dylan said. "Again and again, but they had already made up their minds. And with the way they were acting, I don't want anything to do with this place any more. It killed the whole 'freedom' business for me, the stuff Mevlana says about the importance of the individual. It was fascist, not like a spiritual thing at all."

How was one to comprehend this baffling paradox, that the ashram was such an indescribable paradise, yet the sum of it included these glaring exceptions that couldn't be discounted. A bruised paradise that now didn't include Dylan among its delights, let alone to think what the tantra group would be like without him.

Leela fondled the teardrop hanging from the chain around her neck, then let it fall between her breasts. "What are you going to do?" she asked.

Dylan picked up his empty glass and set it down a little too hard. "I don't know. It all just happened." He scanned the café again. "Go home, I guess. I mean, what else?" He banged the glass down, this time on purpose. "Go to Goa first, maybe, travel over to Hampi, then back to the States. Or check out Sai Baba in Brindavan, or the houseboats in Kerala . . . ."

Leela looked at Dylan's hands around the glass. It had seemed like something real was happening between them, but once again she had been mistaken.

"Look," Dylan said, getting up. "I've got to go take care of some things, be by myself for a while. I'll see you later, okay?"

Leela fingered some of the graffiti etched into the tabletop. Her stomach had wrenched into a shredded rag.

"Fine," she said. "See you later."

"We'll have dinner before I go. Promise." He had moved a bit toward the doorway, but hesitated a moment. "Is everything all right?"

"Oh," Leela said, willing herself to look up at him and smile. "It's all just kind of a shock, that's all. I'm sure it's all as it's meant to be." She watched as he smiled, and then he was gone.

She sat barely breathing. A few stragglers had come in while she and Dylan were talking and had spread themselves around the café. The Nepalese boy walked by delivering a coffee. Leela took a deep breath. *I don't think I can take this,* she thought. *What had been happening between them had apparently been just another 'tantra' adventure.* She didn't think she could endure it, but she would, because she had to. *Nothing was permanent. All relationships ended. It had only been a matter of time anyway.*

He didn't seem to have any qualms about short-circuiting whatever had been developing between them. Their encounter would end up as just another memory of the fabulous vacation in India. Tantra men were just into screwing whomever they could. The Perfect Beloved dream was a farce, always had been. She had been such a fool.

N O WHITE MUSLIN SHEET RIPPLING IN THE breeze. The foyer was blazing with sunlight and bereft of furniture, as always, but the silence seemed uncannily loud. "Hellooo?" Leela called out. No answer. "Gyeltsen? Dawa?"

The words echoed into a lonely oblivion. No one answered. No one came out. Leela walked down the hall, trepidation marking each step. The room staring back at her lay abandoned except for the massage table: no starched white sheet, no maps of Tibet or the acupuncture meridians. The hooks hung deserted.

Leela raced all the way to Dr. Tsenpo's, dodging in and out of traffic and the beggars who lined the sidewalk. The waiting room was full to capacity with Westerners anxious for help with their digestion. Leela hurriedly waved to Paloma who waved back, then she sat down in the only available seat. She certainly didn't feel as patient as everyone else looked. After what seemed like forever, Dr. Tsenpo came out to signal another patient back for treatment.

Leela stood up. Her hands were clammy, and she wiped them on her trousers. "Dr. Tsenpo, what happened to Gyeltsen?" she called out.

The doctor turned his attention from the next patient to Leela. His white coat and slicked-back hair made him indistinguishable from any doctor back home. That is, until he spoke. "He go back to Dharamsala," he said.

"Why? What happened?"

Dr. Tsenpo motioned to the patient. "You go back to Room 3. Lie down wait for me, okay?" Turning back to Leela, he spoke in hushed tones.

"Gyeltsen very disappointed. Wanted to go to ashram, can't go. Living here too expensive. Can't make enough money for family, so go back."

Gyeltsen, who had treated her for free. Leela looked at Dr. Tsenpo and at how sleek and modernized his whole operation was. He certainly had figured out how to rake in the money. Gyeltsen must have had an ambition to create as rich life for his family as his cousin had. But it was impossible for him to see four patients at a time, and he didn't possess Dr. Tsenpo's entrepreneurial skill. How she wished she could pay him now for all those sessions he hadn't charged her.

"I didn't even get to say goodbye." Leela looked down at her hands. "He was so important to me. Did you know he straightened my back?" She turned to show him. "Look."

"Look like always been straight."

"I wouldn't have been able to . . . nothing would be possible that I'm doing now without it being straight. He gave me a whole new life."

Dr. Tsenpo returned to treat his patients. Leela walked over to Paloma and picked at her sleeve.

"You lose your *amigo*?" Paloma asked. She reached over and stroked Leela's cheek. "Shh . . ." she said. "Let's go out to the garden—nature will help."

Paloma sat on the bench under the tree, her feet firmly rooted on the slate tile underneath. Leela knelt down and rested her arm along the older woman's thigh. "Yes, my *amigo*," Leela said. "My very good friend."

"*Dulce*," Paloma whispered. She smiled and put her hand on top of Leela's. "Although you don't want to hear it, this loss is a blessing."

They sat together in silence. Leela wasn't sure where to

look, or how to best place her legs. Everything felt to be encased in cotton.

Paloma brushed her hand gently over Leela's hair. "Everyone wants life not to change," she said. "Especially love. We want our relations with others to be frozen moments in time, perfect, never changing. Neither person growing apart, nor going their own way. That's the common desire for all types of love, yes?"

Leela nodded.

"But that desire kills it, *mi dulce*. For love to be alive it must breathe, and it requires allowing ourselves and others to be free. The partings are difficult, yes. It hurts, but we must keep breathing and ever opening to the flow of life."

Leela felt the pain stabbing her solar plexus, but she couldn't avoid saying what was next. "Wait, there's more," she blurted out. "I didn't pay him when I could have. I took advantage of his kindness. I'm so ashamed of myself."

"Well, then," Paloma said quietly. She stroked Leela's head. "Let the shame burn. Let it extinguish your selfishness for good. You have to learn to give, to give in excess of what you are given. Learn to become a giver instead of trying to get away with whatever you can. You must take full responsibility for creating the world you want to live in. You'll pay your karmic debts when you're ready.

"Now go my little *dulce*. Pay back. Give, give. Give of yourself, your love. Follow your heart. Love wildly and freely and honestly, with as much integrity as you can muster, even if to do so breaks your heart."

34

"Leela! There you are! I've been looking everywhere for you."

Leela looked up from her magazine. Dylan was standing right in front of her. He must be here to invite her to the Last Supper. She looked back down at the article on South Indian cuisine and silently called out to Dr. Tsenpo to appear and summon her for her appointment.

"Leela, I'm leaving tomorrow, and I have to see you," Dylan said. "Come to dinner with me tonight. I want to have my last meal with you."

Leela turned the page. "Sorry to miss," she said. "I've got dinner plans with Jack." She gave him a crocodile grin and a faint wave. "Have a great trip back to the West."

Dylan knelt down beside her chair and wrapped his hand around her bare foreleg. "Leela," he said. "We have to talk."

Dr. Tsenpo appeared at the doorway and motioned Leela to come back for her session. She was definitely not up to one of those breakup conversations that always ended with the woman assuring the man that everything was all right. "Email me," Leela said. "I've got to go."

"I'm going to wait for you. I'll be right here when you come out."

Leela tried not to think about Dylan as the doctor inserted a needle into her scalp. As he placed one in her third eye, her body jolted though it didn't hurt at all.

"You very nervous today," Dr. Tsenpo said. "Relax. Relax."

When she came back out to the waiting room, Dylan sat watching for her return. The sun poured into the room making the whitewashed walls luminous. He stood up. "Let's go over to my place," he said. "We can talk there."

"No," Leela said. "Not your place."

He looked at her and pursed his lips. "All right," he said. "We'll talk here." He came over, took her hand, and led her out to the garden by the side of the building. They sat down next to the banyan tree.

Dylan turned to face her. She dreaded hearing what he had to say.

"I really like what has been happening between us," Dylan began. "I don't want it to end." Leela swiveled her head to face him. "Just because some assholes at the ashram have told me I can't go there any more doesn't mean we have to lose each other. This thing with you is the best I've ever known. I knew it from the first time I saw you." He covered her hand with his. Leela looked down at the back of his untended hand, so unlike Andrew's immaculate ones. She squeezed it and smiled at him.

"The group will be over in two weeks," he continued. "I want you to meet me in Goa when it's finished. I'll have a hotel right on the beach waiting for you. We can go to the Anjuna Flea Market on Wednesdays, dance all night, drink beer, and sleep late. It'll be frigging awesome. What do you say? Or, better yet, so you don't have to travel alone, I'll be happy to postpone going until you're done, so we can go together."

Leela looked into Dylan's eyes. They were limpid and kind, and the expression on his face was tender while at the same time full of resolve. She thought about the strength of character she had seen in him, and remembered his caress along her thighs, his full deep kisses. There was nothing she would like more than to luxuriate in the seaside heaven of Goa with Dylan.

"I'm ready to go over to your place now," Leela murmured, bending in to kiss his neck. He smelled of clove cigarettes and a hint of coconut oil. "I think we need to communicate about this some more."

"Perfect," Dylan said. He leaned in and returned her kiss. "I'll get us a rickshaw. And afterward, when we get around to talking, I want us to make plans about where we're going to go—together—after Goa."

SCRAMBLED EGGS AND TOAST WITH EXTRA butter and jam. The thickest, richest, blackest coffee, the only kind the Mozart served. On three sides of her, the musical mix of languages ranged from French to Japanese, while directly in front of her, the newsprint pages of *The Indian Express* formed a wall. *Merely a more exotic version of the predicament of 1950s housewives everywhere,* Leela thought, as she knocked on the panel that kept Dylan hidden from view.

"Hey there," she asked, "anything going on in the world I should be aware of?"

"Um, I'm not sure you want to know this," Dylan said, appearing from behind the paper and taking a drink of his lukewarm coffee. "This item is about the trial of some farmers in Tamil Nadu for killing their baby. The villagers don't want girls and, you know, with female infanticide being rampant in India and all—"

"I know the drill," Leela interrupted. Her stomach lurched and it occurred to her she might not keep her breakfast down.

"Sorry, babe," Dylan said, reaching out and covering her hand with his. "This shit sucks, I know."

"How about you go back to the latest cricket scores?" she said, frowning, and then smiled so he knew it wasn't about him. "Sometimes the less I know about the world out there the better."

He nodded. There was the sound of rustling newsprint, and the blockade was back in place. Leela looked around for a glimmer of diversion. The café was rolling along at a pleasant hum. She didn't have to search for long, as Travis slid into the seat behind her.

"Hey, gorgeous," he said, lips close to her ear. "Alone at last." He was wearing a fuchsia singlet with a large black *om* symbol on the chest. His chestnut hair brushed his shoulders, and there was a tattoo of the dancing Shiva on his bicep.

Leela's eyes darted to the newspaper fortress. Nothing had shifted. "Not exactly alone," she said, glancing back at Travis. "Dylan's here. You remember Dylan from group." Upon hearing his name, Dylan moved the paper to one side. "Dylan, you remember Travis."

"How you doin', man," he said, nodding.

"Great," Travis said. "It's a pleasure seeing you people out in the real world now that the group's over. That is if you can call the Mozart Café the real world."

"More real than real," Dylan said. "Good to see you." He disappeared again behind the paper.

Leela turned to face Travis. For a whole year she had been anticipating this moment, waiting for him to drop the assistant role, fantasizing what might come of those sly winks, desirous looks, and delightful private jokes. She looked at the way his naked skin glistened from the layer of sweat on it. She loved his long hair, admired his full lips. Was it too late to get something going with him? She glanced at Dylan. Dylan was preoccupied.

"You too," she said, quieting her voice. "Good to see you outside group. Are you still hanging out with Emma?"

"No," Travis said. "She and Rolf have gone back to Germany."

"What?! She and Rolf? They're together? But . . . in the group . . . she was with you . . . he was partnering with everyone."

"I know, right? They have an agreement about how they spend their time here every year. They both 'take their space.'"

"Whoa. That sounds great." Leela laughed. "Although, you know, I'd like to 'take my space,' but I'm not sure I want my partner to."

"Yeah," Travis said. They fell silent. Leela felt his eyes run up and down her body, taking her in. Was it her imagination, or did he move in a little closer?

"What will you be doing, now that the group has ended?" she asked.

"A bunch of us are headed up to Dharamsala." He rubbed his hand over Shiva's face. "It's a way to escape the heat, and the Dalai Lama is in residence for the summer." He leaned in close and put his shoulder right up flush against hers. "Maybe you want to come along?"

Dharamsala, where Gyeltsen was. Maybe she could have a thing with Travis and catch up with Dylan later. She remembered how arousing she had always found his presence throughout the group. She pictured him curled around Emma, and what a friendly lover he appeared to have been. *Why*, Leela thought, *I could be the Shakti to his dancing Shiva, the divine consort down through the ages.*

Maybe Dylan wouldn't mind one last fling. No, that wasn't right, men had a funny way of thinking that then he

would deserve one too. Maybe they could get something going so that if she and Dylan didn't work out, she could meet Travis in Manali in the summer. Go to the Himalayas together and look for the immortals who were rumored to live there. Now was her chance, her only chance, if she was ever to have one. She looked up to see if Dylan was listening, but the paper hadn't moved.

"I've got plans," she said in a low murmur. "But one never knows, do they? Give me your email address, and if things change, I'll meet you there." She reached into her purse and handed him a pen, waiting while he scrawled on a napkin.

"Well, hope to see you," he said, sliding out from his seat. "In any event, I'll be back here for next season. Hey, Dylan, see you around."

"See you, man." Dylan waved and resubmerged behind the paper. Travis bent down and kissed her forehead as he left.

Leela lifted her cup to her mouth but no coffee remained. She glanced at the wall of newsprint, then over at the Nepalese boy emptying an ashtray. She was happy with Dylan, but you never knew, did you? Always keep at least one in your back pocket, just in case. That's one thing she had learned from her sex addict friends.

Dylan put the paper down, calmly folded it and laid it beside his plate. "If you ever do anything like that again, I'll get up and leave and never come back."

EELA LOOKED AROUND THE MOZART ONE last time. The Nepalese boys were emptying ashtrays, and a cat walked the tables searching for scraps. She smiled as she saw Ian chatting up a new arrival, her backpack on the seat beside her and a confused look on her face. *I'm really going to miss this place*, Leela thought.

Down in the druggie corner, she spied a woman her own age looking sad and disheveled. "Hey" she called out. "Angie? Is that you?"

The woman lifted her head as if it weighed fifty pounds. "You," she said. "Where do I know you from?"

Leela left the counter and walked down to her table. The pungent smell of *ganja* and cigarette smoke reeked in that part of the café. "It's been almost a year now," she said, "at the all-night party in Goa. I never got a chance to say 'thank you.' You were right, being at the ashram totally changed my life."

"Cool." Angie's head fell back down to her chest. Her hair was matted and a smear of something was on her face. Her cup had an inch of coffee left in it, and there was a half-eaten piece of dried-up day-old strudel.

"What's been going on with you?" Leela asked. "Let's see, when we met I think your boyfriend was in Israel for the summer?"

"Him. He never came back."

"Oh. But that wasn't the end of the world, right? Plenty more where he came from."

"I don't know; things change. Getting older now . . . not so easy. Sure, sure, it'll be all right." She rubbed her arm. As she did, Leela saw the scratches on her arms, only that's not what they were. They were scarred bubbles on skin gray with bruises.

Angie saw Leela looking and pulled her sleeves down to her wrists. "Do you think you could spot me a few *rupees* so I could get something to eat?"

"No worries," Leela said, digging into her purse. *Where was that wallet?*

"At first we were just smoking *charas*, like everybody else," Angie blurted out. "A little Ecstasy, everything was fine. But then we got into the China White pretty heavy— sometimes I think I should just go home. But this is the life, right? Nothing's like India. It's paradise here."

"To go san-wich!" yelled out the Nepalese boy behind the counter.

Leela handed her a wad of rupees. "I've got to go. Take care of yourself, hey? Get yourself cleaned up and go home, or go home and get cleaned up. Most of all, try to remember what you learned at the ashram. It revolutionized my life, as it did yours. What you learned is always inside, waiting for when you're ready."

She picked up her food and headed out into the sunlight. A beggar's voice immediately rang out, "*Baksheesh*, madam, *baksheesh*." Leela automatically ignored it as she had been acculturated to do, but then Gyeltsen's generosity floated into her consciousness.

"Here," she said. Her wallet was still open from sharing with Angie, so it was easy to hand the woman a few bills. As predicted, as everyone visiting India is warned, when you give money to one beggar, a whole crowd of others will descend on you. The swarming individuals had wants and needs that were heartbreaking, and for once Leela did not steel herself against it, but instead looked into their eyes, person to person. She distributed all her money and food to the hungry people, then opened her backpack and handed out her clothes and toiletries until they were all gone.

Leela headed for the bus stop. Time to go to Goa.

35

TEELA WALKED ALONE TOWARD THE BEACH. She and Dylan had just had sex, and he was snoring loudly in their room upstairs. Rather than wake him, she left a message with the maid that she had gone for a walk, and that he was welcome to join her if he wished.

She slipped easily past the vendors selling hats, wall hangings, jewelry and junk spread out along the pathway. As she stepped beyond their row, the entire vista of unrelenting white sand spread out before her eyes. Only a few people were enjoying the beach that day: two Indian men in suits and ties with their shoes off standing in shallow water, talking; a badly sunburned rotund English couple from a package tour lying on beach chairs, getting even more sun. She thought she'd stroll to Vagator, although she'd never make it there and back before supper.

When she got down to the water, she saw Andrew approaching her, wearing one of the tiny string bikinis the men here wore. His chest was browned from many weeks seaside, and the hair on his chest glinted in the sun. *What a good-looking man for his age*, Leela thought, *for any age actually*. He carried that aura of mastery and invisibility wherever he went.

When he saw it was her, he cocked his head to one side. "Welcome to Goa," he said, embracing her. Leela took in his strong smell of sea air, sweat, and Indian hair oil. He felt and smelled divine.

"This may be the last time we'll see each other," she said, touching his waist. She was wearing the bra top of her swimsuit and a sarong about her hips. Her hair had grown long, and the humidity brought out a previously hidden curl. "We're leaving in three days, back to the West." Didn't he wonder who 'we' were? "I'm going with the one you said was 'a keeper,' remember? We're going to check it out, who knows, even try living together."

Andrew shook his head, turning to look out over the water. "About a half an hour till sunset," he said. "Time to get back to the Shack Bar for the evening's entertainment."

It was the highlight every day in Goa, watching the magnificence of the sun as it sank into the ocean. Every patron in every bar on the waterfront would stop mid-drink to turn toward the setting sun, watching until only a bare orange stripe lay against the horizon. A countdown would begin, then a big cheer as the sun finally dropped out of sight. Someone, a different person every day, always called out, "The Greatest Show on Earth!" or "Author! Author!"

"You haven't even congratulated me!" Leela chided.

"You recognized him immediately yourself. You said he was for me for the long term, that he was my mate."

Andrew looked straight ahead as they walked toward the bar. "I don't remember saying anything like that, and I certainly don't remember the incident or the fellow."

"It was in the food line—ooh—aren't you even happy for me?" He said nothing, so she added, "At least you could offer me best wishes."

They walked along in silence. Andrew picked up a stone which he skimmed across the water. A Rajisthani woman bearing pounds of colored scarves billowing in the wind approached, trying to sell to them. Another gypsy came up out of nowhere on the left, and suddenly Leela and Andrew were surrounded. Leela picked out a finely detailed batik from the one with the most rings in her nose, while Andrew bargained for a deal in Hindi. The women continued on their way, scouting for more Westerners. Leela looked back and saw the brightly hued scarves flapping in the air around the women like kites.

"Well, I've been waiting," Leela said. "What do you think? Really?"

Andrew turned in the direction of the bar and they resumed walking. He shrugged. "You were just starting to get somewhere, and now you want to throw it all away." They began the ascent up to the bar. "Just when you were beginning to learn something, you want to become some *hausfrau* in the West. Don't you know when you go back, your pussy will dry up? What a waste." He shook his head.

"Everyone goes back to the West with the best intentions. They think they will be unique, the one who stays alive, then one day they wake up and wonder where it all went." He looked at her for the first time since they had run into each other. "You will have lost everything you struggled so hard to gain."

"You've never understood me," she said, sitting down on the stone wall leading up to the bar. A light breeze blew her hair over her eyes, which she pushed back. "All I was ever trying to do was find the Perfect Beloved. When I surrendered that day at the very beginning, I swore I was willing to do whatever it took, no matter how painful my learnings might be, no matter what the cost.

"Now it has been revealed who the Perfect Beloved is. Funny, isn't it, he's someone my ego would never have picked, but that's a lot of what I've learned here, to trust existence. To let go. To let go of you! You never realized that I never wanted what you have; it was you I wanted! I so hoped and prayed for it to be you. When it was obvious you were not to be had, I had to continue on experiencing whatever was needed to be learned in order to be able to be found by him."

"Don't go home," he said. The lines on his face were slack, and he suddenly looked tired. "We'll lose each other. Stay here and be one of us." Leela noted without surprise that he didn't say, "Stay here and be with me."

"One of us," she said. "You can all have this 'love the one you're with' attitude, all this 'casual sex.' Casual sex doesn't exist. The term really means that the participants are so out of touch with their feelings they can't measure its impact on them. It dehumanizes everybody. I don't want to be around it. I don't want it at all."

It had been a long time since she first saw him when he bowed down to Mevlana under the bamboo tree. She remembered the first time they made love, and the many times thereafter. She looked into the face that she loved so well. He was so alone, no matter how many women he had. She would never forget him or all that she had learned from him, and she felt a rush of appreciation. "That's not to say that I'm not eternally grateful for all that you taught me."

She dropped onto the ground in front of him, and knelt at his feet. "I have been so blessed to have known you, and to have loved you. I extend my full gratitude that you have taken the time to teach me. I don't know how I will ever thank you. It is beyond the beyond what you have given me."

Andrew gently raised her up by her arms until she was standing before him. "If it is your path to go back to the West and become a *hausfrau*, what can one do," he sighed. "Here's what you can do to thank me. Number one, don't ever forget that this—" he touched her *yoni*—"this is your enlightenment. Center in it; relax. Allow your man to rest there. It is the source of your aliveness.

"Number two: Share what you have learned here, with both your brothers and sisters. Back in the West they are starving, and they are getting close to the point where they will kill for sustenance: for the food of meaning, aliveness, and connection. Share with them, help them in whatever way you can."

He took her face in his hands at last. The look in his eyes was so full of love, Leela's eyes began to tear. "If you must leave, come back," he said, running his tongue around her lips, kissing her fully and deeply. "Come back as often as you can."

ʟEELA AND DʏLAN SAT AT THE SHACK BAR sharing a last *Kingfisher*. Within minutes, the rickshaw would take them to the train, which would take them to Mumbai airport, which would deposit them stateside twenty hours after takeoff. Leela looked one last time at the Goan paradise: the endless cerulean ocean, the blinding white sand, the cloudless sky edged by palm trees. She turned a half circle and looked inside the bar at the wooden tables, and the Indian men who ran the place dressed in starched white shirts and black trousers. The smaller one smiled when she looked at him, and he started toward them to take another order.

"No," she said. "We go back to America now."

"America!" the Indian man said. "A very great place." `

"Yes it is," Leela said. "But in many ways, not as great as India." He grinned, obviously pleased.

Leela nestled closer under Dylan's protective arm. "Are you almost ready to go, baby?" he asked. He took the last sip of beer.

"Ah, do we have to?" Leela was suddenly racked with

fear. What if this was a mistake? What if it all went away? Everything she'd learned about how to exist living in the heart instead of the mind? She barely knew Dylan, and even though it had been unmistakably revealed that he was the Perfect Beloved, and that her destiny was to be with him . . . maybe she should stay here where the living was cheap and sweet and magical. What if Andrew was right?

"You promise me if we go back, my pussy won't dry up?"

"What are you talking about?" Dylan's chest puffed up like a bullfrog. "With the way I fuck you? Ha!"

Oh dear, he has so much to learn about how to please a woman, she thought. *It will take some doing because he has so much ego about it.* The fear came pouring back through her veins. What if she couldn't maintain in the West? She would have lit a cigarette if she smoked.

"I'm afraid to go back!" Leela's hands and voice were tremulous. "What if I forget everything, and I go back to sleep?" She was really frightened now. "What if I go back to a place of not trusting existence? What if the blissbody becomes only a memory?" The pain of it was excruciating.

"I promise you that won't happen," Dylan said. He put his fist down on the table in emphasis. The rickshaw driver had arrived, and was picking up the bags to carry out to the waiting car.

"You promise it won't happen? How can you be sure?"

"I'm sure. I won't let it happen to you." She could see his strength, his commitment, and his nobility. He had promised to protect and provide for her. Now this trust was the trust to which she would surrender. She turned to him and smiled.

"Ready?" he said, standing up and extending his hand. "Let's go home."

the end

about the author

CATHERINE AUMAN, LMFT (Licensed Marriage and Family Therapist) is a spiritual psychotherapist and the Director of The Transpersonal Center. She has advanced training in traditional psychology as well as the wisdom traditions. Catherine lived for a year at the Osho ashram in India—a full-time immersion in tantra and meditation—and she has studied and practiced tantra, love, sex, intimacy, and seduction with numerous teachers. She lives in Los Angeles with her husband, Greg Lawrence, with whom she teaches tantra and relationship enhancement.

acknowledgements

tHANKS TO AN INTERNATIONAL CAST OF CHARACTERS:

Friends at Home:
Leslie Keenan, Maureen T. Smith, Elizabeth Kelley, Katie Darling, Sandra Giedeman, Margaret Drewry Walsh, Lilly Penhall, Emma Moylan, Michael Weiss, Greg Lawrence, Ziri Rideaux, Lynn Hightower, Aurora Brackett, and Dean Santomieri.

Friends Abroad:
Amano, Ananta, Akhila, Kranti, Peter, Margot Anand, Gitama, Radha, Vismay, Pratiyan, Siddhika, Vinit, Vartman, and all the intrepid, courageous travelers from around the globe in search of personal and spiritual growth.

Friends in the Beyond:
Osho and Megha

stay in touch

Websites	catherineauman.com
	thetranspersonalcenter.com
Facebook	catherineauman.author
Instagram	@catherineauman
YouTube	catherineauman
Eventbrite	thetranspersonalcenter

works by catherine auman

books

The Tantric Mastery Collection: The Complete Tantric Mastery Series 3-in-1 Compilation

The Tantric Mastery Series (also available in Spanish)

   Tantric Relating: Relationship Advice to Find and Keep Sex, Love and Romance

   Tantric Mating: Using Tantric Secrets to Create a Relationship Full of Sex, Love, and Romance

   Tantric Dating: Bringing Love and Awareness to the Dating Process

Mindful Dating: Bringing Loving Kindness to the Dating Process

Guide to Spiritual L.A.: The Irreverent, the Awake, and the True

Shortcuts to Mindfulness: 100 Ways to Personal and Spiritual Growth

Fill Your Practice with Managed Care

workshops

Tantra: The Science of Creating Your Soulmate

Tantra: The Foundations of Conscious Touch

Tantric Secrets about Women

Tantric Secrets about Men

Tantra and the Psychedelics of Sex

MDMA and Couples: The Promise of Ecstasy

audio recordings

Tantric Embodiment Induction

Deeply Relaxed

Awareness Breathing

Create the Sex, Love and Romance of Your Dreams with
The Tantric Mastery Series

Imagine yourself in a perfect soulmate relationship full of sex, love and romance. Open yourself to love and awareness. These three beautiful books teach you how.

Catherine Auman's *Tantric Dating: Bringing Love and Awareness to the Dating Process* was named one of the **Best Dating Books of All Time by BookAuthority**. *Tantric Mating: Using Tantric Secrets to Create a Relationship Full of Sex, Love and Romance* follow up this success by teaching what to do next after attracting your perfect love to maintain the magic. *Tantric Relating: Relationship Advice to Find and Keep Sex, Love and Romance* is about how to communicate both verbally and non- to keep the love fires burning.

Buy Now online or at your favorite retailer
Print, Ebook, or Audiobook

Made in United States
North Haven, CT
04 September 2024

56963796R00193